Chasing Clouds

KATHRYN ANDREWS

Chasing Clouds
Copyright © 2018 Kathryn Andrews
Published by Kathryn Andrews LLC
www.kandrewsauthor.com

Cover Image – Perrywinkle Photography
Cover Design – Julie Burke at Heart to Cover
Formatting by Elaine York at Allusion Graphics

First Edition: July 2018
Library of Congress Cataloging-in-Publication Data Andrews, Kathryn

Chasing Clouds
ISBN-10: 1722355573 13: 978-1722355579

Chasing Clouds

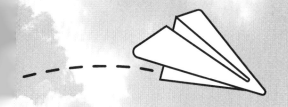

To Megan . . .

For always loving my stories.
They wouldn't be the same without you . . . xo

Chapter 1

Camille

EVERY LITTLE GIRL dreams of her wedding, that one magical day with endless arrangements of sweet-smelling flowers, family and friends, and a big white dress with a skirt so gauzy and beautiful it's meant to be twirled in, as if she were a princess. Music will play, birds will sing, and at the end of the aisle will wait a tall, dark, and handsome man who is so in love with her he'll have tears shining in his eyes.

That's the dream, right?

After all these years, my dream has become my reality, and today is the day.

Today is my wedding day.

A cool breeze drifts across the bare skin of my shoulders, I shiver, and goose bumps race down my arms. My eyes flick to the left, where one of the side entrance doors to the church was left open, letting in the southern February winds. The sunlight from beyond the door looks luminous and inviting, unlike in here, which is cloaked in darkness and shadows. The foyer is empty and still, with only the sounds of the organ playing from behind the two white wooden doors that will soon open and forever cement my fate.

I spent most of the morning quietly by myself, which is how I wanted it. No one understands—how can they? This is supposed to be the happiest day of my life, but what they don't realize is . . . it's not.

I take a deep breath and let my eyes fall shut. The smell of pine wood fills my senses, reminding me just how old the church is and what my getting married here means to my family. Built in the mid-1700s, it's one of the oldest churches in Savannah, and for more generations than I care to remember, my family has celebrated births, marriages, and the passing of life here within these walls. Just like all the other expectations bestowed upon me, there was never a question about where I would be married, just to whom.

Well, maybe not even that. Patrick has been their choice for years, and they slowly groomed him to understand what it means to be part of the Whitley family in Georgia as they pushed him my and Clare's way.

Swaying my hips back and forth with the distant weight of hundreds of ancestors' eyes, I focus on the rustling of my skirt as it swishes around me, the boards groaning under my feet.

"You don't have to do this."

Startled by her voice suddenly breaking the silence, my head shoots up and my eyes lock onto Clare's. The concern and worry etched in her expression and the tension in her posture pull on my heartstrings. Even with as close as we are, she's another person who doesn't understand. I do have to do this.

"Yes, I do."

"No, Camille." She shakes her head frantically and takes a step toward me as my eyes sweep down over her and the

2

pale blue strapless bridesmaid dress she wears. She's so beautiful, just like I knew she would be, and I feel the sting of the tears welling in my eyes. "I don't want this for you. This is not the life you were meant to have."

Letting out a deep breath, I reach for her hand and squeeze. A warm buzz tingles my fingers, and it's so familiar and comforting I find the strength I need to continue—to not walk away. She has to see that I'm doing this for her . . . for us, two halves of a whole that split apart and became the mirror image of the other.

"You're the one who always says our destiny is written in the stars." I smile at her. "This is my destiny."

"And you always respond that the stars don't move, we do. Therefore, you could just walk away. I'm begging you to please walk away. You'll never be happy with him."

"It's not about being happy, you know that. It's about being loyal to our family and doing our duty. We all play a role, we always have, and it's time I step into mine."

Her frown deepens, and her shoulders sag forward. She's making me feel as if I'm letting her down, when the truth is I owe her this.

"Camille, this moral responsibility to our family is not you. It *never* has been, and there's a difference between loyalty and being coerced. Please, I'm begging you, don't marry him."

Before I can respond, the organ stops, and Clare's hand tightens around mine. The panic that fills her flows into me, and my heart starts racing as I think about her words. She thinks I'm being coerced? That's the same as being bullied or threatened—is that how other people see it, too? With our eyes locked onto each other, she parts her lips as if to say something . . . but then the doors sweep open and she drops my hand.

No!

My fingers instantly cool and my ears burn to hear her unspoken words. What was she going to say? I need to know!

Her chin trembles, but she pastes on a smile as she slowly turns and walks down the aisle.

"Please—wait," I whisper.

She hears the pleading in my voice and glances back but doesn't say anything else. The muscles in her face suddenly relax, her concerned eyes seem to warm, and for the first time ever I'm unable to decipher her thoughts. Her expression has done a complete one-eighty, and she looks almost happy, content. Given the conversation we just had, I don't understand. I'm confused.

What just happened?

Does she know something I don't?

With a wink and a small smile, she turns around and walks forward. I follow, stepping into a scene that's my childhood dream brought to life.

The foyer is no longer drafty and dark. Golden light is pouring in through the stained glass windows that line the perimeter of the church, illuminating it and making it almost magical. The air is delicious with scents of honeysuckle, orange blossoms, and roses, and the classical melody of Mendelssohn slowly makes its way past the thrumming of my heart. The string quartet, the flowers, the candles . . . all of it is just so beautiful.

"Camille, it's time."

I tear my eyes from the sight before me and see my father standing next to the last pew with his hand outstretched. The magic of the moment fades away as I realize the beauty is only surface deep, and this wedding isn't what I've dreamed about. It's for show, not for love. His face doesn't shine with adoration and happiness for his daughter on her wedding day; it's full of arrogance. He's not smiling, but his lip is curled in a way that appears more like a sneer, and it's this tiny expression that reminds me I'm just a pawn for others to move as they please. My heart sinks.

Maybe Clare is right. Maybe my loyalties to my family are misguided. Being loyal implies the presence of support, trustworthiness, and faithfulness, but not a single family member reciprocates those things to me. Instead, they antagonize, lie, and boss me around.

Not wanting to waste any more time, my father walks over to me, wraps his arm around mine, and pulls. As if on autopilot, I let him lead me down the aisle. I was at peace with my decision, but now, after one conversation, I feel like this might just be my death march.

The entire church is packed, both sides of the sanctuary and the upper balcony filled to the brim. Along with the ghosts of my ancestors, I can feel every set of eyes on me. The weight of judgment falls upon my back and shoulders, and although some look happy for me and are probably thinking, *She looks so beautiful*, I know others are mocking me behind fictitious smiles.

From left to right, up, down, and all around, I'm assaulted by a stampede of emotions. Panic becomes the strongest, and then nausea sets in.

"I'm proud of you, sweetheart," my father says just loud enough for others to hear as he squeezes my trembling hand. Maybe he is, or maybe he isn't; I don't know. I lost the ability to really believe anything he says five years ago. What I wouldn't give right this moment to have the man in my memories and not the man currently walking me down the aisle.

Patrick moves into my line of sight. Terror streaks through my body, and the crowd becomes a blur. He isn't exactly smiling—more like smirking—and my legs begin to shake.

Feeling the change in my steps, my father wraps his arm around my waist to steady me, and my breathing picks up. The air won't come in fast enough, and my lungs feel as if they're on fire. Squeezing the bouquet, I pull it against my chest and press as hard as I can.

Can't people see there's something wrong with me? Can't they see this isn't normal bride behavior? But then again, I've never been one for crowds, and they must think it's just nerves.

Sliding my eyes off Patrick, I find Ali, my best friend from New York, and Brittany, my cousin. Ali's eyes are sad, and she's smiling at me in a way that screams pity. Brittany isn't smiling at all—she's crying. It's then I realize I'm crying, too.

Moving my gaze back to Patrick, he sees the tears, and his expression falls.

For months I've been telling myself I can do this. I know how to do it. I was born and raised in this life, and I really don't know any other. That doesn't mean I don't secretly want more, the thing every girl dreams about—true love—but right now, right this moment, looking into Patrick's eyes, I feel nothing but fear. This can't be all there is for me, can it?

I do deserve more, don't I?

Then I remember.

I remember the real reason I'm here, and regret sinks in.

I know why. He knows why. Hell, everyone in this room probably does. And, here I am.

With his eyes locked on mine, his carefully constructed wall slips, and staring back at me is the boy I've known most of my life. Before all of this—the expectations, the planning, the political aspirations, the lying—we were friends, and underneath it all, even after all of this, he still wishes I were someone else, and he knows I desperately want to be anywhere else but here.

As my father and I reach the end of the aisle, the strings stop, and a deafening silence blankets the inside of the church. Patrick and I continue to stare at each other, lengthening the moment until my father clears his throat. This is his way of letting us know it's time, and Patrick's eyes slide from me to him as if commanded. The muscles around his eyes tighten as the two men communicate nonverbally, and I watch Patrick's wall re-erect as he slips into the role he's meant to play. His lips twitch at one corner, the telltale sign of a smirk, and just like that, whatever emotional moment we were having is over. He smells victory for the one thing he wants most in his life—his career.

"Who gives this woman to this man in marriage?" the minister calls out.

"Her mother and I do," my father says.

Turning me to face him, he gently lifts my veil, kisses my cheek, and then returns the sheer curtain to its proper place. He avoids making eye contact, and given our opposing stances on this marriage, I understand why.

Stepping toward Patrick, my father shakes his hand and then places my right hand in his left. Patrick's hand is cold, and I find this fitting since he's become so coldhearted and disconnected. A shiver runs through me.

My soon-to-be husband leads me up the steps to the altar. Ali reaches over for my bouquet, my other bridesmaids fluff out the back of my dress, and we come to stand in front of the minister.

"Please be seated."

There is a soft chorus of clothes rustling behind us, but not a single person says a word. Brittany sniffles from over on my left, and Patrick's grip on my hand tightens.

"Dear friends and family, we are gathered here today to celebrate the union of Patrick Easton Walker and Camille Odette Whitley in marriage. Over the years, these two have built a friendship and a commitment to each other that grew, matured, and eventually turned into love. Today, they have decided to create a new bond together, a new sense of family as they become husband and wife. If any of you has reason why these two should not be married, speak now or forever hold your peace."

Silence fills the sanctuary, and it's at that moment I realize this is truly wrong and I desperately don't want it. I thought I could do it. I thought I'd come to terms with the situation and could be loyal to my family, but as the lump in my throat grows larger, I know I can't. Waves of panic crash into me, each one stronger than the last, and my heart pounds so hard it's as if it's trying to beat right out of my chest. The fallout will be excruciating and irreparable, but that's a chance I'm willing to take.

I don't want to get married to him. In fact, I don't want to get married at all.

Looking for a way out, I glance around the altar toward both of the side doors. Patrick pulls on my hand to grab my attention, and his dark eyes sharpen just enough to tell me he's onto me. His fingers tighten around mine even more, as if his hold alone could keep me from fleeing, and his whole body tenses. There's a warning in his stare, and it causes me to pause. An unprecedented feeling courses through me: fear. I'm afraid for more reasons than I can count.

The minister flips a page in his book, and the silence that follows seems to stretch for years. Is this extra time my chance? Am I being given one? Can I walk away? My eyes again shift to the side door, and I can't help but wonder how many steps there are from the altar to freedom. If I took this chance, would anyone try to stop me? Or would they let me go?

Oh, who am I kidding . . . I can't leave.

My eyes blur and with each passing heartbeat, I know my opportunity is slipping away, and Patrick is one step closer to succeeding in this. When I try to pull my hand from his, he just holds on tighter, sending pain shooting through my fingers. I stop breathing, waiting for the guillotine to fall, and he holds his breath with sweet anticipation.

"I do," says a male voice, the words echoing from the back of the church.

What?

Shock reverberates through me like lightning striking, but it quickly dissipates as I exhale slowly, feeling nothing but relief.

Instant, all-consuming relief.

The noose around my neck unravels as my body experiences a visceral reaction to those two words, and I suck in new air, fresh air that tastes a lot like hope.

But wait!

Who?

A collective gasp from those in attendance zips around the sanctuary and seems to pull the air, along with my attention, toward them. Whispers and movements begin as people turn in different directions, looking for the speaker. It's then that, from the back of the room, the man behind the voice steps out into the aisle.

Slowly, he begins to make his way toward us with his eyes locked on mine, and my breath catches. He's incredibly handsome.

Patrick's hand moves off mine and to my wrist as I face the beautiful stranger and watch him approach.

Do I know him? I don't think so. He looks familiar, but it's a vague recollection, as if I may know someone who looks like him but not this man specifically. He has olive skin, a shade on the darker side; dark hair, short on the sides but longer on top; and pale green eyes that make me feel certain I've never seen him before, because I would remember a gaze as striking as his.

"This has to be a joke," Patrick spits out as the man comes to a stop at the bottom of the steps.

"I can assure you it's not," he says, the light color in his eyes darkening to an emerald hue as he continues to hold my gaze.

I don't know where he came from or who he is, but right now I don't care. Relief washes over me. I just know this is a sign, and I'm being given a second chance. My skin tingles as I jerk my arm out of Patrick's grasp and start grinning.

"Sir, what objections do you have to this marriage?" the minister asks, looking confused, his gaze bouncing between the three of us. Neither Patrick nor I turn to acknowledge him. Instead, we both stay locked onto the unexpected guest. I don't know him, and it doesn't appear that Patrick does, either. So, who is he?

"You can't marry him," he says, his voice deep and confident, his regard intense. I don't understand what is happening, even though I feel like I should.

I don't respond—I don't know how to. All I can do is return his stare.

"I love you. Marry me."

A laugh bubbles out of me, and his eyes smile back with a mischievous glint at my obvious amusement.

This is absurd!

The murmurs through the crowd pick up in volume. Patrick says something to someone—presumably my father— but all I hear in my head is, *I love you*, and the more I repeat it, the more the voice sounds familiar. I've heard it before, but I can't place where.

"Look, pal, I don't know who you are or what you're doing here, but I think it's best if you leave," Patrick says as he moves to stand in front of me, shielding me from the mystery man's view. I quickly step around him and move down two steps to put myself at eye level with the beautiful stranger.

That's what he is—a beautiful stranger.

"Camille," he whispers, reaching for my hands. His hands are warm, solid, dotted with calluses and coiled with a strength like I've never felt before. He looks down at our entwined fingers, and his thumb rubs across the white line where my engagement ring usually sits.

I nervously glance at Patrick then find my way back to eyes so green they warm me like the sun on a long summer day. This guy looks nothing like Patrick. Patrick is tall, lean, fair, and wearing a classic black tuxedo, whereas the beautiful stranger is taller, layered with thick muscles, and wearing a charcoal suit that looks expensive and perfect on him.

"Camille, this is insane. You can't possibly be considering this!" Patrick stammers, pulling one hand back to him and clinging to it like a life vest.

When the stranger tugs on my other hand, my eyes return to him, and butterflies take flight within me. "It's time to make that move," he says, and a gasp slips through my lips as my eyes widen.

That phrase . . .

The voice . . .

It's him.

A flush burns in my cheeks as I absorb and memorize the details of his face for the first time. His lips tip up into a lopsided grin, and my eyes are drawn to how full and pink they are. I dreamed about these lips last night, and by the way his eyes smolder at me, he knows exactly what I'm thinking about . . . and he's pleased.

"Ms. Whitley," the minister calls out, and I force myself to look at him. "Are we going to have a wedding today?" he asks calmly. "And if so, with whom?"

I turn to Patrick, whose eyes are wild and frantic with fear. It's not a fear of losing me—well, maybe a little—but I think it's more a fear of this hurting his political dreams. I know marrying him is the safe choice, the choice that was made for me, and that's the reason I'm wavering. We've known each other a long time. He'll take care of me, provide for me, and I'm certain we'll do great things together. I love Patrick, I do; I'm just not *in love* with him. Regardless of our relationship recently, I never want to hurt him, but is all this enough? I don't know.

I turn to the man with the most alluring green eyes, and I see not only an escape, but also an opportunity—an escape from a life I've felt chained to for the last five years, and an opportunity for a different path . . . a life I've only dreamed of and never really thought was in reach. Maybe it was there all along. Maybe I just need to stand up for myself a little bit more, or maybe my whole life has been leading up to this moment.

Is it a risk? Yes.

Is it a gamble? Yes.

Am I okay with strapping enough scandal to our family name to last for generations? I don't know.

Then, just past his shoulder, I see Clare standing in the aisle watching us. My heart rate slows, and I find comfort in just the sight of her. Without her even having to say the words, I know she'll stand behind whatever decision I make, even if my decision is neither of the two men—but is that what I want, to walk out of here? Even if I did, I'm not sure I'd find myself in a different place. Patrick and my father would chase me down and demand a redo. Am I strong enough to stand up to them? I don't know. It's been a long time since I tried.

What I do know is that ten minutes ago I was suffocating, and now I can breathe. I'm certain that whatever I choose in the next minute or so, I'm forever cementing or changing the course of my life, and I'm surprisingly okay with it.

"Camille, have you decided?" the minister pushes, and I briefly close my eyes, gathering myself.

Taking a deep breath, I drop both their hands and turn to face him. A smile splits across my face and I stand a little taller as I answer.

"Yes."

Chapter 2

Reid

The day before

SLOWING DOWN, I pull up to the entrance of the plantation, glancing again at the navigation screen and Nate's text to make sure I'm in the right place. In front of me is a sprawling wrought iron gate with the name Whitley scripted into it, and there's a guard house just before manned by four police officers, two standing on each side.

As I roll down the window, a cool earthy breeze fills the inside of the car, reminding me I'm no longer in Tampa, and one of the officers approaches. He doesn't smile or frown, his demeanor neutral, but there's something about an officer walking toward you, no matter where you are or what you're doing, that's unsettling.

"Evening, sir, how can I help you?" He leans over to get a better view of me.

I look away from him and down the long oak-canopied driveway. For a split second, I wonder what the hell I'm doing here, and then remember I promised Nate, my younger brother, I would come see him.

"I'm here for the rehearsal dinner and the wedding," I say, looking back at him and forcing myself not to stutter or shiver on the last word.

"Identification, please." He holds out his hand.

Reaching into the center console, I grab my wallet and pull out my driver's license. When he takes it from me, my fingers tighten around the steering wheel. Growing up where I did, it was never a good thing when cops were involved, and although this is a completely different situation, old memories stir up old feelings, and some things never change.

The radio of one of the officers crackles and a garbled voice comes through. I don't understand what the person is saying, but it's enough to make my already agitated nerves even more jumpy.

The thing is, in addition to hating cops, I also hate weddings. Just the word alone makes me want to turn around and drive the other way. I'll never understand why people feel the need to legally attach themselves to someone else. Don't get me wrong, I love relationships—the kind that are easygoing, free of expectations, and filled with hours of endless fun. Why anyone wants to give that up for a joint bank account and shared bills, I'll never understand.

Watching the cop, I see his eyebrows rise in surprise and his eyes flicker back to me. He recognizes my name, and his gaze quickly travels over me and my car for confirmation before typing something on the iPad he's holding. This is crazy. Where am I, and who are these people that they need this type of security?

Nate called three days ago to tell me he was flying from New York City to Savannah for a wedding. His friend apparently surprised him last minute with a plane ticket, so when he asked me if I would drive up and be his plus one, I didn't hesitate in saying yes. Savannah is only five and a half hours from Tampa at the most, an easy drive, but what he didn't tell me is that this friend who's getting married appears to be some kind of Southern royalty.

Grabbing my phone, I shoot Nate a text, and he replies almost immediately.

Me: Meet me out front in 5, at the gate.

Nate: K

"All right, sir, you're all set." He hands me back my license. "If you'll just follow the drive about a mile down, an attendant will be there to assist you with overnight parking."

I nod, roll up the window, and begin to drive forward as the gate swings open.

Large oaks line the driveway. They're beautiful but covered with moss, making the canopy thick and dense. Sunlight streaks through the branches here and there, but since it's late afternoon, the drive is mostly dark and creepy. I should have asked who this friend of Nate's is, but I was so excited at the possibility of seeing him, the details were unimportant.

As the trees begin to fade away, a massive white mansion comes into view.

"Holy shit, I've entered the Deep South twilight zone," I mumble to myself.

There are huge white columns running the three levels of the structure, each of which has a wraparound porch. Aside from the massive double front door, there are several sets of French doors on each level leading out to perfectly placed rocking chairs. The lawn is manicured, the interior is lit up, and it couldn't look any more different from where Nate and I grew up if it tried.

I spot the parking attendant at the fork in the driveway, and he uses a lighted wand to direct me to the right toward a building that looks like a stable but is actually a garage.

I stop next to the valet and climb out of the car. My nose scrunches at the smell of the nearby paper mill faintly lingering in the air.

"Good evening, Mr. Jackson." The valet tucks another iPad under his arm and hands me a ticket. "What would you like brought to your room?"

"There's a bag in the back seat."

He smiles and moves toward my open door. "Perfect. You're staying in the Magnolia room, and when you're ready to retire for the evening, someone will direct you."

"Thank you." I nod to him and shove the ticket into my pocket. Magnolia room—is that meant to be cute or cliché? I can't decide.

Following a lighted path, I'm walking toward the front steps when Nate comes strolling out, and his face splits in half with the biggest grin when he sees me. Man, I love this kid, no matter how old he gets.

"Bro!" He skips down the steps, meets me in the circular drive, and throws his arms around me. "Thank you so much for coming."

"Of course." I pat him on the back and give him a once-over. He's muscled up even more since I last saw him over the holidays. "I'd never pass up an opportunity to see you! Especially when you're so close. You're sure your friend is cool with me being here?" I look past him at the grand double doors. We sure are a long way from the Bronx.

"Absolutely. Wait till you meet her—she's awesome." He slaps me on the back as we enter the home, and I can't help but eye him suspiciously.

"Awesome, huh?"

His gait slows and he pins me with a fierce scowl. "No, dude. It's not like that—at all."

"Whatever you say." I chuckle and he rolls his eyes.

Quickly, we walk through to the back of the house and out onto a terrace that overlooks a large lawn completely decked out for a party. There are large white tents, tables scattered about, and waiters wearing black tie attire walking around with drinks and hors d'oeuvres. Beyond that are acres and acres of rolling fields with more sprawling oaks.

The buzz of people talking and a five-piece band playing in the background slowly distract me from the sheer awe I feel of this place. I glance at Nate and he smirks.

"It's nice here, right?" he asks me.

"I feel like I've been transported to the set of an old Southern movie. Jesus, Nate, what do these people do for living?"

"Camille, my friend who's getting married, is the daughter of one of the current senators for the state of Georgia."

"You're kidding, right?" I glance at him and then back at the crowd. Georgia is predominantly a red state, and looking around, Nate and I definitely stand out as the minority with our darker olive skin.

He shakes his head and grins.

"How in the hell did you become friends with a Southern Republican socialite?"

"You know my buddy, Beau? His sister-in-law—well, future sister-in-law—dances with her. They're friends, he and I are friends, and we just kind of ended up in the same circle." He shoves his hands into his pockets and shrugs his shoulders.

Last year, Nate headed off to Columbia on a tennis scholarship, and Beau was on the team with him before he decided to go pro. I met him once, but I never met any of his other friends.

"Hold up." I lean in closer to him and lower my voice. "She's a dancer?"

Nate busts out laughing and shoves me in the arm. "Not that kind of dancer! She's a ballet student at Juilliard."

"Juilliard," I mumble.

Nate is five years younger than me. Right after I signed my letter of intent to play football at Syracuse University, I took Nate around to the different colleges in and near New York City, wanting to show him what life was like outside of the Bronx. I wanted him to see opportunities for another life, a better life. All he had to do was pick one thing and work hard at it, every day. When we stopped at Juilliard, he asked me if I had ever dated a girl who looked like the ones we saw there, and I said, "Not yet, but one day we both will." Of course it was meant to be symbolic, but as I look at him now, I really take him in.

Fingering the sleeve of his suit coat, I smile. "You're moving up in the world, kid. Looks good on you."

"Yeah, feels good, too—but hey, so are you. I bet that new five-year contract with the Tarpons looks real pretty in your bank account." He laughs, but I have to agree with him; it really does.

"So, who all is here with you?" I glance around, searching for a group his age but seeing mostly older people.

"From the city, it's Beau, Leila, Ali, Drew, and Charlie." He points toward the bar at the back left.

"Charlie—that name rings a bell."

Nate's eyes light up and he laughs. "You've signed some things for him before."

"Oh, yeah. He's your friend who's like a super fan?"

"You could say that, and he's the dude walking this way now."

I glance over and see a tall lanky guy speed walking toward us, wearing a seersucker suit and a pink shirt, grinning from ear to ear. "Get prepared, he's really excited to meet you."

A groan rumbles out of my chest as I frown at Nate. "Then our first stop needs to be the bar."

⸻

Three hours pass and more people have recognized me than I expected would. It happens everywhere I go and I understand it's par for the course, but here at a wedding in a different state, I just wanted to spend some time with my brother and not be bothered by people wanting to get autographs and talk football all night. Kill me.

Desperately needing a moment of silence, I wander back into the house and dip into a dark empty room. I think it's a library or a sitting room, but with houses like this, who knows.

Over and over, I was asked why I'm here and who I'm friends with. Not wanting to look like a wedding crasher, I repeated that I knew the bride, saying we'd met in New York City and hoping she'd just agree with my story if approached. After all, Nate did say she said it was okay for me to come.

Moving over to one of the bay windows, I look out across the party and search for the bride. Nate pointed her out not too long after I arrived, but she was busy being social and playing the part of bride-to-be, so she never made it over to us. I hate to admit it, but I've watched her throughout the night more than I should have. She's not the type of girl I typically go for, way too proper and fancy, but there's something about her that kept drawing my eye. Maybe it's because she's strikingly beautiful with her white blonde hair and porcelain doll face, or maybe it's because if you look long enough, it's easy to see she hates every minute of this.

I first noticed the unease through her repetition: smile, stiff hug, clasp hands in front of her, repeat. With each passing person, she'd tuck her hair behind her ear, even if it was already there, and the charade would start all over. Not one of her conversations appeared genuine, and a few times, she looked downright sad and uncomfortable.

Then again, if I had to stand next to that inattentive dick she's been with all night, I'd be sad too. For a dude about to get married, he certainly didn't strike me as gushing with love for his bride-to-be, but then again, what do I know. I'm never getting married.

Behind me, the door opens, quickly closes, and giggling hits my ears.

Great. Just *great.*

"Shh, you don't want anyone to hear us, now do you?" asks a male voice.

"Maybe I do," a girl replies, a little louder than I'm sure this guy wants.

There's a brief pause and then she moans.

This. Is. Not. Happening. I scowl.

Glancing through the darkness, I try to get a glimpse of who might be in here, but from where I'm sitting, it's just too far. I can see them, but not a whole lot of their details.

"Britt, we've talked about this. You know this is it, this is all I can give you, so why don't you just stay quiet for a few minutes and let me enjoy the feel of you."

She moans again, "Yes . . ."

They bump into something, and the sounds of them making out echo around the room. Letting out a sigh, I sit down on the window seat and lean against the wall hidden behind the long drapes. How I found myself in this situation, I don't know, but hopefully it'll be over quickly.

Looking back outside, I spot Nate laughing with his friends, and I can't help the surge of pride that fills me. He's done well for himself, looks genuinely happy, and I'm glad

I came. I didn't realize how badly I needed to know he was doing okay.

The door opens again, light streaks into the room, and this time there's a loud gasp met with dead silence.

"Get out!" The voice is low, feminine, and packed with a rage I wouldn't want directed at me. I'm assuming this voice is from the person who just entered the room. What a dumbass this guy is to go somewhere and get caught.

"Camille," says the other girl with desperation and panic.

Camille?

"Now!"

There's some mumbling, some shuffling, and then the door slams shut.

Peeking out from behind the curtain, I can't not watch, even though it's dark. It's like riding in a car you know is about to crash, and my emotions just elevated along with hers in anticipation.

"How could you? My cousin, and tonight of all nights." Her words are slow, her voice is thick, and my chest suddenly fills with fury for this poor girl.

"Oh, come on!" says the guy. "You know all of this is for show. I don't love you. You don't love me. You shouldn't be so surprised."

What a dick!

"I know you don't love me, but what about loyalty? Faithfulness? Family? Doesn't that mean anything to you?" Her voice is strained, an odd mixture of anger and betrayal.

"Why should it? We both know why we're here, and it's not because of me," he snaps.

What's that supposed to mean?

She gasps. "Wrong! All of this is for you! It always has been. Please, *please* tell me what part of this situation is for me. What do I get out of this?"

Movement comes from her darkened image—she's thrown her arms out, and I watch as she edges closer to him.

The guy chuckles lowly. "Oh, Camille, there's the girl with the fire—and here I thought she died, too."

The sharp sound of Camille's hand hitting this guy's face reverberates around the room. Silence stretches between them, and then she whimpers as he jerks her toward him. My hands tighten into fists and I stand from the window seat.

"That is the one and only time I will ever allow you to hit me. Do it again and you'll regret it." He shoves her backward and she stumbles, reaching for an end table.

"I can't marry you." She shakes her head, breathing hard between each word.

"Yes, you can, and you will." He steps forward, crowding her aggressively.

"No." She tilts her head up, the motion just barely noticeable in the darkness.

"Camille, I'm warning you. Think long and hard before you open that pretty little mouth of yours and say something you can't take back," he threatens.

"Are there others?" she asks.

Silence follows as he thinks about his answer, relaxes his posture, and steps back.

"Does it matter? Look, come tomorrow, it's all over, all of them. I know what the stakes are and what the end goal is. You don't need to worry about this."

She doesn't answer him, just wraps her arms around her middle.

Moving away from her, he walks to the door, pausing with his hand on the knob.

"Just stick to the plan and remember your family. You're a smart girl, so you'll do your duty. You owe them, and besides, it's not like you're the one getting the raw deal here—you're getting me, whereas I'm only getting you."

What!

This guy is delusional, and my anger for this girl pulses through me. What could possibly be so bad that someone feels obligated to marry someone else? And someone like him, too?

He opens the door and her head jerks to the side at the onslaught of light.

"Forget about this, Camille. Get some sleep. Tomorrow is a new day." He pauses and his voice shifts to a definitive tone. "I'll be waiting for you at the altar, and I expect you to be there." With that parting note, he walks out, leaving her alone, and the last sliver of light disappears as the door clicks shut and the air in the room stills.

She doesn't move, and neither do I. I think my shock about this situation almost equals hers.

What the hell is the matter with that guy? How can anyone be so impervious to reality and arrogant at the same time?

A choked sob echoes around the room, pierces my ears, and burns its way down to my toes. Camille's hands fly to her mouth as she bends over, folding in on herself, and lets out a strangled moan. I know I need to make myself known. Not wanting to add to her humiliation, I step out from behind the curtain of the bay window.

"Well, can't say I saw that coming." I'm trying to remain calm, feeling like I'm approaching a wild animal.

She gasps and turns toward the sound of my voice.

Shoving my hands into my pockets, I cross the room and stop a few feet in front of her.

"Wh-Who are you?" she stammers, stepping back a few paces.

I can see her much more clearly now with the moonlight shining directly on her, but I doubt she can see me with the light hitting my back. There are tear tracks running down her face, and the muscles across my shoulders tighten as I silently seethe over her heartache.

"What are you doing in here?" she asks, voice shaky.

"I slipped in for a few minutes of quiet. For the record, I was in here first, and it really doesn't matter who I am. What does matter, though, is whether or not you want me to kick that guy's ass, because I absolutely will."

She looks me over from head to toe, realizes I'm not joking, and then laughs. She laughs so hard emotion twists and turns into tears . . . more tears.

Oh, damn.

Approaching her slowly, I pull her into me. She tucks her arms between us and buries her face in my chest. I shouldn't be touching her, much less holding her this close, but right this moment, I don't care.

Sobs rack through her. As terrible as it is, all I can focus on is how she feels pressed up against me. I'm probably a foot taller than her and she's less than half my size, but she's warm and feels perfect. Taking a deep breath, I catch a whiff of how she smells, my eyes slipping shut. She's been outside for who knows how many hours and she still smells sweet, clean, feminine.

"What do I do?" Her voice is small and unsure.

"I can't answer that for you."

"What would you do?" She pulls back a little and looks up at me. The moon has shifted, so I can no longer see the details of her face, and I'm certain she can't see me at all.

"For me, I think it would be time to move on."

"Move on," she repeats, testing out the sound of the words. "But, what about my family?"

"That's the thing about family, they'll love you no matter what."

"I'm not so sure about that." She looks down and rests her forehead on my chest, her hands gripping the lapels of my suit jacket.

"Well, to me, that's another reason all in itself to walk away. Maybe it's time to find people who will."

Sliding my hand down to her lower back, I squeeze her a little tighter, and she lets out a long, slow breath.

"How did I get here?" she asks, although I know she's not asking me. She's asking herself.

A clock chimes from somewhere in the room and she flinches then slowly backs away. I miss her instantly.

In what feels like slow motion, I watch as she pulls her shoulders back, tucks a piece of hair behind her ear, and stands a little taller. Moving into the role she so clearly knows how to play, she clasps her hands in front of her, and although I can't see it, I know plastered on her face is some semblance of a fake smile.

"I'm sorry you had to witness this . . . me."

"I'm not sorry, Camille."

Her breath catches at the use of her name, and I can't help myself as I lean forward, lightly grip her elbow, and lower my lips next to her ear.

"Better to know now, rather than later." I kiss the corner of her mouth, lingering for just a second longer than necessary. Her lips part and she turns her head as I pull back, brushing her mouth over mine. In another place, another lifetime, I might take the leap to walk out of this room with her, but what she doesn't know and I do is that we come from two different worlds. We don't fit, and with that thought, I take a step back and drop her arm.

Standing in the dark, nothing else to be said, I tuck my hands into my pockets and we stare at the darkened shapes of the other. A small noise comes from Camille, but instead of speaking, she abruptly turns around and slips quietly out of the room.

Chapter 3

Reid

I DIDN'T SLEEP at all last night. I spent half of it tossing and turning due to the anger I feel for the situation this girl is in, and the other half chastising myself for thinking about how good she felt in my arms, a girl who isn't mine and never will be. I didn't tell anyone—I wouldn't since it's her business—but now, I'm sitting in this little church next to Nate and his friends, and every single muscle in me is coiled so tight I feel as if I'm about to spring open and burst.

I know in the background there is music playing, and I should be checking out the bridesmaids as they walk down the aisle—after all, bridesmaids are about as easy as they come—but instead my eyes are glued to the very smug face of that asshole from last night.

Sure, he's playing his part. He's smiling at the guests and winking at family members, but it isn't until I watch his eyes shift toward one particular bridesmaid that I see the real him. I'm certain that other than the girl the look was intended for, no one but me saw the lustful expression cross his features or the deep blush burn through her cheeks.

The organ stops, and all around me, people shift to look at the closed doors. The groom and the girl lock eyes one more time and he smirks while shoving his hands into his pockets to adjust his pants.

What an asshole!

An unidentifiable fury pulses through me, and if I were anywhere else but here, there's a good possibility I would rip his face off and teach him a few things. Guys like him don't deserve this life, and they certainly don't deserve girls like the one who's about to walk through that doorway.

The string quartet sitting in the upper balcony begins to play, and the rear doors whoosh open.

Collectively, everyone stands, and there's a delighted gasp from the guests. I turn to see her and am momentarily astounded. *Damn.* I thought she was beautiful before, but this image of her in a white dress . . . it's indescribable.

Seconds tick by, but she doesn't move. She's gripping her bouquet like it's a lifeline, and behind the short veil over her face, her eyes are darting all around the church. Eventually, her father approaches her and urges her on. What I wouldn't give to know what she's thinking right now.

With her eyes trained on the altar—or him, I'm not even sure—she walks by, the pounding of my heart keeping beat with her evenly paced steps. The expensive smell of her perfume lingers as she passes.

Jesus, what's wrong with me? I don't know this girl, or really anything about her, but I'm completely pissed off at this entire situation and one hundred percent affected by her, more so than I even realized. Maybe it's a case of wanting-what-I-can't-have syndrome, or maybe it's the protective nature I've always had for my family and friends; I just don't know.

They reach the end of the aisle, the music stops, and the minister begins speaking, but I can't hear a single word. Everyone sits and my hands ball into fists as they rest on my thighs. Tension must be radiating off me because out of the corner of my eye, I see Nate looking my way. He bumps me with his shoulder, trying to grab my attention, but I shake my head, because I can't take my eyes off her.

Unexplained heat rises and radiates from my back. I feel like I'm going insane, and then through the screaming in my brain, the minister's voice comes across clear as a bell.

"If any of you has reason why these two should not be married, speak now or forever hold your peace."

I stop breathing and my mind starts jumping. Do I, or don't I?

No, wait—what am I thinking? I can't object to this wedding. Granted, I don't believe in weddings, but what am I going to do, take his place? Fuck no. Besides, she doesn't even know me. Objecting would just cause drama, and I abhor drama. The press would have a field day with this, and the team's PR department would have my ass.

Then I watch as her shoulders sag and her head drops. Defeat. This isn't the reaction of someone who's excited to be getting married—hell, she can't even maintain the fake act she paraded around last night. She should be all smiles, and instead, she looks like she just accepted a prison sentence. My heart squeezes and I let out a slow breath, knowing I've just made up my mind. I can't let her do this, consequences be damned.

"I do," I hear myself saying.

The entire crowd turns toward the back of the church in search of the speaker, in search of me, shock etched on every single face.

"What. Are. You. Doing," Nate growls under his breath, but I don't respond to him. I can't.

I rise slowly and he pulls on my jacket sleeve, but I step out into the aisle and begin making my way toward her. The glares being directed my way prickle over every inch of my skin, but I don't care, because the only eyes that matter now are hers. They're wide, stunned, and light blue, and she's trying so hard to place who I am.

"This has to be a joke," the asshole standing next to her stammers.

My eyes skip from Camille to him and narrow. There's only one thing I know for sure about how today is ending, and it's that she will not be married to him.

"I can assure you it's not."

His face reddens, but I don't care. I look back at Camille and give her a small smile, hoping to break some of the tension.

Camille's eyes widen even farther, and then she jerks her arm away so he's no longer touching her.

"Sir, what objections do you have to this marriage?" the minister asks.

My brain stalls. I hadn't thought about that, and Camille raises her eyebrows in question. She wants to hear what I have to say, and the words just slip off my tongue.

"You can't marry him." We stare at each other so intently, and I'm praying she can read my mind. "I love you. Marry me."

I've never told a girl I love her. It's funny how, as impossible as I thought it would be for those words to ever come out of my mouth, there they are. Even though this is fake, it's scary as hell, and sweat drips down the middle of my back.

Silence falls over the church. It's so quiet I can hear both Camille and the prick next to her breathing, and then she laughs. She laughs at me.

Something in my chest cracks and my already racing heart feels like it's dipped in warm water, slowing it down. Beautiful isn't a strong enough word to describe her laughter.

Murmurs slowly pick up in volume and bounce around the space behind us.

"Look, pal, I don't know who you are or what you're doing here, but I think it's best if you leave." Patrick tries to stand in front of her, but Camille isn't having any of it and moves down a few steps, putting us at eye level.

"Camille." I swallow and reach for her hand. She lets me take it and her fingers wrap tightly around mine. Hers are cold, smooth, and pale, matching her perfect pedigree, while mine are warm, large, and darker, another stark difference between us. As my thumb automatically starts rubbing circles on the inside of her palm, she relaxes and loosens her hold.

"Camille, this is insane. You can't possibly be considering this!" The arrogance from last night is gone, leaving him sounding desperate. He grabs her other hand, like an absurd game of tug of war, and her conflicted gaze travels back and forth between the two of us.

I pull gently, and her eyes return to mine. "It's time to make that move," I whisper, recognition lighting her up as a gasp slips through her perfect lips. A smile tips the corner of my mouth in hopes of reassuring her, and her expression fills with a growing reverence.

"Ms. Whitley," the minister calls. She tears her eyes away, but her fingers clamp down around mine. "Are we going to have a wedding today?" he asks calmly. "And if so, with whom?"

She looks at Patrick; he's shaking his head, imploring her not to do this, not to change her mind. The color has drained from his face and he's deathly pale. Maybe if he had given this girl the respect she deserves, he wouldn't be reduced to begging right now in front of a room full of people, but then again, something tells me this entitled prick won't ever change his ways.

She looks at me, and I can't help but wonder what she sees. The blue in her eyes shifts from light to dark; whatever she's about to do, she's decided absolutely. Her backbone has lengthened, her head is held higher, and then she looks past me. Her eyes lock onto someone behind me, and affection for this person floods her eyes. There's a faint smile on her lips as she blinks then looks back at me.

This is quite possibly the stupidest thing I've ever done. I can already feel the crushing weight of the repercussions this is going to cause, but there's nothing—not one thing—that will change my mind.

"Camille, have you decided?" the minister asks again.

She closes her eyes briefly, looks once more at the prick and at me, and then she drops our hands.

"Yes."

Chapter 4

 Camille

LOOKING AROUND THE beautiful church, I know this will be the only real wedding I'll ever have. After all of this is over, if I ever do find someone worth marrying, I will never have a big formal wedding again. Grandfather is already eighty-five, and for years he has talked about watching Clare and me marry and getting to dance with us at our weddings. Part of me feels like I need to do this for him, but I know in the end I must do this for me.

Looking back at the beautiful stranger, I see there's a tiny bit of fear etched in the lines around his eyes, but there's a lot of confidence backing this position he's found himself in. I'm not sure what it is—he's certainly not the escape plan I had in mind—but there's something about him that I'm drawn to, a calmness that makes me feel safe and a strength in his grip that tells me he's not going to change his mind and back out now.

Through the fear, he gives me a one-sided smile, and deep down I know everything is going to be okay.

"Yes, I will marry you." There's no waver in my voice, no pitched inflection, just relief and determination.

Gasps come from the guests, and from behind him my father stands, pure rage rolling off his body.

"What? No! You're marrying me! That's why we're all here!" Patrick bellows, grabbing my arm.

My gaze snaps back to him, and his grip on my arm tightens to the point of pain. Wincing, I stumble in his direction as he yanks me out of the stranger's grasp and toward him. His groomsmen step up behind him, glaring at me, and that's when I realize Nate and Beau have stepped up behind my stranger.

Nate and Beau?

Alarm bells start sounding in my head, telling me I should know who this is, but with all the commotion going on around me, I can't think, and therefore I don't.

"Let me go!" I yell at Patrick, my voice echoing around the church.

"No," he roars. "I wouldn't do this if I were you."

The fear and wariness so present a few minutes ago are now completely gone, and anger has taken their place. Anger is an emotion I can relate to; it's been lying dormant, just waiting for this moment for the last five years, and it won't be silent now.

"And why not? Now you're free to go be with your mistress in public. Oh, Brittany darling"—I turn to glare at my cousin, contempt dripping from my words—"bless your heart, he's all yours."

More gasps from the audience as Brittany steps closer to me, both embarrassment and hope written across her face. She's so stupid to think this is going to end with her and Patrick walking off into the sunset.

"Stop this, Camille." He shakes me. "I don't know what you're talking about, but you will be marrying me today!" His fingers dig into my flesh and the pain shoots up my arm.

"No, I will not." I try to pull free, but he just squeezes harder, and my eyes blur with tears.

Having heard and seen enough, my mysterious library guy steps up to the altar. His eyes are locked onto where Patrick is grabbing me, and his hands are clenched into fists.

"You will take your hand off her immediately, or I'll remove it for you by breaking every bone in it." His voice is so low and deep only those right around us can hear him, but the threat is clearly legitimate. Patrick's nostrils flare and he reluctantly releases me, one finger at a time. The new guy wraps his hands around my waist and pulls me into the hard wall of his chest, putting distance between Patrick and me.

Commotion is increasing. More people are standing, and things very quickly start getting out of hand. Out of the corner of my eye, I see Dale, Patrick's best man, step around, charge forward, and pull back his fist. Jerking left toward the minister, my mystery guy twists us just as the punch flies by. Because Brittany has moved in a little closer, when Dale loses his balance on the altar steps due to the sudden change in everyone's position, his fist crashes into her face. The impact and her scream are near deafening, and blood immediately begins pouring from her nose and mouth.

The entire audience is now on their feet as Brittany hits the floor, silence once again enveloping the church. Patrick falls to his knees and in this moment, everyone now knows what I discovered last night: she's his side piece.

As the murmurs and conversations slowly start up again, Grandfather walks up to the altar and hands Patrick his handkerchief for Brittany. "I think it's best if you all left now." This isn't a suggestion; it's clearly an order.

"But . . ." Patrick scrambles, hopping up to his feet and looking for my father, who's standing at the end of his pew, shaking his head, his face beet red, while my mother wrings her hands next to him. He's so angry, but he'll never add to the scene; I know he's going to try to distance himself from it as much as possible. There are too many influential people in this room, and if anyone is going to be cast in an unfavorable light, it's going to be Patrick or me, not him. He crosses his arms over his chest and glares at Patrick disapprovingly. Part of me wonders if it's because he was screwing around with someone else behind my back, or if it's because he got caught and their master plan has now been disrupted.

Security steps up behind my grandfather. They've been called in from the outside, and now they're looming in the middle of the aisle.

The volume of our guests lowers as Grandfather turns and raises his hand to silence them. Whimpering from Brittany can be heard across the room as she's still crouched on the floor.

"So, it seems we've had a slight change in plans today. We appreciate your patience as we settle on a few *minor* details for today's festivities." He smiles and light chuckling rises up, instantly lifting the heaviness of the room. "We will begin again in fifteen minutes, so hang tight. If there is anyone who wishes to leave, now would be the time. Thank you for coming." He nods toward the groom's side of the church then turns back to Patrick and his groomsmen.

Patrick's immediate family gathers up their things and quietly exits out the back of the church. The door clicks behind them and all eyes swing toward the front to see what happens next.

"Patrick, it's time to go," my grandfather says firmly.

"N-No," he stutters, slightly panicked and confused. He looks around the room, then at the guy standing behind me, and then at me. Every emotion flees as his desperate eyes bore into mine. My heart aches for what this is doing to him—after all, we were friends once upon a time—but I can't really feel for the person he's become over the last couple of years, and deep down I know he's only going to get worse, not better.

"This isn't over," he spits out then turns to walk away. Dale lifts Brittany off the floor, and as he and the groomsmen follow, each one scowls and issues us a glare that says revenge is coming. With every step they take, I relax and sink back deeper into the arms of a man who's a complete stranger and now my hero.

Bending down, he rests his mouth next to my ear and whispers, "It's going to be okay. I've got you."

I nod in agreement, but am unexpectedly more caught up in the sensation of his warm breath floating across my neck than I am in what's going on around us. A shiver runs through me and his arms tighten. I like being close to him, and as Grandfather reaches for my hand, I'm reluctant to move away.

"Darling, head to the back of the church and wait for me there. Don't go into the foyer." He shakes his head and I understand his concern that Patrick might still be there. All of my bridesmaids except for Ali move to the front pew, and on the groom's side, Nate steps up to stand in for the best man. Recognition flickers in the periphery of my brain, but all thoughts stop as I see Grandfather pinning his boutonniere onto the guy I've agreed to marry. Not looking at my father or any other guests, I numbly make my way to the back of the church and remind myself to breathe.

A short time passes before my grandfather joins me, and again the string quartet begins to play. In a matter of fifteen minutes, I feel completely different about what I'm about to do, and I wonder if I look different, too. As we make our way down the aisle, I know without a doubt I could have walked by myself, but the smile on his face is priceless. He whispers that he's proud of me, and although this moment is fleeting, I'd do it all over again just to hear those words from him.

Green eyes smile at me appreciatively as I approach, and more than once I watch his gaze fall over the length of me. He likes what he sees, and so do I. He's incredibly handsome, tall, and strong, and based on the way he carries himself, fearless. I can't help but wonder where he came from, who he is—not that it matters. I'm so thankful for this man in front of me, and it's quite possible I would follow him just about anywhere.

When we reach the end of the aisle, Grandfather lifts my veil, gives me a small kiss, and tucks my hand into the warmth of my new groom's. "Well done, son." He pats him on the shoulder and leaves the two of us staring at each other. I refuse to look anywhere else, not that I'm sure I could.

This is crazy—absolutely *crazy*.

Nervous butterflies take flight, but I don't care. His eyes are bright and excited, and I'm certain mine mirror them.

Lacing our fingers together, we simultaneously take a deep breath, turn, and walk up the steps toward the minister, who smiles warily at us but winks at me. I get the feeling everyone knew I shouldn't be marrying Patrick except for Patrick, my father, and me.

No, that's not true—I knew, too.

He leans over and quietly asks, "Sir, what's your name?"

"Reid Harrison Jackson."

A jolt hits my body at the recognition of the name, and all other sounds are drowned out as understanding settles in and roars through my ears.

I glance past him at Nate. Our eyes lock and hold as his narrow and his lips press into a thin line. His brother, who lives in Tampa . . . his brother, who he said was coming as his plus one . . . his brother, who he backed as Patrick bore down on him. His *brother*. Shock must register across my face because Reid's grasp on my hand tenses, his fingers tightening around mine.

Leaning forward, he asks me if everything is okay.

Shifting my gaze from Nate to him, I whisper, "Yes," shaking off the confusion and again feeling spellbound by the depth of his green eyes as they capture mine.

"Ladies and gentlemen, we have gathered here today to join this woman, Camille Odette Whitley, and this man, Reid Harrison Jackson, in holy matrimony. If there is anyone here who objects, speak now or forever hold your peace."

The church is so silent you can hear the cicadas outside in the trees. This time no one answers, and as the minister continues, I let out a sigh of relief.

The ceremony proceeds, but every word is lost on me. I'm going through the motions, but I can't focus on anything other than the man across from me—his striking eyes, the way his fingers are constantly moving against mine, how delicious he smells, and that he's doing this for me. I know this wedding isn't real, but I'd be lying if I said it didn't feel completely surreal and I wasn't living in the moment. It feels like what I would imagine a wedding to a soul mate would feel like—magical.

"Do you have the rings?" the minister asks. I shoot Reid a look of panic just as Grandfather, who has already risen, walks over and hands Nate two wedding bands. As Nate passes them to the minister, I glance at them and see they're his and my grandmother's. A small gasp slips past my lips—why does he have hers? I look over, and he just winks and nods.

Repeating the offered vows, Reid and I slip the rings onto each other. Reid pauses as he looks at the one circling his finger, squeezes his hand into a ball, and then raises his eyes to collide with mine as the minister says, "You may now kiss the bride."

Kiss the bride!

Stepping closer to me, one side of Reid's mouth tips up in a smile. I know this because I have to tear my eyes away from his lips to catch his eyes, those beautiful green eyes that make me feel giddy, safe, and excited for the first time in a long time. Gently, he lifts my veil, and instead of flipping it back over my head, he slips under it to be close to me. What had acted as a filter is now gone, and everything about him is vivid, sharp, and—just for today—mine.

Taking my face in both his hands, he lowers his lips to brush them against the corner of mine then pulls away, but only by the most miniscule distance. Memories of last night's kiss flutter through my mind. Wonder is immediate, and heat races through me. Wanting to be closer, I grab the lapels of his jacket and inch up on my toes. Feeling me shift, he moves one hand to my lower back and gently pulls me flush against him. His lips connect with mine again and slowly, deeply move in a way that lets me know, up until this moment, I have never really been kissed. This is a fairytale kiss to complete my fairytale dream wedding. Every part of me tingles, and although this kiss is simple and crowd appropriate, in an instant I lose myself to his hands, his mouth, his taste. This isn't something put on as an act just to keep up the pretenses; this kiss is real, and he feels it, too.

Applause erupts from the guests, reminding us where we are, and the moment is over.

Reid takes a small step back but continues holding me tight.

"Wow," I mumble, and I'm rewarded with half-lidded eyes and a smile that's just for me.

"Ladies and gentlemen, Mr. and Mrs. Jackson!"

Reid pulls the veil off us, flips it behind my head, and pats it down. He turns us to face the audience and we both smile as, hand in hand, we walk down the steps, up the aisle, past the rows and rows of people, and into an empty foyer.

"I can't believe we just did that," I whisper, his gaze shooting down to me as the church bells begin ringing and the front doors of the church are thrown open wide by people outside.

I pull on Reid's hand and we duck into a small coat closet. I need a few minutes to myself, and I'm certain he does too.

"Are you okay?" he asks, running one hand down my arm and turning the light on with the other.

"Shouldn't I be asking you that?" I peruse his face to see if there's any hesitation or regret, but I find none, just concern—concern for me, someone he doesn't even know.

His lips twitch like he wants to smile, and all of this is so overwhelming I think neither of us knows how to act or what to do.

"Why did you do this?"

Instead of answering, he shrugs his shoulders and runs his thumb along the edge of my jaw. I'm in awe of this man . . . complete awe.

Tilting my head so it falls into his hand, I step closer to him and rest my forehead on his chest, just like last night. How crazy it is that all this started not even twenty-four hours ago.

What if he hadn't been in the library? No, I can't think like that. I can't think about the what-ifs; I can only think about how grateful I am.

Reid wraps his arms around me, and this is how we're found when it's time to go.

Stepping outside, the sun is so bright Reid and I have to squint to see what is going on around us, and I find Clare. She's standing next to Ali, and there are tears of happiness shining in her eyes. She blows me a kiss just as Grandfather guides us farther forward and shakes Reid's hand.

"Congratulations, son. I know the two of you will be very happy together." He smiles brightly then leans over to kiss me on the cheek. "I'm very proud of you. Things always have a way of working out for the best—never forget that."

I nod, not sure what to say. People have started to gather around, so neither Reid nor I say anything, just stare at him and then at each other.

"Why don't the two of you head back to your house, change your clothes, and spend a little time together before the reception this evening." He ushers us down the church steps and into the parking lot.

I turn to face him. "But, Grandfather—"

"No buts. You two will see tonight through," he whispers, "and then we'll talk about what's next." He pauses and pats my cheek. "Smile, it's your wedding day."

A 1960s Rolls Royce Silver Cloud pulls up, and Reid, who's still holding my hand, guides me over, then we climb in the back.

As the car pulls away, people cheer and wave behind us. The cool, slightly pungent southern air hits my face, and my free hand reaches for my veil to keep it from flying away. My mind is racing; it won't slow down, and for the next ten minutes until we pull up in front of my house, neither one of us speaks.

Chapter 5

Reid

ADRENALINE IS A funny thing. One moment you feel on top of the world, and the next you want to be buried within it.

As we pulled away from the church, I glanced over to find Nate standing on the top steps with his hands shoved in his pockets. He wasn't smiling or frowning; if anything, his expression was unreadable, and that feels even worse than him showing disappointment.

Did I disappoint him?

Part of me feels guilty, because if he did have any type of affection for this girl, I broke the number one rule between brothers. But, at the same time, if he cared for her in any sort of romantic way, he should have been the one to step up and stop that wedding. He's her friend. He should have seen the signs, should have known how she truly felt about that guy, and he should have done something.

Then again, between the two of us, I'm always the one to do something. It's just who I am, and I know that. I'm incredibly protective of those close to me. I can be impulsive and assertive, and I can't stand to see people bulldozing those who appear weaker than them—not that I think Camille is weak, though I don't actually know anything about her, and she *was* going to marry that guy. Just thinking of him has frustration and tension running across my shoulders and up my neck.

Minutes pass. Neither of us acknowledges the other, each lost in our own thoughts as the car comes to a stop in front of a colonial brick house covered in ivy, just off of Johnson Square in the historic district. The home sits on a corner lot on a tree-lined road, and we're the only car occupied as it idles. The driver gets out and walks around to stand next to my door but doesn't open it.

"What are we doing here?" I ask, looking around as people walk by. I thought we were headed back to the Whitley mansion; that's what I get for not paying attention.

"This is my house—this is where I live." There's pride in her words, but her voice fades off, almost like she's hesitant, shy.

My head whips toward her. "What do you mean? I thought you lived in New York."

"Well, I did." She looks past me and out the window at the house. "After Patrick and I got engaged, he and my father thought it would be best if I moved back. Although I loved living there, I guess I kind of agreed. If I was going to be his wife, I should be where he is. I belonged here." Her eyes find mine again and I can see she's nervous. Is she nervous about the misunderstanding, or nervous because she mentioned Patrick? I'm not sure, but I hate that she is, and I can't help but grit my teeth as my mind sticks on his name and an indeterminate feeling courses through me.

"So, do you own this house with him?"

Her eyes widen and her lips twitch as a small smile makes an appearance. "No. My grandfather bought this house for me and my sister years ago."

"You have a sister?" My brows rise, and she nods. Nate never mentioned she had a sister—not that he talked about her much.

"Clare." Her expression turns solemn and she drops her gaze, looking down at our hands. I had forgotten we were still holding hands, and my thumb involuntarily starts rubbing her soft skin. I swear every emotion this girl has today is making itself known. Where were all these expressions last night? I watched her off and on for hours and she looked like a porcelain doll the whole time, so stiff and shiny.

"Was she at the wedding?" I mentally scroll through the bridesmaids to see if I recollect any of them resembling her.

She lets out a sigh. "She was."

"Huh. I don't know if I saw her. Where is she now?"

"Who knows." Lifting her head, she looks down the road in front of us and pauses before asking, "Reid, why did you do this?"

It seems her adrenaline has worn off, too. She's asked me this twice now, and I wonder if she regrets it. Does she regret saying yes to me? Then again, those are the same questions I keep asking myself.

"Honestly, I don't know. I kept replaying over and over in my mind how that prick spoke to you last night, and then there was this look on your face as you walked down the aisle, and I just reacted. Probably wasn't the smartest idea, but there's no going back now."

"No, no going back now." She frowns. "Thank you." Her eyes lock onto mine, and nothing else needs to be said.

My lips press together as I squeeze her hand and nod.

"I am curious, though—why didn't you tell me who you were?"

"When was I going to do that?" I chuckle. "It really didn't seem relevant last night."

"I guess not, but you know what I mean. I hope the shock on my face wasn't too obvious."

"It wasn't, and really, I'm a nobody unless you follow football, and those who do saw me last night. I wasn't a surprise to them. I'm actually surprised you didn't pick up on it sooner, especially when Nate stood up behind me."

"I should have. I knew you were coming, but there was so much going on, I couldn't think."

"I stopped thinking, too."

My mother and my coaches have always both chastised and praised me for this. In stressful situations, there's no happy medium; I always react first and contemplate later.

Suddenly feeling claustrophobic in the back of this tiny car, I glance over at Camille's house. "Come on, let's go inside." I release her hand and pat her leg.

"Okay."

The driver sees us moving and he opens the door. I climb out, breathing in the fresh air to calm down, and help her out of the car. People passing on the sidewalk stop to take us in. A few camera phones go up and she smiles, always playing the part, except this time it's with me. I hate that she knows this part so well.

"So, this is where you live?" I ask, our fingers finding each other and linking together once again. It really is a very nice looking house from the outside, larger than anything I've ever lived in.

She smiles as she opens the small gate leading to the front steps. "It is. As much as I loved living in New York City, I love this house even more. It was built back in the 1850s and was originally a hotel. It was then bought by a Northerner who worked in lumber and redesigned it to be a house. It's obviously gone through several rounds of restoration, but I couldn't possibly love it any more."

While she unlocks the front door, I run my free hand down the white portico column beside it. With the history of this house, the history of her family, I feel way out of my league.

Entering the foyer, I'm immediately taken with the architecture and details. A lot of thought and care has clearly gone into each aspect, like the intricacies of the crown molding, the arched doorways, the elaborate curved stairway, and the colors. It's beautiful, and it's easy to see why she loves it so much.

"Please, make yourself at home." She stops us at the base of the stairs and looks around nervously. "Just wander wherever. There's food in the kitchen, a TV in the living room, and a guest bedroom on the second level. It's yours if you want it."

"Okay," I murmur.

She's unsure about what to do with me here, about what's supposed to happen next.

The house is completely empty and still, and a heavy silence falls between us as she takes a step away from me. Our hands finally drop, and in a way, I feel like the connection we've shared over the last hour is now broken. I feel like it's now her and me, two separate entities.

"Will your sister be arriving soon?" I rub the back of my neck, trying not to feel completely out of place.

Her brows scrunch down in question and she tilts her head just a little.

"You said your grandfather bought this house for the two of you."

"Oh. Yeah, he did, but no, she's not stopping by. She doesn't live here. It's just me."

I look up at the top of the winding stairs that go up three levels and then at the rooms on each side of me. One is a formal sitting room, the other a library. "This is a large place for just one person."

"It is, but it's mine and no one can take it from me." Her tone is a little sharp. After meeting her douchebag ex and her father, I can see why this would be important to her.

"I'm going to go upstairs for a while to rest and get changed for tonight, if you don't mind." Her cheeks turn pink; she's putting space between us, and I guess I realize I'm grateful. I need to sort through the shit in my own head and think about what comes next.

"This is all I have." I hold my hands out, thinking about my small bag and my car back at her parents' house.

Her gaze drops and slowly runs over the length of me. My stomach muscles tighten; I think I like her eyes on me. "You look great," she mumbles. "Really great." Finally, she reaches my eyes. "It's too hot outside for this dress, and besides, I have another one to put on for tonight." She picks up the long layers of her skirt and sways her hips back and forth.

"You looked beautiful today—I hope you know that."

Her cheeks and neck flush red as she inhales, her chest expanding. My eyes drop to the swell of her breasts and I have to force myself to look away. No need to make this more awkward than it already is.

"Thank you."

I briefly wonder if anyone told her that this morning then silently curse myself for not telling her sooner.

"Do you mind helping me with the buttons?" She turns around and presents her back to me.

"Sure."

I step toward her as she pulls the veil from her head and tosses it onto a console table. Gently pushing her hair over one shoulder, I look down at the row of pearls waiting to be undone. Sliding my fingers under the fabric at the top, one by one they unfasten, leaving the full length of her back exposed. She grips the front of her dress, keeping it up, and I can't help running my finger down over each bump of her spine, lingering on the last one. She has the softest skin, and under my touch, she starts trembling—and I know it's not because it's cold in here, but because this affects her, and the entire day is catching up to her. Instinct takes over and I step closer, wrapping my arms around her. Pulling her back flush with my front, I drop my head next to hers.

"Reid—" Her voice breaks as she breathes out my name and her arms layer over mine. The trembling has turned to shaking and she starts breathing harder.

"Deep breath, Camille. I've got you."

I can't imagine all the things going through her head. This situation only inconveniences me a little bit, but her— she may as well have thrown a bomb at her family, her friends, her life.

In and out, I take deep breaths, and slowly her breathing returns to normal, then we're breathing in sync. Her shoulders relax and curve as she folds herself into me. I hug her even tighter.

"Everything is going to be all right. We only have a few more hours left today, and we can do anything for just a few hours. So, go on upstairs, do your thing, and I'll be down here when you're ready."

She twists around in my arms so she's facing me, still holding the front of her dress, and her eyes find mine. So many emotions swim in her watery crystal blue eyes, but the one that stands out the most is reverence. Bending down, I kiss her forehead. She lets out a sigh, and then she's gone.

Somewhere up above, I hear a door click shut, and the vast emptiness of this gorgeous old home surrounds me.

Reality sets in and I cringe as I think back to what I've done. If walls could talk, I wonder how disapproving they would be. Hell, even I disapprove. Rubbing my chest, I look down at my feet, needing a moment to compose myself.

Seriously, what have I done?

This girl knocks me on my ass and I don't even know her. In real life, I would never know her. Yes, she is unequivocally the most beautiful girl I have ever seen by far, but that's because she's in a different class level, which has never been my type at all. I've never wanted a girl like her: rich, proper, sophisticated. I like girls who are relaxed, confident, and not materialistic . . . yet when I'm near her, I seem to have zero self-control—*zero*. I don't know her, but after this morning, it seems I would do anything for her.

Shit.

Moving through the house, I find myself in the kitchen gulping full glasses of water. It's one thing to keep myself pulled together when she's near, but now that I'm by myself, I allow the roar of emotions in my head to take over.

Looking down, I cringe at the sight of the ring on my finger and try to pull it off, only to find that it seems stuck. Her grandfather isn't nearly as large as I am, and I was surprised it slid on at the church. I have large hands—really large, perfect for catching a football—and of course now it won't come off. It's like a bad omen, one I brought upon myself.

Bracing my hands on the counter, my head drops, and I let out a harsh sigh.

"This isn't real. This isn't real. This isn't real," I chant to myself, trying to remain calm. People get married and divorced all the time; it's just a matter of paperwork. We can do this. I mean, maybe we can just annul it. It's not like it's a real marriage anyway.

It's not a real marriage.

Letting out a sigh, I roll my shoulders, crack my neck, and attempt to pull myself together, thinking back to what I just told her: it's only a few hours, and I can do anything for a few more hours.

Spotting a large bag of chocolate gummy bears on the counter, I take a handful and begin eating them one at a time. I've never heard of chocolate-covered gummy bears. Really, I never eat sugar—ever—but right now, I forgive myself and indulge.

Wandering into the living room, I flop down on the couch and take a look around the room. Of course, this place is just as beautiful inside as it is outside. It's a little girly, but it fits what I'd imagine her home would be like. I bet her interior decorator cost her a pretty penny. Then again, she can probably afford it.

To the left of me is an ornate brick fireplace with a large flat-screen television above it, and across is a heavy wooden white bookshelf. Every inch of it is stuffed with books, but it's the complexity in the details of the carving that catches my eye. It's a beautiful piece of furniture. I've never seen one like it, and it fits in here perfectly.

Getting up to explore the house, I wander from room to room and take in everything from the brightly-colored original paintings on the walls to the rugs, the chandeliers, and the furniture. There are no pictures of people anywhere, but I do take a closer look at her books, hoping to find out something about her, something she loves in particular like mysteries or autobiographies, but there's a really broad selection covering everything from woodworking to romance to *The Alchemist*. So far I haven't stumbled across anything to tell me who Camille Whitley really is.

Returning to the kitchen, I grab more gummy bears and refill my glass one more time before leaving it in the sink.

Everything here is so put together and clean. This place has the makings to be an amazing family home, but it all feels more for show than actually lived in. I guess as one person, how many rooms do you really need? She probably only uses three, maybe four, and that's when I draw the parallel between her, her life, and now her home: always perfect, but secretly screaming for some chaos.

After a while, I head back to the couch and decide to lie down and close my eyes. She didn't say how long she was going to be, and frankly, I'm beat. In my back pocket, my phone buzzes. Pulling it out, I see a text from Nate and five missed calls from my agent. It's only been a little over an hour, and he already knows. Groaning, I turn off my phone and scrub my hand over my face. I'll deal with him tomorrow.

Two hours later, the sound of Camille's heels alerts me that she's heading down the stairs, and I stand up to greet her. My heart rate increases with each step she takes, and I feel ridiculous until I see her and my jaw drops. I'm again shocked by how gorgeous she is—the kind of gorgeous that definitely says, *You can look, but don't even think about touching.* She's wearing a skintight white lace dress with long sleeves and tall gold heels. Her hair is pulled back off her face into a knot behind her head, and her lips are painted dark red.

"Wow. You were beautiful earlier, but this . . ." I shake my head at the ludicrousness of the situation. "You take my breath away."

Her cheeks flush pink against her pale skin and she looks away. Unless this girl has the personality of a rock or is witchcraft crazy, Patrick is an idiot, a complete dumbass.

"What's that?" She points toward the coffee table, and my eyes follow.

"I found an empty notebook on the bookshelf, so I hope you don't mind. I know this"—I gesture back and forth between the two of us—"today . . . isn't real, but I still wanted to give you something. It's the best I could come up with on short notice."

"You made me a paper airplane?" She looks at me then back at the small folded piece of paper. Suddenly, I feel stupid. Paper airplanes are childish, not wedding day gifts.

"I did." I move to pick it up and now regretfully hand it to her.

"It's a really fancy paper airplane." She turns it around and looks at each side of it. "Thank you," she says, her eyes returning to mine, large and happy.

I shrug my shoulders and give her a tight-lipped smile.

Gently holding the paper creation, she puts it on top of a stack of books on a small table by the window. Staring at it for just a moment, she turns back to me and smiles, not one of her fake expressions, but a genuine one. It's so different from all the others I've seen on her, I feel jolted and six inches taller. Maybe it wasn't a foolish idea after all.

"I love it. I really do."

"I'm glad."

I hold out my hand, and she walks over and slips hers into mine. I've never been one who particularly cares about hand-holding, but hers . . . I think I could hold on to it for a really long time.

"Ready to go?" I ask.

"As ready as I'm going to be."

Chapter 6

Camille

HE GAVE ME a paper airplane, a small sheet of paper folded into tiny angles, and I can't think of one other thing in my life that has ever meant so much. No bribery, no sinister plan, no strings attached, just a genuine gift from him to me, because he thought I would like it. How thoughtful is that? I know in my head I'm being irrational, silly, but he's already done more for me than he knows, and then to top it off he wanted to make sure I got a gift from him on my wedding day—our fake wedding day. Who does that?

My fake husband does, that's who.

I'm so distracted thinking about this man sitting next to me, I don't realize we've pulled up to my father's house until Reid is leading me out of the car. Dread settles into the pit of my stomach. It's not that I'm unsure about him, more that I'm unsure about the reception we're going to receive from those behind the door.

I used to love this house. I imagine most do love their childhood home, but as I've gotten older, I see it now for what it is: a tomb, a place where souls go to die. Yes, I'm being dramatic, but originality isn't welcome here. It's all a false front for a life you want others to believe is real. Perfect politician, perfect wife, perfect twin girls . . . perfect perfect perfect—only, none of us is. It's because of this expectation that over the years, this house just got colder and colder. No one wants to live in a place that's devoid of warmth.

As we move up onto the porch, with each step it becomes harder and harder to move my legs. Reid feels the change in my stride and looks down at me. His forehead wrinkles in concern and he's about to say something when the doors are swung open by a hired staff member and he presses his lips shut.

Walking inside, he redirects us into the vacant library. I find it a bit ironic that we're back in here, where all this mess started just about twenty-four hours ago. The door clicks shut behind us, but this time there's light from the dusk sky filtering in. I can see him perfectly.

Releasing my hand, he wraps one of his around my face and tilts my head back to look in my eyes. *God*, those stunning green eyes.

"Talk to me." His voice is calm and smooth, but even so, my anxieties about being here surge forward.

"Reid, I don't know what to do." I reach up and grab his wrist, anchoring myself.

"What do you mean?"

My eyes trail over his nose, his lips, the stubble across his jaw, every detail so much more masculine than Patrick. If I allowed myself, I could get lost in him, but I know better. This isn't about that; it's about him helping me out of this situation.

"Them . . . out there." My eyes blur with tears I refuse to let drop, and he shakes his head.

"No. Just stop for a minute and take a deep breath. Let's talk this through." His thumb swipes back and forth across my cheek. I push the uneasiness and the hesitation from my mind, because although I don't know him, a stranger in every sense, I feel like I do. He's on my side, I know he is, and I'm not doing this alone.

"Remember what we said earlier." He pulls me into his warm body and tucks my head under his chin. "This is just for a couple of hours. Everything is going to be all right."

"How do you know?" I plead for him to give me an answer, my eyes dropping to his chest . . . his very broad and muscular chest. I move my hands and slide them under his suit jacket, around his waist to fist the back of his shirt. The body heat trapped there seeps into me and spreads up my arms.

"Because I know nothing has to be decided today," he says calmly.

"Well, we kind of did make a huge decision today."

He chuckles, and the feel of it vibrates through him and into me. Leaning back, I look up to see his warm eyes humoring me while one hand spans my lower back, pulling me closer, and the other still cradles my head.

Why is looking at him like looking at the sun? Being held by him, the feel of him, the smell of him—it's distracting and blinding as the heat spreads through me and curls in the bottom of my stomach.

"Listen, your family and friends are waiting outside for you. There's nothing scary out there, just people who love you. I'm getting to spend time with my brother, there's going to be some great food, and if you're lucky, I'll ask you to dance." He winks.

"It is scary out there. You don't understand . . . those people don't love me. They're social climbers and gossipers in the worst way. I feel like I'm being fed to the wolves. I always do, and especially after today. They'll all know this is fake—if they don't already—and it's more humiliation for my family. That's why I don't know what to do."

"So let's make it real," he says, his tone so casual.

"How do we do that?" My stare bounces back and forth between his eyes.

"Go on a date with me." He grins.

"A date? What?"

"Be with me tonight. We're already in this together, so why not? For tonight, be mine." He shrugs one shoulder.

Be his.

Could I be his for one night? I haven't been on a date in so long, or out with another guy in over five years. I don't even know if I know how to act.

"What do we tell people?" I ask him.

"Nothing really. I think less is more. It's not anyone's business, and the more details we give, the harder it will be to remember them all."

"Yeah, I think you're right, but we will get asked."

"Okay, we met late last summer after your semester started. I was visiting my family and went out with Nate and his friends. You and I instantly hit it off and secretly kept in touch."

Three sentences . . . three sentences of a lie that now has to give proof for my erratic behavior . . . three sentences that do sound believable.

"Okay, simple enough. I like that."

"It's going to be fine." He gives me a smile and my gaze lowers to his mouth. There's a small scar on the top left side of his upper lip, and I decide I like it.

"They're going to clink the glasses and expect us to kiss."

"So I'll let you kiss me." He laughs. My eyes dart back to his, and they're filled with amusement.

"It has to look real." I laugh with him and tug on the back of his shirt.

"Do you think it didn't earlier?" He cocks an eyebrow as his thumb slides across my jaw and brushes across my bottom lip.

"I don't know," I whisper, watching those green eyes sparkle and then become heated.

His hand on my lower back presses and my body pushes more into his, the buckle on his belt feeling like the only thing preventing complete contact of his body with mine. Both his stomach and back muscles are flat and hard; he feels amazing, and I can only imagine he looks amazing too.

"Come here, princess." His voice pulls me from my thoughts.

Butterflies take flight. He's going to kiss me, here, in the library. I know we kissed earlier, but that was for show. This is here and now, with no one watching, and it feels real, like this is going to be our first kiss.

Leaning down, his nose runs alongside mine, and he drops a kiss on the corner of my mouth. Earlier I was so caught up in the moment and what was happening, I didn't take the time to memorize the details, but I sure am now. His lips are full and soft, and my heart rate picks up as I start breathing faster. He's so close. He smells so good, and I bet he'll taste exquisite.

"This has officially become my favorite first date ever." He pauses, and I feel the side of his mouth tip up as the day-old stubble on his cheek brushes against my skin. "Kissing at the beginning instead of the end, mmm." The sound rumbles from his chest and into mine. I like the way it feels more than I should, and deciding I don't want to wait anymore, I push up on my toes to seal my mouth to his.

If there's one thing I've learned about Reid today, it's that he doesn't do anything halfway. He's either all in or all out, and with this kiss, he's all in.

When he licks across my bottom lip, I gladly open to him and allow his warmth to sink into me. Part of me thinks I should feel bad about wanting this kiss so much—after all, I'm supposed to be married to someone else—but I don't. I want this kiss. No, I *need* this kiss, and I can tell he does too as his hand on my lower back moves to cradle the other side of my face. He holds my head, angling and moving me to just where he wants me, and I'm more than happy to comply. Over and over his tongue twists with mine as his mouth, lips, and breath take what they want. Every part of me is tingling, and I'm in complete euphoria as I surrender to this moment and just feel . . . feel him, his fingers, his heart beating against his chest, and how he's wordlessly promising me he's got this and everything is going to be okay.

Patrick never kissed me like this. He was soft, tentative, and now I'm wondering if he just didn't want to or wasn't into it, because this kiss is the kind stories are written about, the kind that will ruin me for anyone else.

The door opens and slams against the wall.

"Camille!" my father bellows.

Reid and I jump apart and my father stops dead in his tracks. Both of us are staring at him as confusion slips across his face.

"Wait. I thought . . ." He trails off, his eyes bouncing between the two of us and narrowing in on Reid.

"You thought what?" he asks, moving to stand closer to me, wrapping his arm around my shoulders. Mine slips around his waist. I roll my lips in between my teeth and inwardly smile at how full and swollen they feel.

Grandfather walks in, stands next to my father, and grins at us.

"Nothing. Camille, I need to speak to you." He again glances between the two of us. "In private," he sneers.

"Not tonight, sir. She's all mine tonight." Reid looks down at me, smiles, and kisses the top of my head. "Do I have lipstick all over my face?" he asks.

Feeling emboldened, I quirk a mischievous smile, and he minutely raises his brows. "No. Darling, you know I prefer lip stains over lipsticks."

One side of his mouth tips up. "I do know, but I'm just making sure." He bends down and lightly kisses me again. I can feel the anger radiating off my father from across the room.

"I don't know who you think you are, but you can't come in here—" he yells, moving closer to us in an attempt to grab me by the arm, and I squeeze Reid's hip, hard. He responds immediately and pulls me tighter against him.

"I can and I will," he says, cutting my father off. "I'm her husband now, and unless you want us to leave and be rude to *your* guests, I suggest you take a step back."

Reid is glaring at him, and I swear he's grown three inches taller and two inches wider. He well outsizes my father, who, like the smart man he is, moves away from us.

I know people don't see me as a strong and independent woman, but I've always thought I am. I know I am a people pleaser. I don't like conflict, and I want to make others happy. I prefer to go with the flow and keep the harmony between us all rather than rock the boat. But, when needed, I've always been able to make decisions for myself and own them, just like today at the church. Standing here with the two of them in a face-off, though, now I don't know. Maybe I'm not as independent as I thought I was. Securing my grip on Reid's side, I willingly allow him to take over for me, to speak for me. What kind of person does that make me?

"All right now," Grandfather says as he walks to stand in the middle of my father and Reid. "We're here to celebrate tonight. We have a house full of guests and we're going to remember that." He looks pointedly at my father, his tone very much stating that all this needs to be handled another day when there aren't one hundred and fifty sets of eavesdropping ears just outside these walls.

"Fine, but this isn't over." He pins me with a look I'm certain is meant to intimidate me, but I'm over it, completely done with his overbearing ways. I lengthen my spine instead of cowering, and I swear Reid beams with pride. I know I have some tough questions to ask myself about the type of person I am once the dust settles on all this, but I do know one thing: I will no longer be anyone's doormat. I am not a pushover, and I refuse to allow people to treat me this way anymore.

Holding my head high, I release Reid's side and reach for his hand. His fingers lock around mine and I pull for him to follow me. As we start to walk past my father, Reid stops us, and I know he needs to get the last word in. After all, my father did just issue a threat of more to come, and I can tell Reid doesn't like this dynamic. He doesn't like it at all.

My father's eyes widen as Reid leans toward him a little, his nostrils flaring like a bull's as he breathes in and out. If my father has any question about who he's dealing with here, Reid squashes it immediately. He has no intention of ever letting my father have the upper hand.

"Stay away from us," he growls. He doesn't even need to say *or else*; it's implied, and my father knows it.

Glancing once more at Grandfather, who is grinning at us, I shake my head in disbelief.

I never thought I'd be happy to say I'm glad I caught Patrick cheating on me, but I am. If I hadn't walked in on him, I wouldn't have met Reid, and for the first time in a long time, I feel like things just might be okay.

Remembering Reid's words—*just a few more hours*—I grip his hand, pull us out of the room, and think to myself, *Never again.*

Chapter 7

Reid

I KNEW WE'D get some speculative glares tonight, but I never would have guessed there'd be so many. As bride and groom, we were fortunate enough to have a table to ourselves, but maybe it would have been better if we had moved over to Nate's table. Hardly anyone spoke to us, and when they did, jabs came at us from right and left about what we did to "poor Patrick" and how he must be handling all of this. With each ticking minute, I became angrier.

I mean, what is wrong with these people? Now I see why she was so worried to be here tonight. Hell, I'm giving her props for even showing up. I would have given the one-finger salute as I drove away as fast as possible. No wonder she married me; why would anyone want this life?

Even still, although I feel like she owes them absolutely nothing, Camille plays her part, the one she's perfected, but I see the heartache lying under the surface. The only family member to speak to her is her grandfather, and thank goodness for him. The only time she lit up was when he acknowledged her. He even took over the father-daughter dance, claiming they needed to appease him because he's an old man. Of course, Camille and I danced too, cut the cake, and kissed, but I also saw how many glasses' worth of champagne passed through her lips.

I know she's not mine. I don't even want her to be mine, but for tonight, she is, and I've had enough.

"Hey, are you ready to go?" I lean over and ask her as we're taking a break from dancing and sitting at a table just off the dance floor. The few friends she does have here look exhausted, and it's only a matter of time before they say good night as well.

Blurry, sad eyes find mine. Slowly she nods and lets out a relieved sigh. Pulling her hand to my mouth, I kiss it lightly, and the two of us stand. She links her fingers through mine then leans into my arm and hugs it. This girl is killing me.

"Excuse me, ladies and gentlemen," says a voice over the speakers.

My eyes whip across the lawn to find Nate standing on the stage looking directly at me. *What is he doing?*

"Thank you to everyone who decided to stay tonight and share in this unexpected, but certainly not unwelcome turn of events." *Is he giving a best man speech?* "For those of you who don't know my brother, and I'm sure that's most of you"—he chuckles—"there's no one in the world like him."

My heart rate slows as I stare at him. He knows this whole thing isn't real, so is he just trying to make it look more authentic? Is he doing it because he knows he'll never have another chance? Or is he doing it because he's my brother and he's supporting me?

"What people see on TV, the dedicated athlete and teammate—sure, that's a huge part of who he is, but that's not all he is. Reid is the best person I know. Growing up, he filled every role I needed filled, from father figure to best friend. He taught me how to tie my shoes, he bought me my first tennis racket, and he showed me how dedication, hard work, and determination can help you achieve your dreams. He's selfless. He gives one hundred percent of himself, and he never asks for anything in return."

Warmth trickles into my veins as his words sink in. It's one thing to know someone loves you, but it's entirely different when you hear them speak it. I mean, Nate and I have never had flowery type conversations. We push each other, hard, because that's what brothers do.

"I never thought I would see this day, but then again, I shouldn't be surprised. It's in his nature to care for others, always has been." He shakes his head and presses his lips together.

I don't understand. He should be surprised. I've told him repeatedly I never plan on marrying, and I don't really care for other people, I just do right by them.

"Camille." His eyes shift to her. There's an unnamed emotion in them that again makes me feel guilty, but I shake it off, because I can't and I won't. "You will never find a better man than my brother. He will be loyal, honorable, and generous, but he needs someone to continually show him it's okay to be vulnerable, and that it's also okay for someone to take care of him for a change. He doesn't always have to distance and numb himself. He can let go of the facade, because those who truly love him will never leave and will always stand by him."

I don't know why he's saying this. Vulnerable? That's not even a word in my vocabulary. No one should ever be vulnerable, and it's being strong and secure in my ways that has made me the man I am today. I don't need anyone to take care of me; I take care of myself. Also, I wouldn't say I distance myself. What I do is keep a pulse on reality so I can make the most informed decisions. That's how I run my life on and off the field, and it makes me a great leader.

"Treat him right, because he deserves the world and then some." Nate briefly drops his head then swallows to gain composure, and I can't help but frown. Man, he's sure making this sound and look real. "So, if you would, please raise your glasses. Here's to Reid and Camille. Together, may you both find your way, fall in love every single day, and always listen to what your heart has to say—it'll never steer you wrong."

Everyone raises their glass and takes a sip.

"Now, go make me an uncle!"

Laughter erupts, but the lump in my throat is so large I can barely breathe.

Stepping off the stage, he walks to Camille first and gives her a kiss on the cheek. They don't exchange any words, just smiling at each other with a warmth that comes from an established friendship, and I find I'm slightly jealous, which is just dumb. In front of me, he stands eye to eye, and I'm at a loss for words.

I'll be the first person to admit I have a marriage phobia, but that's not what this is. This is fake, a means to an end. Chivalry is not dead. I did it for her, so why does this moment with my brother in front of me, Camille holding my hand, tucked into my side with the stars above us suddenly feel so real?

"N-Nate," I stammer.

"Not here." He claps me on the shoulder. "It was good to see you. I'm glad you were able to make it." He chuckles, glancing at Camille and back. "Make sure you tell Mom sooner rather than later. I don't want to be there when you do."

Mom. I haven't even thought about her yet. He laughs at my expression, and Camille's hand tightens around mine.

Looking down, I see tired lines are etched around her face. Her spark has faded, and I know it's time to go. I let go of her hand and wrap my arm around her shoulders. She wraps hers around my waist.

"We're gonna take off." I clear my throat. "Thanks for the toast. It was unexpected, and it meant more than you know." It's true, although I'm still trying to sort through his words.

He wraps his arms around both of us, slaps me on the back, winks at Camille, and then walks away.

Today has been a long day.

Seeing our chance for escape, Camille and I walk quickly through the house and out the front door.

The car is still parked out front, and the driver jumps when he sees us.

"Should we say goodbye to your grandfather?" I glance at her to gauge her thoughts.

"No." She shakes her head. "He'll understand."

We slip into the back, and the car pulls away very quietly. I wonder how long it will take them to realize she's not even there anymore. *Oh well. Good riddance.* She's better off with me, a complete stranger, than that horrible crowd.

"Reid." Her voice is soft, but I hear her and look down. "Can we just drive around for a while?" she asks, leaning into me.

"Of course, princess."

The driver nods to let us know he's heard then rolls the windows down. Slipping off my jacket, I pull Camille onto my lap and wrap her up to keep the chill off her skin. She lets out a contented sigh as she curls into me, and we let the sound of the wind whipping through the car take over.

By the time we pull up to her house, she's fast asleep, whereas I'm wide awake. The driver opens the car door then the front door as I carry her into the house. She's so small and light in my arms.

At the top of the stairs there are several rooms, but only one has an open door. Inside the dark bedroom, I spot her wedding dress hanging up and know this is the right one. Everything about this space looks like her and doesn't at the same time. The taste of the furniture looks high-end, as I would expect, but none of the pieces match. Each one is different in style and I assume color, even though I can't tell with just the moonlight.

When I set her on her feet, she leans her weight against me as I pull the zipper on the back of her dress. It slides down easy enough and the dress slips to the floor. Even standing in only her underwear, this girl is class personified. She's elegant, graceful, and comes from a pedigree I'll never understand. Me, I'm from eight hundred square feet in the Bronx.

Shaking my head at the world of difference between us, I remove my dress shirt, pull off my T-shirt, and slip it over her head. She looks around the room, up at me, and then turns to climb into her bed, patting the spot next to her for me to follow. Of course I do, because when it comes to her, I can't not. I watch as she takes off her shoes and they drop to the floor, and then she pulls the rubber band at the back of her head and all her hair comes tumbling down.

I don't realize I'm holding my breath until I breathe in through my nose and the air fills my empty lungs. She shifts around, moving the covers. My T-shirt slides up, and my eyes cling to her long, toned, gorgeous legs. The vision of this girl is almost too much. I know I shouldn't be here, but wild horses couldn't drag me away. She slides under the covers and lets out a deep sigh as she drifts back to sleep.

Kicking off my shoes, I sink into my side of the bed and settle down next to her. As exhausted as I am and as much as I wish I could sleep, I can't. Minutes tick by, turning into hours.

Sometime early in the morning, Camille stirs. Rolling to my side, I look down at her just as her eyes open and find mine. I don't know what to say to her; I'm afraid she'll ask me to leave, and I really don't want to.

Shifting to face me too, she whispers, "I'm sorry."

"What are you sorry for?" I reach out and run my hand down her side then lightly grip her hip.

"Getting you involved in my mess." She squeezes her eyes shut and a tear falls down the side of her face.

"Trust me when I say, I don't do anything I don't want to do."

Large, remorseful eyes blink at me, and I move my hand to brush her hair off her face and behind her ear. Leaning forward, my lips graze the corner of hers, and she lets out a soft sigh.

"Do you want me to sleep in the other room?" I ask her.

"No, please stay." She scoots closer, tucking her face under my chin and her body right next to mine.

"All right then."

As I wrap my arm around her, her leg tangles between mine. She's so small, but so perfect—too perfect for me, but I guess we'll deal with that another day.

Chapter 8

Camille

I SHOULD BE surprised to wake and find myself in the arms of a guy I've only known for a day, but I'm not. Vaguely, I remember him carrying me inside, and I kind of remember having a conversation with him in the middle of the night, but what I know for certain is I'm glad he's here—really glad.

Closing my eyes, I rub my forehead to try to ease out some of the lingering effects of last night. I know I drank too much, more than I ever have in a social setting before, but no one stopped me. Maybe they understood, or maybe not; I remember the unabashed stares from my father's friends.

At one point in the evening, I had gone to the bathroom to find a few minutes of reprieve, and I was just sitting in a closed stall when a couple women walked in and started talking about me.

"It's really a shame what she did to her family after everything she's put them through and all they've continued to give her. I mean, how ungrateful." The sound of a zipper filled the room as one of them dug through her bag.

"I know, and poor Patrick. Why he ever thought she was going to be good enough for him, I'll never know. He's going places and will ultimately do so much better than her."

And that's the core of it right there: no one has ever thought I was good enough, for anyone or anything. My vision clouded with years of repressed anger. As much as I had felt uncertainty leading up to the wedding, in making the decision to leave this life, these people, I have complete clarity. Everyone has their breaking point, and it turns out I've reached mine. *No more.*

Pushing the stall door open, I walked over to the sink to wash my hands. The two women, both of whom I don't know but have seen at other functions, froze up. My guess is they're the spouses of my father's colleagues, political wives, something I never ever want to be. Looking at them once in the mirror, I tucked a few strands of loose hair behind my ears, smoothed down my dress, and brushed past them as I walked out. Nothing needed to be said. They knew I heard them, and for the first time, I realized I didn't care.

Not caring—such a strange concept to me.

I didn't care about any of it—the politics, the cattiness, the expectations—and for the first time, I felt free.

Letting out a sigh, I release years of unwanted disappointment into my pillow, and Reid's arm tightens around me as he scoots a little closer. He's behind me, cuddling with me, and I like it way more than I should. He's warm, still smells good a day later, and I swear he has the biggest arms I've ever seen.

Patrick and I hardly ever shared a bed, maybe a few times in the beginning because we needed each other, but after a while, that need faded and so did we—or maybe his need didn't, he just satisfied it somewhere else.

Oh, Patrick.

Just thinking about him has me squeezing my eyes shut, wishing for a few more minutes of sleep.

Over and over, I keep asking myself if I'm shocked that I found Patrick cheating, and I'm torn right down the middle. Half of me isn't surprised at all; it's easy to see how he's become that guy. I mean, we attended different colleges, we were hardly ever together, and when we were, it was never fun, never about us. Even I have no problem admitting to being miserable. But, the other half of me is shocked, because I thought I knew him and his character. I've known him my entire life, and we've been together for so long. Where is the respect for me that should come with all that time? I was willing to spend my life with him, giving us all I had, because I thought we were solid. I guess not, and that hurts more than I would like it to.

Sneaking out of the bed, chills run over my bare legs, and I look down to see I'm wearing a large white T-shirt. Relief and gratefulness fill me as I tug down on the hem. I already feel awkward enough about this entire ordeal; I don't need to add being naked in front of Reid without remembering it to the list.

Glancing at the bed, I see he's lying half on top of the covers, on his side, facing me. No shirt, no shoes or socks, just his pants and layers of muscles running underneath the smooth tanned skin of his chest and back. He looks nothing like Patrick, and I find myself visually tracing the lines of his shoulder, neck, and face, hoping to sear it into my memory. My beautiful stranger . . . man, is he something else.

Needing a little space, I brush my teeth, change my clothes, and make my way downstairs to the living room. More than once last night, my mind drifted to Reid's paper airplane, the thoughtfulness in the small gift bringing a smile to my face each time. Finding it by the window, I pick it up, contemplate throwing it to see if it flies, and decide, *Why not?* Pulling my arm back, I flick my wrist and watch as it soars across the room. My heart lifts in joy as it takes flight and also drops the moment it nosedives toward the ground. Racing after it, I grab it to keep it off the floor then put it back on top of the books. It's too perfect, and I plan on keeping it forever.

Glancing out the window, I see the sky is bright blue today, my favorite shade, and I search it for clouds, but there are none. It's vast and bright. Looking around the back yard, I admire all the blooming camellias along the perimeter of the property and watch as a bird lands on an old marble birdbath fountain I found at a garage sale. It's a peaceful morning, a beautiful morning, and for the first time in a long time, I don't feel a loss at the absence of clouds.

Most people have something, that one thing that's a source of constant comfort to put them at ease, and clouds have always been mine. They're always moving, always changing, and their freedom to float by uninhibited soothes me. The thought that somewhere someone else was looking at them too makes me feel like I'm not trapped and alone in this world, but today, I'm not watching the freedom in the sky—I feel it inside me. I feel like I can breathe. I don't know what's going to happen next, don't know if I'll stay here or where I'll go, but I do know that yesterday I made the right decision. Today is a brand-new day; today, I am free.

Feeling inspired, I grab a cup of coffee and head out to my workshop in the carriage house.

The weekend after Grandfather gave me the house, I found myself in the carriage house that wasn't home to cars, but several pieces of old large forgotten furniture. I immediately went to the store and bought a book on restoration, paint remover, a hand sander, wood filler, and a few other things. Hours turned into days, and very quickly I had made a workshop that became my place of solace.

Of course my father hates what I've done with the space and how I'm spending my time, but my grandfather loves it. It's funny how they are so different, yet their professional goals were always the same—the same goals Patrick has. I feel a slight twinge of sorrow for how I've probably set him back quite a while, but then again, maybe he'll rally some sympathy and use this to his advantage. It's in this moment, thinking back to all the conversations we've had about the future and goals, that I realize not once did he or my father ask me about mine. They just assumed they knew best and planned everything for me.

How did things go so wrong?

Walking around a China hutch I recently brought in, I lightly drag my fingers over its newly sanded surface and feel each of the imperfections that make it so unique. I found it in an estate sale over off of Forsyth Park. The only things wrong with the piece are a few scratches on the front leg and the fact that it looks a little outdated. In my mind, I saw it transform to a distressed gray color with chunkier legs, new drawer pulls, and lighting. It's going to be stunning.

Hearing the creak of the back gate, I turn and see Patrick striding into the back yard. My skin starts crawling; what I wouldn't give to have Reid here with me. It's not that I need him here—I can handle Patrick on my own—but there's nothing wrong with wanting some backup.

He stops short when he sees me standing next to the window of the carriage house, likely having expected me to be inside. His eyes widen and then narrow.

"Patrick, what are you doing here?" I ask as he opens the screen door and enters.

"We need to talk," he says, shoving his hands into the pockets of his perfectly creased pants.

"No, we don't. I have nothing to say to you." Attempting to put some distance between us, I move to the little coffee machine I keep in the back corner next to the sink.

"Camille, you can't be serious. Look, I'm sorry you found out about Brittany, I really am, but that's over. It's all over. I need you to stop trying to prove whatever it is you're trying to prove and come back to me."

What *I'm* trying to prove . . . am I trying to prove something? My first thought is no, I just want out, but then I realize yes—yes, I am trying to prove to myself that I'm worth more than this. My life deserves more. Keeping my back to him, I drop a pod into the machine and let my anger boil right along with the water.

"Camille," he says impatiently.

"Patrick, I'm only going to say this once"—I turn to face him—"so you need to listen and listen good: I am never coming back to you, ever. I never should have let this charade go on as long as it did. I'm sorry for you, and I'm very sorry for me, but it's time to let this go. It's time to move on—I have."

I know shoving in his face that I'm now with someone else isn't very nice, but I honestly feel it's the quickest way to end this.

"Charade?" He tilts his head. "You know, two nights ago you were the one who was preaching to me about faithfulness, loyalty, and family. Does that all of a sudden mean nothing to you? Are you really going to choose him over me and your family? I'm truly sorry I hurt you, but you don't want this life, a life with him. I know you—we're cut from the same cloth."

"How do you know what I want? You've never even taken the time to ask me. Everything for the last five years has been about you and your future. Also, in case I need to remind you again, it seems to me I already chose him."

Adding some cream to my coffee, I pick up the mug and walk toward him. I move into his space and he steps back, which is exactly what I want. *Keep going, pal—right out the door.*

His cheeks splotch red as his irritation increases. "You don't even know him! Me, Camille—you've known me your entire life." He throws his hands out.

"You're right, we have known each other a very long time, but you're wrong—I do know him. What on earth would make you think I don't?"

His brows furrow down. He's trying to decide if I'm lying or not, and I find I don't really care. I may not have known Reid for a long length of time, but I do know that in the last thirty-six hours, he's given me kindness, safety, honor, and my freedom. That's more than Patrick has ever given me.

"You've never mentioned him, not once."

"Funny, I could say the same about Brittany," I say quietly, calmly taking a sip of coffee.

"I told you, that's over. Wait . . ." He takes another step back and his eyes pierce me—hard. "Were you with this guy the whole time you were in New York?"

"Does it matter? It's not like you can stand there and all of sudden tell me you were completely faithful in Boston. You'd be a liar, and we both know it. Besides, you've told me plenty of times that I'm not the love of your life."

Guilt flashes across his face and he lets out a deep sigh.

"That's not true. You know I love you. I need you, Camille."

"You love a version of me that doesn't exist. I am not now, nor will I ever be her, and how selfish of you to stand there and tell me you need me. What about what I need? Have you ever thought about that?"

His expression goes blank as he stares at me like I'm a stranger. Reaching up, he rubs the back of his neck then looks around the coach house like it's the first time he's seeing it—and who knows, maybe it is. Just like my father, he's always hated this space, hated that I like to work with my hands. I keep my fingernails unpolished as they'd just chip anyway, and I frequently have calluses. To me, they're proof of something beautiful I've made, but to him, they're a mark of something below us.

Whatever.

They can disapprove all they want.

I didn't care then, and I definitely don't care now.

Chapter 9

Reid

THE SOUND OF a saw or something wakes me. Somewhere nearby there is construction happening, and my eyes burn as it feels way too early in the morning—or maybe it's because I haven't slept much for the past two nights. Squeezing them tight, hoping to relieve some of the tension, I crack my eyes open and see that Camille is gone. I didn't really expect her to be here as things are awkward enough, but a strange and unwanted longing to be near her sinks in.

Rolling to my back, I throw my arm over my face and think about all the shit that happened yesterday. I still can't believe I married a girl I don't know, and part of me expects film cameras to jump out and say, *Just kidding!*

The thing about marriage is I've always considered myself allergic to it—like, break out in hives at the mere suggestion of it—but today, I don't really feel itchy, just more uncomfortable about the unknown. Maybe it's because this marriage is fake, or maybe it's because deep down I know I have nothing to lose . . . like my heart.

Grabbing my phone off the nightstand, I see there are four missed calls from the team's PR director and a ton from my agent.

Shit.

Sitting up, a sense of dread fills me. Despite the fact that I had an out-of-body experience yesterday when I willingly volunteered to be in this position, it never occurred to me to think about how bad the ramifications of this might be for other people in my life. I was singularly focused on her, and now that reality has set in, I know the hammer is about to fall.

A huge part of our team mission is "keepin' it real." We pride ourselves on setting ourselves apart from others in the league by no drugs, no arrests, and no scandal. This definitely has scandal written all over it, and suddenly I feel like this is the walk of shame times a thousand.

Swinging my feet over the edge, I crack my neck and mentally prepare myself for whatever is coming. I tap my agent's name, and he answers on the first ring.

"Hey, Derek," I say, my voice chipper. He knows I know why he's been calling, but I refuse to lessen what yesterday meant to Camille, nor will I bow my head like a child being scolded.

He chuckles, but it doesn't sound friendly—more sarcastic, with an edge to it—and I cringe. "So, I hear congratulations are in order?"

"Good news travels fast," I say with a pleased and upbeat tone. There's no need for him to make this more than what it is, and I will not feel bad about it."Want to tell me what's going on?" He sips from a drink and there's a clunk as he sets it down.

What's going on? That's very similar to the question I've been asking myself for the last two days, and if I had a solid answer I would give it to him, but I don't. I don't feel like explaining myself, and I also don't want to make things worse for her. The expression *less is more* is the best approach here.

"Not really." As much as being shoved into the public eye comes with the territory of playing a sport on a professional level, this is nobody's business, end of story. I rub my free hand across my thigh to shake off some of the uneasiness this conversation is provoking in me.

"Is she pregnant?"

A laugh breaks free and echoes around the room. Kids are great and all, but since I never planned on getting married, I've never really thought about them. In fact, I've spent years making sure all precautions were in place to prevent them.

"Not that I'm aware of." My eyes skip to the wedding dress hanging on the back of the door and then to the one she wore last night, which is draped over the back of a chair. Both dresses fit her like a glove, and she looked incredible.

He lets out a sigh. "Well, that's good. I'm not going to lie, I'm shocked."

This is the reaction I'm going to get from most everyone. Yes, I'm shocked, too, but I can't help but wonder if their shock is because they've not heard of us together, or because they have a hard time believing we'd end up together—someone like her with someone like me.

"You and me both," I mutter.

"You're aware of the organizational policies, Reid. They don't make allowances, as you know." Although the ink is barely dry on my five-year contract, that doesn't mean much if they view me as a wildcard and a liability to the team. There's always someone waiting in the wings, ready to prove how hungry they are and how replaceable we are.

"I do." It's the second time in two days I've said these words, and whereas yesterday was spontaneous and all for her, today feels leaded with expectations and is all about me.

"Here's what's going to happen: I've spoken to your publicist and the organization's PR department, and everyone is in agreement on releasing a statement about you and your new bride. We are very happy for you both, and we respect the privacy you've requested since the very beginning of your relationship and encourage others to do the same. We wish you and Mrs. Jackson a long and happy marriage."

"We appreciate that, Derek." *We.* I've never been a *we* with anyone in my life. "If you need anything, you know how to find me."

"Will do." He hangs up.

Fuck me.

What the hell do I do now?

Think, Reid. Think.

Pacing the room, I run my hand over my face and shake my head. People are going to blow this situation out of proportion, and instead of viewing me as some type of chivalrous hero, they'll paint me as a public embarrassment. I did a good thing for her, but somehow it has already turned into a bad thing for me.

That's when I see it: a five-by-seven framed photograph sitting on top of the nightstand on her side of the bed.

Picking it up, I study the two girls in the picture. Both are wearing dance clothes, like they've just come from practice, and they're both the same height and shape. This has to be Camille with her sister; they both look young, but that's where the similarities stop.

Camille's hair is pulled tightly in a bun on top of her head, her feet are in a dance position, and she's smiling at the camera with that expression she wears to play the proper part. She looks a little different, but it's still her; it must be the age difference. The other girl, however, has her hair dyed cotton candy pink, it's in a sloppy ponytail, she's not standing any way in particular except her arm is thrown around Camille, and her head is thrown back with her eyes squeezed shut as she's laughing. Camille is gorgeous—she can't help but be—but my eyes keep drifting to the sister. Whatever she's laughing at, I find I want to laugh with her.

I think back to the guests at the wedding and the other bridesmaids. Did I see this girl there? Maybe I did, I don't know. I was so focused on Camille, a herd of elephants could have run through and I wouldn't have noticed.

Also, if she was dying her hair pink at this age, rebelling against her upbringing, there's no telling what she looks like now. Good for her for getting out and doing her own thing. I can't say I blame her for not wanting to stick around for last night.

Putting down the frame, I walk over to the window, look down at the carriage house, and see them.

Oh, hell no.

I'm up here trying to figure out how I'm going to deal with this shitstorm I've just landed myself in and she's down there with him? No way. Anger ripples across my skin as I grab my shirt, throw it on, and head down the stairs and out the back door.

Neither one of them hears me approach, and I know I should interrupt their conversation, but I don't. Instead, I lean against the wall between the door and the window, giving me just a small view of them, and eavesdrop. I've officially stooped to a new low.

After we shut him out yesterday, he and Camille haven't had a chance to talk. I realize they need to, and hopefully he'll hear her loud and clear. Also, if she has any lingering doubt about leaving this guy, I need to know.

"I can't believe you're doing this," he says animatedly. "All our plans!"

"Again, all *your* plans," she counters. "You stopped including me years ago."

Throwing his hands on his hips, he lets out a deep sigh, and a tense silence hovers over them as they stare at each other, neither backing down.

Using this opportunity, I take a good look at him to try to see what it is she liked in the first place. Sure, he's tall, but there's hardly any muscle on him. He's dressed nicely, if you like that country club collared shirt look, but there's something about him that's not right. Maybe it's because he's found himself in a situation he doesn't want to be in, but he seems on edge, anxious and antsy.

"Whatever. We'll figure this out." He crosses his arms over his chest like his decision on this is final.

Hate seeps into my veins, and Camille and I simultaneously ball our hands into fists.

"No, we won't! God, I'm so sick of this. No more, Patrick. No. More." She takes two steps away from him, but all he does is smirk as if what she just said has no bearing on reality.

"I really don't know what's gotten into you. You've never talked this way or behaved like this. You know better, so shaking off whatever this is sooner rather than later will definitely be in your best interest. You know what all of this means to families like ours, and now we're going to have to clean up another one of your messes. Enough. Also, I've told you before—stop dressing like this." He waves his finger up and down. "What if someone sees you?"

She looks down at her clothes, and so do I. What's wrong with what she's wearing? Tiny denim shorts show off her gorgeous toned legs, and the black tank top says *Plié Jeté Chassé Every Day*. Her hair is pulled up in a messy bun and she has a bandana rolled up and tied around her head. She looks hot.

Her eyes meet his, and her cheeks flush red with anger.

"Leave," she grits through her teeth as she points to the door.

"She wouldn't want you to be doing this."

Who is *she*? Who wouldn't want her to be doing this? I can't imagine anyone who knows Camille and loves her would want this life for her.

"That's rich coming from you, because I know this is exactly what she would want me to do."

I do love how she's not backing down. She may be little, but she's got fire in her that shows her strength.

"Fine. I'll leave, but this isn't over. You and him will never work, and the minute it ends, I'll be here to pick up the pieces."

"Patrick, for the last time, you need to hear me when I say you and I are done. There will never be an us. No more. Never again."

"I wouldn't be so sure of that if I were you. Your father will be here soon enough. He's already working to clean up your mess, and he spoke to Judge Williams about destroying that whipped up marriage certificate your grandfather produced. Thank God the press hasn't caught wind of this yet so there's still time."

Her father's on his way? Just great. Is it even possible to just destroy a signed and registered document? I don't think so, but then again, I know nothing about this world or these types of people. They can probably do whatever they want and no one would bat an eye. Whatever. She and I will figure it out, and I've officially heard enough.

"Time for what?" I ask as I stride into the room, purposely bumping into Patrick as I head straight for Camille. "Morning, princess." I cup the side of her face and run my finger across her jaw and down the side of her neck. Taking a few seconds to soak her in, I scan over her features to make sure she's okay, and her big eyes light up with relief at the sight of me. My heart thumps hard within my chest. *Damn.* Leaning down, I press a kiss to the corner of her mouth, and her cheeks turn up as she smiles.

Patrick doesn't answer, and I can feel him watching us. As we turn back to address him, his face has shifted into a deep scowl and hate is pouring off him.

"You had better have a really good reason for being here the morning after our wedding." I pin him with a fierce glare and drape my arm around Camille to pull her close. She wraps her arm around my waist.

His eyes widen just a bit but then narrow as he takes us in. He's confused, just like I'm sure the rest of the world will be given our backgrounds and our current lifestyles. Nothing about the two of us looks like we fit together, and I understand that, but somehow we do. She fits perfectly tucked into my side, and I like it.

"You do realize her father will never stand for this," he says, his words shooting daggers at me.

Camille's fingers dig into my side as she grips me hard. As much as I've never considered marriage to be on my radar, let alone getting a father's approval, I think it's normal to want it. Isn't getting it like a rite of passage? It says, *You're good enough.*

Patrick has hit below the belt, and he doesn't even know it.

"Well, it's a good thing I never asked him, and you need to realize . . ." I step away from Camille and stalk toward him. His face blanches, but he straightens his back to stand his ground. "I. Don't. Care."

"Do you have any idea the kind of people you're messing with?" he spits out at me.

I snort and one side of my mouth tips up. Someone else might find that line intimidating, but this guy has no idea the shit I've seen or where I come from.

I crack my knuckles and flex my fingers. He watches the movement as I lean over to get closer to his face. "Leave."

He opens his mouth to say something as his eyes bounce back and forth between me and Camille, but then he changes his mind, turns on his heel, and strides for the door.

"Oh, and, Patty." I move back to Camille, pull her in front of me, and wrap my arms around her. "You'll be happy to know my publicist and my team's PR department have already issued a formal statement congratulating us. Cat's out of the bag now, and we couldn't be happier." I dip down and kiss her cheek. She pushes back against me, wanting to be closer, and I feel her smile against my lips.

"This isn't over." He gives Camille a lingering angry look before he walks out and the gate slams behind him.

Camille and I stand there in silence. Glancing down, I see anguish is written on her face, but I don't know at what. Is she upset that he's upset, that the world will know she's tied to me, or that his threat of it not being over may have some weight to it?

"Did they really issue a statement?" She leans her head back against my shoulder.

"They did. Are you okay with that?"

She smells so freaking good, like strawberries and vanilla. It's almost distracting.

"I guess I have to be." She turns, wraps her arms around my waist, and tucks her face into my chest. "Thank you, Reid."

As I rub my hand up and down her back, the tension slips away from her as she leans farther into me. I've hugged women over the years, but never like this, where they really settle in. It's nice.

Scanning the carriage house over her shoulder, I spot the saw that woke me. It's sitting on a large drop cloth next to a power sander and several other pieces of equipment.

"What's all this?"

She pulls back and I tip my head, surveying the room.

"It's my workshop." She smiles excitedly and looks around to see what I'm seeing.

"Workshop," I mumble. "Do you do all this yourself or do you have someone do it for you?" Around the perimeter are beautifully finished pieces covered with a light layer of dust.

"I do. I love transforming furniture people don't want anymore into something fresh and exciting."

My eyes stop on two headboards leaning against the far wall. Both are wooden, and where one looks like it belongs in a grandmother's house, the other has been stained darker, a fancy ivory padded fabric has been added between the posts, and it looks tacked down with large ornate bolts.

"What do you do with them when they're done?"

"I consign them in shops around town and up into Charleston," she says proudly.

"Really? So this is like a hobby of yours?"

Her face drops at the way I've described something she clearly loves, and she turns away to pick up the tools she was using.

"I guess you could call it that." So quickly she went from being animated to defeated. I'm certain I can guess who's made her react this way.

"Don't do that."

"Do what?" She picks up her cup of coffee and takes a drink.

"Downplay something you love just because it's new to me. Tell me about this. What would you call it? I mean, I know nothing about you other than you were dancing in New York, friends with my brother, and marrying an asshole."

She looks at me and her eyes flare with a tiny bit of the fire I've seen rise up in her. She's mentally debating how much she wants to share with me, and I'm hoping she'll share it all. Setting down her cup, she faces me and stands tall.

"This is something I think about almost every minute I'm awake. It's more than just a hobby to me, so I don't know what I would call it. I love working with my hands, building, creating, taking things no one wants and turning them into something beautiful."

"I know what I would call it: your dream job. I think this sounds great."

She lets out a sigh.

"If this is your passion, why were you dancing in New York?"

"It was expected." She frowns and redoes her hair on top of her head.

Walking to her coffee, I pick it up and take a sip. It's cold; she's been out here for a while.

"Have you always done what's expected of you?" I'm trying not to judge her, but it's kind of hard.

Pressing her lips together, she takes the coffee out of my hands and moves to a coffeemaker that's sitting on a countertop near the back. "No." She doesn't elaborate, just brews another cup, and steam floats out the top.

"Sugar?"

"No, just cream."

She pours it in, stirs, and then walks the cup back to me.

"Thank you."

She nods.

"So, what were you doing before you came to Savannah?"

she asks, changing the subject as she jumps up and sits on top of the dresser she's currently working on. Her feet dangle and she swings her legs. I'm momentarily distracted and clear my throat.

"Not much, since it's the offseason for us. Mostly we spend time catching up on things that are put on the backburner during the year, like traveling. Some get married"—I wink at her—"and others have businesses or charities they run on the side. I'm involved with the Boys and Girls Club of Tampa Bay, which is where I've been spending most of my time, but I don't have to report anywhere until the third week of April."

"Kids, wow. Do you want kids one day?"

I laugh and she smiles along with me. "No. I never plan on getting married or having kids."

Her smile drops. "You don't want to get married one day?"

"No."

There are at least a dozen questions sitting on the tip of her tongue, but she doesn't ask them. Even if she did, I wouldn't answer.

Taking a sip of the coffee, I walk over and lean on the table closest to her. "Have you given any thought to what you want to happen next?"

She lets out a long, slow sigh. "I have, but honestly, I just don't know. For so long I've had this vision of what my life was going to be, and now I feel like I've dumped everything into a blender and things are all muddled and undefined. There's my family, Patrick, and my life here, but now I've been given the opportunity to do and be what I want, and I don't know if this is it anymore. I just need a little more time to figure out how to manage this mess I've made."

"How much time?" I ask, probably a little too quickly, and she misinterprets my question.

Guilt slips across her features and she shrugs her shoulders. She doesn't want to ask, and I'm pretty sure she doesn't feel she has a right to, but what she doesn't realize is this just might work out for both of us. "Honestly, I don't know. I'm the one inconveniencing your life, so you tell me. Whatever you want, whenever you want, I'll do it."

I cross my arms over my chest and decide to just lay it all on the line. "Turns out, the team's PR department doesn't like to be blindsided. The owners and management of our team have a zero tolerance policy for drama or scandal of any kind, and apparently, me marrying a senator's daughter on a whim is just that."

She flinches.

"I stand behind what I said last night—nothing has to be decided today—but . . . how does two months sound?"

"Two months?" Her brows shoot up. I had been worried she would say no, but with that reaction, it might be a yes.

"That's how long I have until I report to offseason training camp. Once I leave, we can figure out the details then—quietly."

"I'm sorry you're stuck in this position." She frowns.

"Don't be. I went into this willingly, and besides, it doesn't have to be a bad thing. I think spending two months with you could be fun. I mean, why wouldn't it be? I train a lot—football is my life—but we have nowhere we need to be, and it'll give you some time to figure things out."

"I really do need time." She breaks eye contact with me and looks at the ground, and that's when I see it: she feels alone, and what she really needs is a friend.

Moving to stand in front of her, I throw my hand out to shake hers. Confusion slips onto her face, but she slides hers into mine. "Hello, my name is Reid. It's nice to finally meet you."

She laughs and my chest tightens.

"Camille. It's nice to meet you too." Her blue eyes lock onto mine and tingles race up my arm from the hand touching hers. "So, we're going to do this?" she asks, looking at me with a mixture of wariness and awe.

"Seems like we already are." I should let go of her hand, but I don't. Instead, I step closer and link our fingers together.

Tilting her head to the side, she looks at me—really looks at me. "I know why I am, but why are you?"

That's a good question, and I can't answer it. Shrugging my shoulders, I answer her with a smile and throw out another idea with a hopeful expression.

"I know this might sound crazy, but what do you say about going on a honeymoon?"

Chapter 10

Camille

SOMETIME DURING THE night, Reid's car and things were dropped at my house. In less than an hour, he's changed into a worn pair of jeans, a long-sleeved T-shirt, and athletic shoes. I have my bags packed, and we're on our way. Although we're calling this a honeymoon, we both know what we're really doing is running away. I'm running from my father, Patrick, and years of passive aggressive comments, but I'm not sure what he's running from, unless he's just running from my father too. The thought makes me giggle, and he glances over at me.

"What?" he asks, his lips curling up along with mine.

"Nothing, I just think we're crazy."

"Nothing wrong with that." His left hand stays on the wheel as his right stretches out to grasp the headrest of my seat. Blues music plays through the speakers, and though I haven't given any thought to the type of music he listens to, this was unexpected. It's nice, and it suits him.

"I feel spontaneous and reckless. This is so not like me," I tell him. It used to be, but I haven't been that girl in a long time.

"Really? What are you like then?" His hand slips down to the back of my neck and his fingers tangle in my hair. I'm surprised by this, and then not at all. We don't know each other, but since he found me in the library, it's been so easy to touch one another, and I like it.

"Boring. Predictable." I rub my hands down my thighs. Knowing we were going to be in the car for several hours, I threw on a pair of jeans and a large, loose T-shirt that likes to slip off one shoulder.

"Ha, I find that hard to believe."

"Believe it."

"Well, I hate to break it to you, sweetheart, as adventurous as you're feeling and all, but we're headed to my place, and other than the view, I assure you it's very boring."

His place. For all intents and purposes, he's a stranger, and I probably shouldn't be traveling five hours away from my home to go to an unknown place without any form of transportation to escape by. Strangely enough, I'm not nervous, not about him at least, more just about the uncertainty of what happens next—next in my life, next in my career, next with my family, and next with him.

The ringing of his cell phone blares through the speakers, and on the console it flashes the name Mom. He winces, removes his hand from my neck, and then glances over at me as he picks it up through Bluetooth. I miss his warm fingers.

"Hey, Mom." There's affection in his tone, and I smile to myself. There's something about a guy who loves his mother; it's endearing, sexy.

"I've waited two hours. Two. Hours, Reid, and I can't wait any longer. I know you think because I'm almost twice your age I don't understand technology, but I do. Twitter alerts about you have been going off all morning, and it seems the world knew you got married before I did. Married, Reid! Explain."

"First off, calm down. Second, say hi to Camille. She's sitting next to me in the car and you're on speaker." He glances at me, his face filled with apology.

"Good morning, Camille. From the posted pictures, you looked beautiful yesterday. Too bad my son didn't invite me!"

"It's not like that." He lets out a sigh. "Look, we didn't plan this. Without getting into all the details, just know this is temporary and a means to an end."

"For who?"

"For me, Ms. Jackson." I can't sit here and say nothing while she berates him. "Reid is helping me, and I'm incredibly grateful."

There's a pause. "Are you in some kind of trouble?" She doesn't sound put off, more like she's gone into mama bear mode.

"Not anymore. At least I don't think so," I answer honestly.

"Well, did Reid tell you we know people? You just say the word."

A laugh escapes me, and Reid smiles. She doesn't even know me, but she's already got my back. Apparently, the apple doesn't fall far from the tree.

"All right, Mom, we're going to go. We can talk about this more later, but if you're asked, we'd appreciate if you played along that this is real."

"Son, if papers were signed, it's real."

My chest tightens and I glance at Reid, but he keeps his eyes on the road, his face expressionless.

"Camille, if you ever need anything, you can call me any time."

"Thank you, Ms. Jackson. I really appreciate that." More than she'll ever know.

"You two stay safe." And then she hangs up.

"Sorry, she can be a little intense."

"I think she's great. My mother would never call me—these types of conversations are left for my father."

"Speaking of intense . . ." He slides his eyes briefly over to mine, eyebrows raised.

My father was in rare form last night. He never loses his composure when there are people around, and he shocked us all.

"You have no idea. That was just a tiny glimpse of my life, and that was tame."

His lips press into a thin line; he doesn't like that.

My phone pings with an incoming text. Pulling it out of my bag, I see there are twenty-two messages from Patrick, and I frown.

"What does it say?" he asks me, glancing over at my phone.

"That he and my father want to speak to me at noon, privately." I flip the phone over so it's face down and hold it against my leg. I'm hiding it from myself even though I've already seen it. I wish I could un-see it.

A weighted silence falls over us, and Reid's hand tightens on top of the steering wheel.

"Do you want to talk to them?" he asks without facing me.

"No." To further prove my point, I power off my phone and toss it back into my bag.

"They're persistent, that's for sure."

"More like not used to not getting their way."

Clare's words from yesterday strike a chord within me. She was right; I shouldn't have relied so heavily on moral responsibility. They were coercing me and have been for a long time. Sure, they played it off as doing my part for the family, but that's not what families do, and I was never the girl to play along. I always did things my way—when did that change? And why did I allow it?

"So, was your mom serious? Does she actually know people?"

"If I told you, I'd have to kill you." He chuckles and winks. "I am from the Bronx."

"The Bronx—that's where you grew up?"

He looks over at me skeptically. "Yeah. Didn't you and Nate ever talk about things like this?"

"No. I knew he was from the city, but it never really came up. Don't get me wrong, I consider him a friend, but we really didn't talk about stuff like that. At least he didn't with me."

"What did you talk about?" His words are monotone. I knew the subject of Nate was going to come up sooner or later, and it's better that it's now. I don't want him to think he's crossed any line between him and his brother when he hasn't.

"Day-to-day stuff—school, ballet, tennis, our friends." Reaching over, I lay my hand on his leg, which is packed with very hard muscles, and he covers it with his own. "Reid, I love Nate and think he's a great guy, but I don't want there to be any confusion about my friendship with him. It was strictly platonic and really only social. I didn't get together with him outside of our friends, didn't talk to him on the phone. It wasn't like that."

"Okay." He squeezes once then links his fingers through mine.

And so begins five hours of driving. He continues to hold my hand as one phone call after another rolls in, the ringing constantly echoing throughout the car, causing me more anxiety than I care to admit: Beau, his friends, his agent, teammates, the team's PR department, his publicist, sponsors, news reporters, magazine reporters—you name it. It's imagining what my phone will be like when I turn it back on that has tension tightening every muscle across my shoulders. In less than twenty-four hours, I've gone from feeling trapped to free, and now, after hours of this—the many, many phone calls—followed.

A few times, I feel Reid's gaze on me, but I just stare out the window. Eventually, he's had enough, gets tired of telling the same story over and over again and turns his cell off, too. The freedom I feel from both of us being disconnected from the world is exhilarating, and a deep sigh I didn't know I was holding in escapes me. If only this could last.

Walking into the sunken living room of his condo, I run my fingers over a thick burgundy plush blanket that's thrown across the back of his couch. I expected a bachelor pad, but this—this is so much more. Dark wood floors with pale gray walls, leather furniture, and silver accents are laid out before us. It looks like it's straight out of a Restoration Hardware catalog; it looks perfect.

"Wow, so this is where you live?" I ask, taking a full spin to get a good look at everything. There are windows stretching across the back wall, giving him the most beautiful view of the city and the water behind it, an open floor plan, a modern kitchen with a white marble breakfast bar, and a chunky wooden six-person dining room set. Of course there's a huge flat-screen TV mounted over a decorative gas fireplace, and the walls are covered with black and white photos of different styles of planes, a few city scenes, and a blues musician—the same musician playing the saxophone, the piano, and the bass guitar.

"Yep," he says, setting our bags down behind the couch. "A friend of mine, Jack, another player on our team, lives across the hall. This unit had just opened up, so right after I signed with the team, he approached me about checking it out. Living near another player makes things easier when it comes to practices, meetings, and games. Plus, it's nice to be near a friend."

"I can totally understand that. I lived on the Upper East Side of Central Park and school was on the west, so no one lived near me. The commute was lonely."

"Do you miss it? The city and the dancing?" he asks as he walks into the kitchen and grabs two glasses, filling them both with water from the refrigerator.

"Yes, but at the same time, no."

"Really? Why?" He's moved back in front of me and is handing me the second glass of water.

"I love dancing, but it was always more of Clare's thing. I just tagged along over the years to be with her, and then one thing led to another and I ended up in New York City. It's like once I was thrown on the path, I couldn't get off."

"Was Clare with you in New York?" He takes a sip of the water and then licks his lips . . . lips that have kissed me.

"No." I clear my throat and glance away. She was supposed to be there, supposed to be the one dancing her life away, not me. I think about our family, the endless expectations just for the sake of appearances, and I frown. My father was so happy when I told him I would pursue dance. He said, "The continued discipline and grace ballet requires will serve you well, especially when you become a politician's wife." Only, I never wanted to be a politician's wife; he just neglected to ask me, or even care.

"I think I saw a picture of her in your room. You're with another girl, you're both younger, and she has pink hair. She looks like you, but she was laughing, so I couldn't be sure."

I know what picture he's talking about. I love that picture of us. Every time I see it I think about putting out a few more, but something always holds me back and I don't.

"Yes, that's my sister in that photo. We're actually twins—identical."

"Really? I didn't see it, but I guess I saw the personalities more than the features."

Personalities. Within five minutes of meeting us, our personalities made us look drastically different. One of us was perfect; the other was the black sheep.

"You'd see it if she were next to me, and it actually goes one step further—we aren't just twins, we're mirror twins."

"What does that mean?"

"It means we have identical but asymmetric features. When I stare in the mirror, I see her. See this?" She points to the dimple on her right cheek. "On Clare, it's on her left cheek. She writes with her right hand, I write with my left. She's more right-brained and I'm more left. Experts say our personalities are more based on life experiences, but I don't know. It just seems like we're opposite in every way."

"Huh," he mumbles, thinking about this and studying me, the different features in my face. "What's she doing now?"

I shrug my shoulders and take a sip of the water to cool off the emotions trying to settle in. "Whatever she wants."

"That doesn't seem fair." His lips press into a thin line, and I realize I'm staring at them.

Moving to the kitchen, I pull out a stool at the bar and sit down. "Well, you know what they say—life isn't fair. Really, though, I was just trying to do right by my family."

Reid follows and takes the seat next to me. "I understand that. Growing up, my mother used to work long hours during the day—well, 'used to' isn't right, because she still does. I have a little sister, Tally. She's thirteen years younger than me. She was unexpected, but I can't imagine our family without her."

"Nate's mentioned her. He helps your mother sometimes," I tell him.

"I know. Tally tells me." He smiles. "I had hoped after I signed with an NFL team she would cut back some with work, and she did a little, but not enough for my liking. I asked her once why she continues to kill herself day in and day out, and all she said was, 'I don't take handouts from no one.' I don't consider me contributing to our family a handout, but in her defense, she's never been able to depend on anyone else for any stability. Maybe I'm like her, but I find that to be a strength in character, not a flaw."

"What does she do?"

"She's a nurse at Calvary Hospital."

I'm not exactly sure where that is. I spent a year and a half in New York City and not once did I venture outside of Manhattan into the other boroughs.

"Well, I think you're both right," I tell him. "There's nothing wrong with wanting to contribute to your family's well-being, but at the same time, there's something to be said for accomplishing things on your own and the pride one has in that."

"Pride always comes with a cost."

"Tell me about it." My eyes meet his and he frowns again at whatever he sees there.

Reaching over, he lays a hand on top of my arm. It's warm, and my skin burns from the contact; I like him touching me.

"You know everything is going to be okay, right?" The soft tenor of his voice and the kindness he continues to offer have my eyes stinging. His thumb swipes back and forth, and I forcefully swallow the lump forming in my throat.

"I do . . . eventually. In the end, this too shall pass."

"It will." He gives me a small, encouraging smile. "Is there anything I can do to help you?"

A laugh escapes me. "As if you haven't done enough already. I'm going to be in debt to you for years to come."

"No, you aren't." He pulls his hand away and leans back in the chair, propping his foot on the bottom rung of mine. "I told you, I don't do anything I don't want to do." He picks up his glass and guzzles the rest of the water down.

"Thank you, Reid."

"At some point you're going to have to stop thanking me." He nods, wanting me to agree with him.

"Maybe." A blush creeps up into my cheeks and I shrug my shoulders.

"You've got this—I know you do." His green eyes penetrate into mine. He's so confident, so sure of himself, it's hard not to believe him, and this support from him makes me feel like maybe I do.

"I know, it's just everything feels gray and foggy. I can't see what happens next, and I don't like that. I have so much I need to figure out, so many conversations to have, and that leaves me uneasy."

"Well, like we said yesterday, nothing has to be decided today."

"I can't believe it's only been twenty-four hours. I still can't believe I walked away from him, from them."

"Believe it. There's plenty of time to think things through. The ball's in your court now, and I'm on your team. You can stay here as long as you want."

"On my team." I grin at him.

His lips tip up, and his eyes sparkle at me, smiling. "What can I say? I'm a sports guy through and through."

Chapter 11

Reid

IT'S WEIRD TO have a girl here in my condo. Other than my mother and sister, Camille's the first one. Granted, I've only lived here for a year, so that's not a lot of time to make a ton of memories, but still, no matter where I am, I have strict rules about not bringing dates home. From the very first day I walked onto the field at Syracuse, I've been warned and heard enough stories to know that nothing good can come from women knowing where you live. It creates extra drama, and quite frankly, there's the issue of security.

But, after this morning, it's security that I'm wanting for her. I don't know why that guy thought it would be okay to come over and walk into her home the morning after our wedding, but hearing her father had the same plan was all I needed to suggest leaving.

I understand they don't know me and aren't happy with how things went down, but to have such a complete lack of respect for her boundaries—and hell, even mine—means the answer is no and always will be no. We do not need that in our lives, period.

I've just given Camille a tour of the rest of the condo and showed her which room will be hers when the front door opens, slams against the wall, and in rushes Zeus. Large black paws thunder against the ground and a floppy tongue heads straight for me—that is, until he sees Camille and changes his course, sliding across the hardwood floor.

"Reeeeid," she yells while backing up, eyes big and frantically looking for an exit plan.

"Zeus, no!" I command, but it doesn't matter. The seventy-pound fur ball leaps into the air, slams into Camille's chest, and they both go flying backward. She ducks her head and rolls into the fetal position to keep from being trampled.

"Oh my God! I'm so sorry." Jack and I both move at the same time. He runs over and grabs Zeus by the collar as he drowns Camille in slobbery kisses. Giggles and squeals peal out from under him as I bend down and pick her up. The dog is almost as big as she is.

"It's okay, no worries." She laughs, wiping her face off before moving to scratch behind his ears. His tail thumps hard on the floor, and I swear the dog is smiling at her.

"Dude, what are you doing here?" I shake my head and give him a look that straight up tells him I'm pissed.

"Zeus heard you come in and wanted to say hi." He shrugs his shoulders then narrows his eyes, as if to say, *What the hell is going on?* I ignore him and instead glare at the dog, who really does look happy to see me. The fury coursing through me recedes, and I squat down so Zeus can pad over and get some love.

Jack and I have always had an open door policy, but now that she's here, it needs to be amended. "Whatever. Camille, this is Jack." I stand and wave at him. "Jack, Camille."

She steps forward and holds out her hand. "Hi. It's nice to meet you."

He looks at her hand, chuckles, and then pulls her into a giant hug as he plants a huge kiss on her cheek. She again squeals and I abruptly move to pull her out of his arms and into mine. She feels so small up next to me, so foreign. Not only do I not bring girls home, I never cuddle with them either, not in private or in public. It gives them the wrong impression, but with Camille, it's different. *She* is different.

"What the hell." I glare at him.

"Just showing the lady here where Zeus gets it from." He grins and she smiles back, one of her real smiles, not the stiff socialite expression.

"Well, stop. Not cool." I rub my free hand across my hip to shake off some of the uneasiness I just felt. All of this is pushing my senses into overdrive, and I feel out of control. We may have played the part yesterday and slept together last night, but touching her is not something I'm used to, and yet I can't seem to stop.

"So, the rumors are true then?" He eyes Camille and looks at both of our left hands, his brows furrowing just a little. "You got married."

He says this as a statement, but his eyes are locked onto mine, his gaze questioning. Jack is my best friend, has been since the day I joined the team. We're with each other daily, and I do mean every single day. If anyone on the team would be suspicious of this marriage and know something is up, it would be him.

"I did."

"Wow, none of us saw this coming, especially me. I thought you were going to see your brother." His tone is a mixture of irritation and disappointment. "I mean, shit, man, I live across the hall from you, know just about everything there is to know about you, and not once have I seen you bring a girl home, much less her." He waves his fingers in her direction almost dismissively.

Camille drops her head and moves an inch closer to me, pressing her side up against mine. I know she feels guilty about me finding myself in this situation with her, and now she's witnessing some of the fallout. She doesn't want the people in my life to be upset with me.

Jack sees her subtle movement and his eyebrows rise in alarm. "No." He throws out his hands. "I didn't mean it like that—I wasn't saying you and him . . . ugh," he groans. "It's just Reid is a private person, and well, I thought I knew him really well, so I'm just not sure what to think of this."

"You really don't need to think anything of it. Just say congratulations." I nod, glaring at him, hoping he picks up on my cues. I'll give him just enough details later to pacify him. He doesn't need to know the whole story; no one does.

There's a weighted pause as he assesses us, and Camille's hand moves around my back and twists in my shirt over my waist. He sees her wrap herself around me, and then all of a sudden his face relaxes and transforms.

"Of course, man. I'm so happy for you both. Congratulations." He smiles at us, his eyes drifting to her, and my arm tightens around her shoulders. She smiles back shyly, and my heart thumps hard in my chest.

She's smiling at him again with one of her real smiles. Jealousy spikes through me that he's on the receiving end of it, and I know this is not good. I shouldn't be caring who she smiles at. She's not mine, at least not really, so it shouldn't matter.

"So, do you have any friends?" he asks, winking at her.

She giggles and Zeus's tail starts thumping against the floor at the sound. He's moved from me to her, to sit at her feet.

"Well, that didn't take you long," I say, shaking my head.

"What! Doesn't hurt to ask." He grins.

"I do, but they're spoken for. Sorry." She shrugs her shoulders and places one hand on my chest. Reaching up, I grab her hand and hold it to me. The move is familiar, kind of intimate. Jack sees it but doesn't say anything more that might upset her. For that, I'll have to buy him a beer next time we're out.

"She has a twin sister." I smirk at him. Camille is gorgeous, and I know he sees that.

"Really!" His eyebrows shoot straight up. "Identical?" He's looking at her so hopefully.

"Yes," she answers.

He clutches his heart like he's in pain. "Please, please, please tell me she's coming to visit."

"She's not," Camille answers tentatively.

"Damn, that's too bad. Well, if she does, tell her to come not this weekend but next. Bryan texted me earlier—mark your calendars, Billy is hosting a newlywed party for y'all."

"Of course he is," I mutter.

I'm trying hard not to feel annoyed, wanting to be appreciative instead. Billy is one of the nicest guys I have ever met. Instead of a team mom, he's like a team dad, and he's always doing things for the guys, remembering birthdays and other random stuff. Plus, his wife, Missy, is just the sweetest. I was just hoping to keep this marriage a little more on the down-low, not shove it out in the open so much.

"I'll text him later and thank him."

Then it occurs to me: the team PR representative will probably be there, and this will satisfy the higher-ups. It'll get them off my back, at least for now. Billy suddenly becomes one of my favorite people.

"All right, I'll get out of the way, but tomorrow we need to be in the gym by seven."

"Yeah, I'm in." I haven't been in two days and I can feel the stalled energy building up in my system. I need to work out, and hard.

"Come on, Zeus, it's time for a walk." The dog's ears perk up and he trots to the door. "We'll catch y'all later." With a flick of his wrist, they're gone, and the door slams behind him.

"I'm sorry about that." I release Camille and step away from her.

"Don't be. He seems nice." She runs her hand through her hair, and the scent of coconut drifts my way.

"He is nice. We're kind of like roommates who aren't actually roommates. I'll make sure he doesn't walk in again, just in case."

Her cheeks turn a nice shade of pink, but she smiles at me gratefully. Really, I just want her to feel comfortable here. I want her to feel like my home is her home, at least while she's staying in it.

"So what do we do now?" she asks, looking around and eyeing the couch. After the shitstorm of communication I've received today, plus Patrick this morning and on her phone—which she hasn't made a move to power back on—it's obvious neither of us wants to leave.

"How do you feel about a Netflix binge and food delivery?"

She lights up. "Sounds perfect. I think I'll change my clothes first and get more comfortable."

The thought of her taking her clothes off just one room away has me fisting my hands. Images of her from last night flash through my mind, and I swallow at the thought of touching her bare skin again. Swallowing down the desire that just came over me, I inwardly scold myself. This girl doesn't need me adding to her already confusing situation or making her feel awkward. As I realized this morning, she needs a friend—just a friend. "Yeah, I'll do the same."

"Thank you, Reid." She smiles, and I can't help but watch as she walks down the hallway and disappears into her room.

Chapter 12

Camille

THROUGH THE WALLS of the condo, I hear Reid's alarm go off. It's six-thirty. In. The. Morning. This is the start of my new routine. I say mine, because I'm pretty certain he already maintained this schedule before I showed up.

Every morning he starts his day with a huge helping of scrambled eggs, vegetables, and a protein shake, a breakfast he's previously made and portioned out. Then he's out the door and off to the team's training facility with Jack. Four and a half hours later they return and he makes another huge protein shake. After that, he and Jack watch game films of other teams and specific players. Usually they eat lunch together then both head off to take a nap. For dinner, I cook for us, not because I feel I have to, but because he's been so kind to me and I want to. We eat dinner, watch some TV, and then head off to bed.

I've never given much thought to what it's like being a professional athlete, but he's extremely dedicated to his career and his lifestyle. From the hours he puts in and the amount of sleep he gets to the total ratio of grams of protein, carbohydrates, and fat, he's totally committed, and I see why he said he doesn't have time for relationships. Plus, this is just the offseason.

As for me, I don't know what I'm doing.

We got here on Sunday, and now it's Friday.

Day after day, I wander around his condo, looking at his things. I try to keep my stuff hidden and out of his way; he was so kind to bring me here, and I don't want to implode his life or wear out my welcome. I've admired all the little things he has that make the condo his, but it still feels kind of sterile, more like a fancy hotel suite than a home. Mentally, I've redecorated some of it with pieces I could make, and maybe toward the end of our time together I'll approach him about it as a way to say thank you.

Eventually, I turned my phone back on and deleted every message and every text. I didn't listen to or read a single one of them, no matter who it was from.

Guilt is a funny thing. Even though I know I wasn't wrong in not marrying Patrick, all week I've been second-guessing how things went down. Mentally, I've been creating pro-and-con lists in my head, like: he was my friend and I loved him, but if he loved me then why did he treat me so terribly? I broke my word when I told him I was in this for life, but he broke his word to me the minute he touched my cousin. I also know Patrick and my father never would have let me leave that church without saying "I do" to someone. Too many of their friends were there, and a canceled wedding to one of their own because I changed my mind about Patrick is way more offensive than me supposedly falling in love with someone else. They would have called it cold feet, and they would have forced my hand. It had to happen this way with Reid, or it wouldn't have happened at all. I keep trying to remind myself that things will be okay, that I will be okay, but by changing the path my life was on, I feel like I've somehow altered my character, who I am at the core.

Maybe that's a list I should be working on: who am I, and what's important to me?

"Camille?" Reid calls from the door of the condo.

"In the kitchen!"

Zeus, who's been staying here with me and keeping me company while the guys are gone, hears the door open and Reid's voice at the same time. Ears perk up, tail starts wagging, and he takes off to find him.

"Hey, Zeus. You keeping my girl company?" he says, speaking softly to him.

My girl.

I know he's just talking to the dog, but hearing him think of me that way, even if it's not in a romantic way, has me unlocking emotions that have been shut away for a long time.

"Let's take you home," he says to the dog in a silly voice.

His leash and collar jingle as Reid grabs them off the counter, and the two of them make their way out of the condo and across the hall. I'm glad for the moment; it lets me soak in his words. Patrick called me his girl once to a group of his friends that were down visiting from Boston, where his college is located, and it felt more like ownership, like I was his possession. Having Reid speak about me this way . . . it makes me feel more like I'm his friend, someone who is adored by him. I haven't felt adored in a really long time, and I didn't realize how badly I needed to. One day, if Reid ever decides to break his rules and settle down, some lucky girl will get to call him her guy. I sure hope she appreciates what she's getting.

Once again, the door opens and closes. Rounding the corner, Reid walks into the kitchen, and just like every time

I see him, I want to swallow my tongue. He's wearing a dry-fit shirt that shows off his perfect huge arms, athletic shorts with a compression pair underneath, and sneakers—all the same brand name, one of his sponsors.

"Hey." I smile at him as he takes a seat at the breakfast bar. "No nap today, huh?" I ask as he eyes the food I'm cooking.

"No, on Fridays we usually have an afternoon offensive team meeting. Strategies, planning, and crap like that for the offseason."

"Gotcha." In a bowl, I whisk together the ingredients for a mustard vinaigrette dressing.

"It smells great in here." He rubs his hand through his dark hair, making it perfectly imperfect.

"Thanks. I hope you don't mind, but I saw where you order your food from, so I opened an account and played around with delivery service today. I thought I'd make something different for you for dinner."

His brows slant together with hesitancy. "What is it?"

A grin slips out as I tease him. "Don't you worry, I didn't deviate from your super strict diet. I made a cauliflower crust pizza and a salad."

He groans. "I haven't had pizza in forever."

"Well, don't get too excited—we haven't tasted it yet." The timer on the oven dings, so I grab a mitt and pull it out. I have to admit, I think it looks great.

"Princess, if that pizza tastes anything like the other food you've cooked this week, it's going to be a slam dunk."

The compliment hits me deep. Patrick never complimented my food. He expected it to be ready when he got home, and that was the end of that.

"Thank you," I say, keeping my back to him so he can't see what his words mean to me.

"I'm the one who should be kissing your feet and thanking you. I haven't had someone cook for me in a long time, and I'm starting to feel a little spoiled." He watches me as I slice the pie then lay it on the bar between us along with the salad.

"So how are you doing?" he asks a little cautiously while loading up his plate.

"I don't know." It's the most honest answer I can give him. He nods, thinking about this as he dives into his salad. Silence falls over us as I sit down across from him and we both start eating.

"What did you do today?" he asks a few minutes later.

I can't look at him, so I pick up my knife and cut my pizza into small bites. I'm not sure why I feel ashamed to tell him I did nothing, but I do. "Same thing as yesterday."

"Hmm," he mumbles as he devours more than half of the pizza by picking it up and using his hands. I can feel him watching me, and I'm torn between blushing because I like how it feels to be looked at by him and blushing because I'm embarrassed.

"I'll get there, I promise. I just need a little more time."

"There's no rush. You've got at least two months here with me."

My eyes lift to his. The green in them is warm, relaxed, not irritated and cold. "Are you sure this isn't a problem for you? I've invaded your space and I feel bad."

"What do you think?" He glances down at his now empty plate then back up at me. I can't help but giggle and feel pleased by how much he liked the food. "Don't feel bad. I don't, and surprisingly, I don't mind having you here."

My eyes shoot to his and he rolls his eyes.

"What I mean is, I've lived by myself for so long, I thought it would be weird having someone else share my space with me, but it hasn't been weird with you at all. It's been easy."

He shrugs his shoulders then gets up to rinse his plate and put it in the dishwasher.

He's right—it has been easy. We haven't tripped over each other at all. In fact, we've just blended together like we've known each other forever.

"Have you talked to your sister yet?" he asks, leaning back against the counter and crossing one ankle over the other.

"I did, a little earlier," I say, shoving the last of my food in my mouth.

"Really! Did she say where she's been?"

Earlier in the week, he asked me if I had talked to her, and I said no. He looked offended for me—hell, I was offended for myself—and then said, "Maybe she's just giving you some space and running interference with the parentals. I'm sure she'll call soon." But that's how Clare is: everything is always on her schedule and never on mine.

"No." I shake my head, swallowing. "But I'm used to it. She's very evasive."

He lets out an unhappy grunt as he takes our glasses and refills them with water. I had been hoping to find some type of clarity once I did talk to her, but that didn't happen. I was so happy just to hear from her, I yelled, startling even myself.

"Where have you been?"

She laughs, and the sound instantly lowers the anxiety that's been building within me for days. "Here and there."

"What does that mean?" I demand.

"Does it matter?"

I can just see her shrugging one of her shoulders and tossing her gorgeous hair over the other as if abandoning me for days isn't a big deal.

"Of course it matters! Everything about my life is in complete chaos and I need you."

"You're being a little dramatic, don't you think?"

"No, I don't."

"Camille, you don't need me. I have eyes. I was there and saw the guy you married. The only part of your life that should be chaotic and messy is his bedroom."

I can hear the humor and the teasing in her tone. I scoff and start pacing the room. "It isn't like that."

"Well, why not? You are married, and he is hot." She accentuates the last word, and deep down I realize I don't want her looking at Reid that way. Between the two of us, Clare always got everything she wanted, and even though I know she and Reid are not a possibility, the thought of it still makes me ruffled. He's the one thing in what feels like my entire life that's mine, only mine.

"It just isn't."

Clare starts laughing again, and I swear if she were here I might just kick her. "Seems to me things might make a little more sense to you if it was like that."

"Will you please stop? I need your help. You're the sensible one between the two of us. Tell me what to do."

"No way. It's time for you to stop listening to everyone else and decide for yourself. What do you want to do?"

I hated that statement, I hated her question, and I also hated how we left things.

"Well, at least she finally called." Reid's voice pulls me from my thoughts. "Feel free to invite her down. I know you told Jack she wasn't coming, but as long as you're here, this is your home too. You can invite whoever you want." His brows draw down and he frowns. "Well, except for other guys. I don't think that would be a good idea, even if you were discrete about it."

"Reid, we are married. It may be a rather unconventional marriage, but I would never bring another guy back to your home. I would never bring another guy anywhere. For as long as we are a we, I'm yours." I roll my lips between my teeth and watch him. His eyes widen just a little, but they never break from mine.

"I'm yours, too," he says, letting out a deep breath.

Eight days—that's how long I've known him, and in that time, he's been kinder than anyone has been to me in the last five years. My eyes scan over the details of his face, a face I've come to revere, and I'm so grateful.

"So, I picked this up for you today," he says, leaning to the side to pull a folded magazine from his pocket. "I saw it and thought you might like to see what's going on around town. Maybe if you knew where you were going, that might help you get out for a bit."

He slides it across the bar so it sits in front of me. I don't say anything, because I know he's right. I need to get out.

"Did you leave at all this week?" He walks back to his seat, sits down, and lays his forearms on the bar in front of him.

I pick up the local magazine and thumb through it to avoid seeing any form of disappointment on his face. "I went out on the porch—does that count?"

"Camille." The tender way he says my name has heat climbing up my cheeks.

"I know, I know," I say, letting out a sigh. "I just needed a few days."

A few days have now come and gone, and with this push from him, it seems time is up.

"A couple of blocks over, there's a park on the water, and most weekends they have some type of fair or festival. Maybe you'll want to check it out. Next weekend is the Gasparilla Festival of the Arts, and I've heard it's amazing. I think we should go."

"We?" My eyes dart up to his.

"Yeah, why not? I think it will be fun." He flips the magazine open to the schedule of events, and then it hits me: he wants to go out with me. With *me*. I don't know why this gets me so excited, but it does.

"Okay." I smile at him and look back at the festival list. "Wait! Tomorrow there's one called the Vintage Flea—can we go to that?"

The corner of his lips twitch and he leans back in his chair. "Yep."

"You knew about this." My eyes narrow.

He shrugs his shoulders but can't help the lopsided smile that slides onto his face.

"Why didn't you lead with this? The arts festival sounds great, and I'd love to go to that, too, but this . . ." I flip through the magazine to find the advertisement for the flea market: *A unique upscale vintage market focused on antique-inspired indoor and outdoor goods and furnishings.* I'm so excited, I run my finger over the page. I even love the logo.

"I didn't want to push you if you weren't ready, but Billy was talking about taking his wife, and it kind of reminded me of your workshop."

Just thinking about my workshop has my hands itching to create something one of a kind and beautiful. Maybe we'll find something tomorrow.

A grin splits my face from ear to ear. "I'm ready."

Chapter 13

Reid

ALL WEEK LONG I watched her. I mean, how could I not? This beautiful girl moved into my space, and surprisingly, things went smoother than I expected. I haven't had a roommate in years and have never had a girlfriend who stayed longer than twelve hours, but Camille was quiet, kept to herself, and didn't try to bother me at all.

During the day, I noticed she moved the furniture around a bit, and I think she was using the floor space to exercise or dance. She has to miss it, right? That's what she did for so long. Then, every night, she cooked dinner for us. The conversations were always light and easy, and afterward we would watch a movie.

If I'm being honest with myself, however, even though she was here, it felt like she wasn't, and that bothered me. I know she's not really my responsibility—after all, she's an adult—but I did disrupt her life, marry her, and bring her here. Frequently, I watched her just stare outside. The back wall of the condo has floor-to-ceiling windows that look out toward the water, and yes, the view is nice, but I'm pretty sure she wasn't looking at anything.

She's lost.

I can't say I blame her—she did just flip her entire life upside down and now needs to figure out what's happening next—but by Friday, I was starting to worry about her. At first she was a zombie, and then she transitioned to anxious, almost like a domesticated animal that's about to be set free in the wild. She knows it's coming but is uncertain about exactly when.

I've never had a serious girlfriend. I've never wanted one, and now that I'm here, in this situation with her, I don't know what to do. To make things worse, she isn't even just some girl; she's a senator's daughter—high society, a true Southern belle.

The complete opposite of me.

For so long, my life was worrying about my family and pushing myself to get into the NFL. I was certain if I finally made it, my mother would take a step back and enjoy her life more, but she didn't.

Every month I deposit money into her account and Nate's, but she rarely touches it, and he's just as conservative, using it only for practical expenses outside of his scholarship. Part of me sometimes feels like I don't know what I'm doing all this for, but if I wasn't doing this, feeling the need to always take care of them, what would I be doing?

It's this thought that makes me somewhat understand how she's feeling. Change is hard, especially when it's sudden, even if it was wanted.

Speaking of change . . .

On Monday, when I headed into the training facility, the dynamic with my teammates had changed, too. The guys fell into one of two camps: happy for me—this came from those currently in a relationship of some kind—and wary of me, almost like I have some kind of plague. The latter came from the uncommitted guys, who just a few days earlier I was one of, and proud of it. Technically, I still am one of them. I stand by the fact that I never want to get married. It's not something I see for myself.

No one was curious or asked for an explanation, but then again, I'm certain they all saw the social media coverage of the wedding. Reporters went crazy over what they are calling one of the biggest Southern scandals of the century. The Whitley family, being one of the oldest and most prominent families in the region, was shocked along with the community that their precious daughter would jilt such a beloved close friend of the family and an aspiring political candidate for an NFL player from the Bronx. Yes, I'm well-known in the football industry, but outside of that, I'm a nobody. Of course they played up Patrick as the victim in these stories and knocked me down, but that's okay. I already knew we weren't in the same league; it just sucks to be reminded of that, and in front of all my friends, too.

Needing some advice on what to do with Camille, I sought out Billy, one of our team captains and an all-around good guy. Without giving him too much detail, I mentioned that I needed to get her out of the condo for some fresh air and to do some sightseeing, and he suggested the festivals. She'd get to see some of downtown while staying close enough to the condo that she could go home if she wanted to. So, I stopped and picked up the city magazine from the small grocer downstairs and hoped for the best. It was time to push the baby bird out of the nest.

"That's a big hat," I state as she wanders out from her bedroom.

Her face lights up as she pats it tighter onto her head.

"You brought me to Florida." She laughs.

I think this is the first time I've heard her laugh since the wedding, and my chest tightens.

"Look at my skin." She holds out her arm. "I'm so pale you could call me Casper."

I glance at her arm and then my eyes trail down to take in the rest of her. She's wearing a denim button-down with the sleeves rolled up, a little yellow skirt, and flip-flops. The only skin that jumps out at me is on her bare legs, which are rock-solid. Every bit of this girl is gorgeous.

My eyes climb back to hers. "Well, we certainly don't want you getting burned."

"No, we do not. I brighten up like a tomato. You're lucky you don't have to worry about that." She glances at my olive-toned skin. "And look, you're wearing a hat, too." She walks over and wiggles the brim of it. Coconut wafts over me. She smells so good.

"It's my disguise."

She laughs again. "You do realize there's no disguising you, right?" Her cheeks tinge pink as she waves her hand from my head to my feet. I know I stand out in a crowd because of my size. It is what it is, but maybe the hat will help.

"Maybe not, but the hat and sunglasses are better than nothing." I tap the aviators tucked into the neck of my shirt.

"Are we meeting your friends there?" She walks into the kitchen and picks up a clutch handbag.

"No. I told them we might wander over, but I wanted to leave that up to you. I can text him to meet us, or we can just do our own thing."

"Do our own thing," she says, more to herself, but then her eyes light up. "Kind of like a date? Friends can go on dates, right?" She meets me at the door, which I hold open for her.

A chuckle escapes me. "Sure, we can call this a date."

She presses her lips together to fight smiling, but her expression tells me this makes her happy. I like seeing her happy.

"I haven't been on a date in a really long time," she states, passing by me and heading for the elevator.

"Technically, that's false—our first date was at the reception." I lock the door and we walk into the elevator.

She turns to look at me, and I'm wondering if she remembers how we started that date—a kiss at the beginning versus at the end. I liked it. "You know what I mean." She spins so she's facing forward. The doors close and we start our descent.

"Yes, I do, and for the record, it's also been a long time for me, princess."

Outside, the weather is perfect. The skies are blue, not a cloud in sight, and the breeze is cool coming up off the water. We stop at the coffee shop across the street to grab a drink then wander down to the park.

Jack and I have come over here a few times in the last year, but those festivals were more night events: a margarita festival, rib fest, and a couple of concerts. I've never come to anything like this, and without Camille, I doubt I ever would. Just walking up, I can feel the excitement pouring off her.

White tented booths are lined up one after another, making rows, and these rows fill up the entire park. It's crowded—really crowded.

"What do you think?" I ask her.

She turns to look up at me from under her hat and smiles from ear to ear. "I don't even know where to begin."

"Here looks as good as any." I point to the first one, which is filled with old dishes, teacups, and teapots. Why anyone would want this stuff, I have no idea, but she's happy, and that was the goal.

Together we walk through the aisles, and she examines everything. Some things she picks up to check the price, and others, I think she's just looking at the fine details.

"The furniture in your workshop—where did it come from?" I ask, curious to know more about her.

"Most of the pieces I find are from estate sales, yard sales, or flea markets." She picks up a plate that looks like china, flips it over to look at the back, and then replaces it.

"No antique shops?"

"No. Things are overpriced there and have usually been touched up in one way or another. At estate sales and yard sales, most of the time people are just looking to get rid of things."

We move on to the next booth, and it's filled with grandfather clocks. "Makes sense to me. What are you doing with the furniture once you have it?"

She walks around each one and looks it over from top to bottom. "Restoration. Over time, pieces inevitably get scratched, nicked, or dinged. See right here." She points to a large gouge on the side of one clock. It looks like something fell on it or hit it. I nod. "Hinges become loose, legs wobble, and oftentimes there are water rings or burns. I repair or replace these things, and more often than not, I modernize the pieces, make them look more current while keeping their authenticity of looking worn, used, loved."

"You want them to look used and not new?"

"Yes. Ever heard of shabby chic?"

"No, thank God."

She giggles. "Basically, it's a style of furniture that looks new and used at the same time. People who like that look will have several pieces in their home as statement pieces, but none of them will match. With so many beach houses up and down the coast, the style sells really well. Beach houses are meant to be relaxed, not formal, and mixing the right pieces together makes the houses feel cozy and complete without the high price associated with furnishing a home. Every piece tells a story, you just have to listen."

"Yep, not something I've ever thought of—not once."

Instead of responding to me, she's stopped in front of a booth called *Through the Looking Glass* and is staring at a large floor mirror propped against the back wall. Walking into the booth, she tilts her head as she runs her fingers down the wooden frame.

"It's a beautiful piece, don't you think?" a man asks as he steps up next to her.

"I do. Where did you get it?"

"Flea market in Virginia. The guy said he found it at a church roundup. They were looking for donations for the furniture, and as the saying goes, one man's trash is another's treasure. He bought it and cleaned it up."

"A treasure indeed," she says sincerely.

Personally, I don't see anything special about it. Sure, it has a wide wooden frame, but one corner is damaged, it's all scratched up, and it's awkwardly big.

"Are you local?" she asks him.

"We have a storefront over in Dunedin, but I spend most of my time on the road."

"I think I need to go check out your store." She's intrigued and looks around the tent at the other items he has.

"Well, we'd love to have you. If you're interested in the mirror, I'm open to offers."

Camille is quiet as she again peruses it. She walks around to check out both sides then wanders out the back of the tent so she can pull up the wall and examine the back. Part of me has the sudden urge to just jump in and buy it for her—it's clear that she loves it—but another part of me is enjoying watching her in her element. Her wheels are turning; she sees something in this item.

Another customer requires the shopkeeper's assistance, and Camille comes back to me.

"What do you think?" she asks.

"I have no opinion. This is all you, so whatever you want."

"I think I want it." She takes off her hat and pushes all of the loose pieces of hair back.

"What would you do with it?"

A slow smile tips her lips up. "Oh, I have an idea." She puts her hat back on and goes to speak to the guy.

After negotiating on a price, he agrees to sell her the mirror for an amount that, to me, seems like way more than it's worth. She, however, is beaming, so I can't help but hand my credit card over.

"No way, Reid."

"Yes way, Camille. You're with me, and you said this is a date, so this is how it is."

She scowls and crosses her arms over her chest. "But it's too much—I can't ask you to pay for this."

"Too late."

The man takes my card and tries to diffuse the tension by changing the subject. "Do you want to take the mirror now, or can we hold it until the end of the weekend and have it delivered to your home?"

The mirror is a really big piece of his booth, so I can see why he wants to hold on to it. "You can deliver it Monday or Tuesday, that works for us," I tell him. She'll be home to receive it, so there won't be any logistical problems. I give him my address, and the guy smiles as he thanks us for our business. Camille squeezes my arm with excitement. She's touching me, and I can't help but look down at her fingers wrapped around my bicep.

"Thank you, Reid." Large blue eyes shine up at me.

"Haven't we talked about you not saying that to me anymore?" I step another inch closer to her, run my free hand down her arm, and slide my hand into hers.

"This is different." She laces her fingers with mine and squeezes then doesn't let go.

Bending down, I tip her hat to the side, kiss her cheek, and whisper, "You're welcome, princess."

We keep exploring for the next couple of hours. She doesn't find anything else she wants to buy, but we stay hand in hand as we walk from booth to booth. She continues looking through the different items, whereas I continue looking at her. There's original art, clothing, jewelry, home decor, homemade items, quilts, indoor furnishings, outdoor furnishings, plants, perishables—you name it, someone's got it for sale—and it isn't until we're down one of the last rows that I spot a long camera lens directed straight at us.

Shit.

I drop her hand, wrap my arm around her shoulders, pull her close, and spin us around to go in the opposite direction.

"What are we doing?" She looks up at me.

"Photographer." My protective instincts have taken over and I want to put as much distance as I can between us and him.

She glances back quickly and stiffens. "Do you think he saw us?" She wraps her arm around my waist and we pick up the pace.

"Yes."

"Do you think he knows who we are?" Our steps fall in sync as we round a corner to move out of sight.

"I don't know. My guess is probably."

She stops us and looks up at me as I look down at her. "Do you think we should go home?" She's frowning, and I hate that her happiness from earlier is gone.

Looking around at the people wandering by us, she puts her free hand on my chest and steps closer. She's so small tucked up next to me I can't help but put my hands on her waist and bring her flush against me. Her hat flattens as she lays her head against my chest.

"That's up to you," I answer her.

Nothing would make me happier than to have the world see us out and together. I have nothing to hide, but I know she does—herself. The whole point of coming to Tampa was to try to stay low-key. We both knew eventually the media would catch up to us, but as this is her first outing and she's still adjusting, a little reprieve would have been nice.

"Well, I'm not ready to go home yet." She tilts her head back. "Maybe we go out for lunch somewhere quiet?" Her eyebrows are raised above her sunglasses.

It occurs to me that I like her thinking of my condo as home.

It also occurs to me that I'm liking all of this just a little too much, things I've never liked with anyone: her in my home, her sharing meals with me, her out in public with me, her touching me, her on my arm for others to see—her, her, her. It's here and now that I remind myself all of this is temporary. I can like it all I want, even savor it, and for now that's okay, because in the end I'll still be me, she'll be someone who lives a completely different lifestyle from me, and we'll each go on our way. Dust in the wind.

Knowing this, I block the sudden assault of feelings and decide not to stress over what it all might mean. I can live in the present, and I can enjoy my time with her.

"Lunch sounds great, and I know just the place."

Chapter 14

Camille

"HOW DID YOU find this place?" I ask, removing my hat and laying it under my chair. Reid stands and lifts his arms to adjust the umbrella over our table, angling it to keep us shaded, and his T-shirt rises a bit, giving me a nice peek of his smooth, muscular stomach. I imagine my fingers tracing over each muscle, dipping up and down. I know I shouldn't be thinking about what he would look and feel like with that shirt off, but I can't help it. He is incredibly handsome.

"Billy brought me after I joined the team." He sits back down in his chair and runs his hand over his hat to pull it down a little then picks up his menu. "He said it's the best place in town to get served fresh fish, and he's right. The menu changes daily based on what they caught earlier that morning."

"That's so great. Savannah has a few places that serve fresh-off-the-dock food, too. I'll have to show you my secret places next time we're there."

From behind his sunglasses, his eyes jump to mine. Feeling a little like a deer caught in headlights, I realize how that sounded and start backtracking.

"Not that you'll be in Savannah with me. I wasn't implying that we'd still be together longer than the two months, just that the food is good there and I think you'd like it. Gah, you know what I mean." Embarrassment climbs up my neck and heats my cheeks. I dig my sunglasses out of my bag. He's wearing his, so I'll wear mine too and hide behind them.

He chuckles and one side of his mouth tips up. "Deal. Next time I'm in Savannah, we'll eat at your favorite places." Reaching over, he tucks a few strands of hair behind my ear, runs his thumb down the column of my neck, and then squeezes my shoulder.

"Okay," I mutter. I can't seem to make any other words form.

Dropping the conversation, we both look over the menu, the waitress takes our order, and pretty quickly, our drinks and the food come out.

Reid is very easy to be around. I don't feel any of the added pressure that comes with constantly being surrounded by people who are just looking for you to make a mistake so there's fuel for gossip. He's laid back, quiet, and genuinely seems like the nicest person I've ever met.

"Tell me something about you," I blurt out between bites.

He quirks a grin. "All right. Yeah, I guess we really don't know much about each other, and that makes this normal date-like conversation. Let's see . . ." He rubs his chin as he stares across the table at me. "My favorite food is barbeque ribs, but I don't eat them very often because they're slathered in brown sugar. My favorite color is green. Growing up in the Bronx, sure we had grass and trees, but not like you see everywhere else. For that reason, I've always been enamored by it."

And here I am thinking green could become my favorite color, too, but because of his eyes.

"I hate the snow. I didn't even know I hated it until after I moved here and got to experience a winter without it. I've never been skiing, so it's not like I miss the sport side of it, but last year I went home for Christmas and it was miserable. There was dirty slop everywhere. So, unless I change teams and end up back up north, I'm never living in snow again."

"A Yankee turned Southerner." I smile at him and watch as the breeze sends the trim around the umbrella waving back and forth. Shadows play across his face, a face I could stare at all day.

"Call me what you want, but I understand now why people move south." He picks up his drink and takes a sip. His hands are so large they cover the entire glass.

"I didn't mind the snow so much, maybe because I had never lived in it before, so it was a novelty, but I thought it was pretty."

Setting the glass back down, he leans back in his chair. "Pretty to look at on my phone while I'm sitting next to the pool." He grins. "I am a Yankees fan, and there's nothing quite like Yankee Stadium in the summer, but now that you mention it, I don't think I could ever fit the mold of a Southerner. There is always Phoenix, though."

"What mold is that?"

"People who drive slow, talk slow, eat fried food, and drink sweet tea."

"That's a terribly cliché description of Southerners," I reply, balking at his words.

"You know what I mean." He smiles. "I'll never sound the part—darlin' just isn't in my vocabulary—and can you imagine the looks on the faces of the stiffs at your father's country club if I rolled up wearing a bowtie and tried to fit in? It's never going to happen."

That's funny, because I think he'd look quite handsome in a bowtie, and whether he's in New York or Georgia, I don't think he'd fit in anywhere. He's meant to be noticed, and I admire that about him.

"Well, in all fairness, I could never be a true New Yorker, even if most of them are transplants. I never could understand the subway system, my manners ensure that I allow everyone to rush past me, so I'm always late, and I'll never eat a hotdog or falafel from a street vendor."

He narrows his eyes. "You never ate a hotdog while wandering through Central Park?"

"Absolutely not. And listen"—I lean forward—"*How you doin'?* It just doesn't sound right coming from me."

He laughs. "No, it sure doesn't."

"As for Phoenix, I could never live there—I like living near the water too much." I look past his shoulder at the marina dock. Lined up on every post is a pelican. Granted, they're waiting for handouts from the fishermen, but still, pelicans are really cool birds.

"I'll keep that in mind," he says, drawing my attention back to him. Lifting his beer to his mouth again, he takes a drink and watches me over the rim of his glass.

"Take your sunglasses off. I don't like not being able to see what you're looking at."

"Only if you take yours off," he challenges.

We both toss them on the table, his eyes find mine, and my stomach bottoms out. There should be rules against how potent a person's eyes are. It's not fair. He could turn me into putty if he wanted to—forest green putty.

"Okay, last one," he says, shifting in his chair to cross his ankle over his knee. "The first time I ever flew on a plane was my freshman year at Syracuse when we had an away game at Clemson. Of course, I didn't tell anyone this at the time, but I sat by the window and gave the poor armrests the death grip."

"You didn't fly on a plane until college?"

"Nope. Never needed to, but now, with the team, sponsorships, and seeing my mom, Nate, and Tally, I'm on a plane probably two dozen times a year."

"We have a family plane. I don't even remember a time when we weren't flying somewhere."

"Of course you do." His lips press together and he shakes his head just as the waitress comes by to clear our plates.

"Would either of you like dessert?" she asks.

He looks at me, and I tell her no. I already know he doesn't like to eat sugar, so there's no point in asking him to share.

"Okay, that's several things about me. Now it's your turn, and I already know your favorite candy is gummy bears, so don't start there."

"I do love gummy bears. Let's see . . ." I pick up my paper napkin and start messing with it. "I don't really have one favorite food per se, because I love all breakfast foods: biscuits and gravy, cheesy grits, corned beef hash, pecan waffles—I could go on and on."

"Every single one of those sounds like a heart attack waiting to happen," he mocks.

"Listen here, not all of us strive to have the perfect body like you." I tear a piece of the napkin off, ball it up, and flick it at him. He catches it easily with one hand. Stupid football hands.

"You were a dancer, so your diet was probably more strict than mine—wait, you think my body's perfect?" His face has taken on an expression like he's just been told the secrets of the universe, and my cheeks flush.

"Um, you know it is, so quit it."

He laughs and the waitress comes over with fresh drinks. I reach for my wine, and he watches as I take a sip then lick my lips. He looks so calm sitting there, whereas I want to squirm under his perusal—squirm my way right over onto his lap. I let out a deep breath, put the glass down, and his brows rise just a little, urging me to keep going.

"So, I don't have a favorite color. As a kid I tried really hard to pick one, but when I did, I felt bad for the other colors. If I have to pick one, I always say orange, because no one picks orange."

"You're right, no one picks orange." He smirks.

"See! But every time I say orange, I immediately feel bad for yellow. No one picks yellow either, but you see it out and about more than orange. Poor orange, the unwanted child of red and yellow."

"Do you always root for the underdog?" He tilts his head to the side.

This question hits a little too close to home. I've felt like the underdog my whole life.

"Yes, I think I do." I shift in my chair and cross my legs.

He leans forward and rolls the stem of my wine glass between his fingers. "Good, I like underdogs, too."

My heart twirls in my chest.

"I've never been to Disney World, although I've always wanted to go, and my favorite childhood memories are of running with Clare through the field behind our house."

"What were you running from?"

"Usually each other, but mostly me from her, because she was mad about something I did and wanted to hit me. We would fly kites, chase the clouds, I don't know . . . that field was our place of freedom."

"Chase the clouds," he repeats as he thinks about my words.

"Yeah, the weather changes a lot and quickly here in the south. Not sure about up north, but being coastal, during the summer we'd have daily afternoon thunderstorms from the humidity buildup, and the dark clouds would chase away the white ones. The coastal breeze makes them move swiftly. I know it's silly, but it was fun for us. It was like the only place where we could be loud, wild, uninhibited, just us."

"I'm glad you two had that place."

I want to say I'm glad, too, but I can't. As much as I love the good childhood memories we made there, it's the backdrop of some of my worst, too.

"Don't look now, but they've found us," he mumbles, slipping his sunglasses back on and lifting his drink to his lips.

"Who found us?" Panic washes over me thinking Patrick and my father have somehow followed me here and will force me to leave. I mean, technically I know I'm an adult and they can't force me to do anything, but they just have this way about them that fills me with dread and jumbled nerves.

"Paparazzi."

Paparazzi.

Groaning, I drop my head forward, and pieces of my hair swing in front of my face, alerting me to the fact that I look disheveled and not put together.

"How do you think he found us?" I whisper.

I close my eyes and fight the urge to freak out, trying to compose myself. Needing to sort out my thoughts, I realize they fall into one of three categories: succumbing to the feeling of propriety that's been instilled in me since birth, rebelling because I should be able to live my life like I want without worrying if pieces of my hair are blowing in the wind, and deciding on what I want to do and who I want to be as I'm trying to start living my life for me.

"I'm not sure. He must have trailed us."

Ultimately, I decide it's a combination of the first and the third. Yes, I am trying to start a new life, but currently there is someone else in this life, and I should put my best effort forward for him as well.

Taking a deep breath, I sit up straight, smooth my clothes down, and cross my ankles, tucking them under the chair. Next, I undo the loose ponytail my hair is in, gather it, and wrap it in a tight bun at the base of my head. I reach under the chair, grab my hat, and put it on. Pulling out some lip gloss, I apply it, return my sunglasses to my face, and fold my hands in my lap. Sitting up straight, I smile. Reid is watching me and frowning.

Through the black tint of his sunglasses, he pins me with a narrowed stare. "What are you doing?"

I give him my perfected polite expression and lightly shrug my shoulders to play off my actions as no big deal. Looking around the patio, I take in where I'm sitting and what the background of the photos might entail.

"Don't you know appearances are everything? I learned a long time ago to always be prepared. I'm actually surprised I slipped like I did by allowing myself to get so casual. Maybe it's because we're here and it's so easy to be with you, I don't know, but in Savannah, I can't go anywhere without being recognized. Here it's probably you. People know you."

His frown deepens as if I've somehow insulted him.

"Reid, one hundred times over, they'd rather have the bad shot instead of the good one. The tabloids and the general public eat that up, which is why I can't give them an opportunity." I'm feeling defensive, and I hate that he's making me feel this way—or is he? Maybe I'm making myself feel this way.

"You know you're being crazy, right?"

"Am I? Messy hair means I'm stressed. No makeup means I'm letting myself go or I'm depressed. A lot of food on my plate and I'm eating for two. I know it shouldn't matter, but it does. You'll be in these photos, and I am now a reflection of your choices, too."

"Camille." At the way he says my name, the tenor of it on his lips, my chest tightens with affection. "Who cares? I certainly don't care what you look like. I think you're beautiful whether you're dressed up for our wedding or climbing out of bed in the morning. It's all the same to me, because all of it is you. You have to live your life, and you can't be worried about what others think all the time."

He said 'our wedding,' and I think a piece of my heart broke off and blew his way.

"That's easy for you to say."

Leaning back in his chair, his fingers grip the edge of the table as he watches me. "Probably, and I'm not trying to take anything away from you. Based on what you've told me, I understand how you've lived your life up until last weekend, but you walked away from that life to find a different one. It doesn't matter anymore. Appearances don't matter to me. Character does."

I want to say it does matter, because even if the photos aren't about me being here, in his world with him, his face and his name are his brand for his profession, and I never want to make him look bad—not that I think I looked bad a few minutes ago . . . oh, I don't know.

Letting out a deep sigh, I break eye contact and look out over the boats in the marina. Back and forth they sway in the water, just like my emotions. Part of me feels justified for what I said and for my actions, and then another part of me feels shame. Since that moment in the library at the rehearsal dinner, he's never tried to make me be anyone but myself, and he seems to want me just as I am, so why do I feel I have to put on the act now?

"I think you have beautiful hair. Take it down."

My eyes skip to him and then away.

Shifting my gaze, I look and see that the photographer is still there, sitting next to a large yacht. He's trying to look inconspicuous, but he knows we know he's there.

Reid is right. I need to worry less about what others will think of me and more about what I think of myself, about my character, as he said, and that's so true. It's the character of the people back in Savannah—that's why I left and why I'm searching to find me. I really am trying, so, taking a deep breath, I keep the hat on but pull the rubber band out and let my hair fall free.

Chapter 15

Reid

TODAY, I WOKE up feeling off. I couldn't tell you why, but I feel on edge and I don't like it.

The condo is dark and quiet as I walk into the kitchen. I heat up some eggs and sit down at the large breakfast bar to eat. Camille's clutch and hat from yesterday are sitting on the other end and as I stare at them, it occurs to me that I like them there. I've always loved living by myself and swore I always would, but I don't mind her things blending with mine. In fact, I don't mind her being here at all.

Why did I think living with someone would be so bad? Granted, our setup is that we're roommates; I still have my room and she has hers. That gives me space, so maybe that's the difference. We aren't on top of each other one hundred percent of the time—although I wouldn't mind if she were on top of me now and then.

Shaking my head to clear it, I rinse the bowl, drop it in the sink, and head down the hallway to peek into Camille's room. She leaves the door cracked, and before I head to the gym, I can't help but watch her sleep. I know that makes me sound like a total creeper, but I need to see her before I leave to remind myself this is reality and I am married.

Man, do I hate that word.

Light from the hallway and her window spills in. She's curled up on her side with one leg sticking out from under the covers, and she's hugging a pillow. She looks tiny, sweet, at peace. I hate that she doesn't look like this during the day, and the thought leaves me feeling very protective over her. I still don't really know why. We aren't a real couple, and none of this should matter as much as it does, but that doesn't change how I'm feeling, nor has it stopped new feelings from taking root.

All week, she stayed in the condo. She wore what girls call yoga clothes, and although she looked a little lost in her head, in her own thoughts, she seemed somewhat relaxed, seemed okay. I got to know her this way, with her messy hair, a smile that got bigger and brighter each day, and a laid-back personality that made us living together effortless, but the second she felt watched at the restaurant, she became someone completely different. All day she felt like mine, and then within two minutes at the end of lunch, she didn't. It's like the air shifted and even though it was warm out, a chill drifted over our table.

The way she transformed and looked around made me uncomfortable. She became the girl from the rehearsal dinner. She looked poised, elegant, and every bit the high society girl she is, a harsh reminder of how different we are and how not real this will ever be. It's not that I want it to be real—because, let's face it, I don't—but listening to her talk about the photos and people's opinions made me feel like I wasn't good enough to be sitting there with her, which had me questioning myself, and I never question who I am or who I keep company with.

Minutes pass, and it's as if she somehow senses me, rolling to her back and letting out a small noise. Something in her dreams causes her to smile, and my chest tightens with an unexplainable longing. Yesterday she smiled. She smiled a lot, and not that fake closed-mouth smile she gives people out of polite obligation, but one that feels like maybe it's coming out just for me. I liked it, more than I should.

A knock on the front door lets me know Jack is ready, so I walk away from her and grab my bag.

Jack and I always ride together to the franchise headquarters, the stadium, and training facilities. It keeps us accountable. Plus, this early in the morning we can both tolerate each other fairly well.

"What's wrong with you this morning?" he asks, glancing over at me in the passenger seat. My bag is on the floor between my feet and one of my legs is bouncing nonstop.

"Nothing."

"Liar. Trouble in paradise?" He grins at me and I shoot him a *piss off* look.

Jack got the full story of what happened at the wedding the morning after he met Camille. I knew there was no way he was going to let it go, so I filled him in on the way to the gym. He of course howled with laughter at the mental image of me stopping a wedding, but not once did he call me an idiot. Instead, he just smiled and kept his thoughts to himself.

"Things are fine."

"Then why are you so antsy?"

"I don't know. I just am." Letting out a sigh, I dig around for my phone in my bag and start searching the Internet for photos of us from yesterday. I can't find any, and that surprises me; usually paparazzi post things immediately. Instead, I type in Camille's name and scroll through the images. I pause when one of her and her sister pops up.

It's older, and they are younger, maybe fifteen? I've never known identical twins before, and it's uncanny how similar and how different they look at the same time. Looking at Clare, I find I'm resentful for Camille that the bulk of family responsibilities have fallen on her while her sister left to do her own thing. What kind of person does that?

"By the way, I plan on doing extra cardio today, so I hope you don't mind sticking around a little longer."

"Not at all. You go ahead and work out all that pent-up sexual frustration you have going on." He smirks.

"That's not it."

"You sure? Because if I were living with a girl who looked like that . . ." He shakes his head.

"Dude." My tone is laced with warning.

"What? I'm just saying." He shrugs his shoulders and his smirk stretches to a full-blown smile.

Ignoring him, I resume looking through the photos. There are so many of her and Patrick, my jaw clenches and my teeth grind together. Extra cardio will be good for me; I really need to clear my head to figure out what my problem is, and I really need to burn off the extra calories from dinner last night.

Three hours turns into five. I rotated through the core areas of my workout: weight lifting for strength, full-body exercises for explosiveness, and treadmill blocks for speed and endurance. Sweat is dripping off every inch of me, and by the end, I'm physically depleted.

"You all right?" Bryan asks as he comes to stand in front of my treadmill. He wraps his towel around his neck as I hit pause three times and the belt slowly comes to a stop.

"Yeah, I'm fine." I grab my bottle and chug the remaining water down.

"You sure?"

That's when I know I need to shake this mood off. It's never a good sign when your quarterback wanders over to check on you.

"Yep. Camille and I went out to dinner last night and I fell off the diet. Needed some extra time today to take care of that."

He cocks an eyebrow at me, and in return I rub my stomach and wink at him. Shaking his head, he walks away, and I drop my gaze to the ground.

All athletes know to leave it all at the door. It's instilled in us as kids to the point that it becomes a habit; that way mistakes aren't made, injuries don't occur, and games aren't lost. Today, I didn't leave it at the door. *Shit.*

Feeling like I need some clarity, insight, or something, I break for the locker room. Throwing my towel down, I reach into my bag for my phone and hit Nate's name.

"Bro," he answers on the third ring.

"How's it going?" I smile, already feeling better.

"Shouldn't I be asking you that?" He chuckles.

"It's going fine." I sit down in the chair in front of my designated space.

"Fine . . . that's it?"

"Well, yeah. What do you want me to say?" I prop my feet up on a shelf inside the built-in cubby.

"You have a beautiful girl living with you who happens to be your *wife*—things should be better than just fine, and I know for a fact this girl is awesome to hang out with." There's a slight tone to his voice, and it causes me to wince. Letting out a deep breath, I brush off the guilt and remind myself that if he'd wanted her bad enough, he would have gone after her.

"Okay, let me ask you: when you've spent time with Camille, how did she act?"

"What do you mean?" Street sounds from around him—sounds of home—echo through the phone.

"Tell me what she was like—what did you do together?"

"This is a weird question."

"I know it is, but I'm trying to get to know her and understand her better. It's easy to see how someone is when they're in their normal environment, but it's not like that here."

It's silent for a few moments as I listen to car horns and muted conversations of other people.

"Are you regretting marrying her? A girl you didn't know?" He ends with sarcasm.

"No, jackass, it's nothing like that. I'm just curious about how she acted around other people."

"I don't know . . . she was always quiet. Unless you spoke to her, she stayed in the background and observed more than participated. The most I ever heard her speak was on New Year's Eve when she told us she was getting married. Don't get me wrong, she's always been super nice, but she reminds me of a beautiful piece of art—pretty to look at, but completely untouchable."

"Is that why?" I rub my towel over my face, wanting to know his answer and not wanting to at the same time.

"Why what?"

"Why you never asked her out?"

"No. I didn't ask her out because she was with someone else. I respected her enough to respect her choices, and I didn't pursue it."

"Even though you knew she didn't really want to be with that guy."

"But I didn't. She never flirted with other guys or gave the impression she wasn't happy, and honestly, it wasn't until months after meeting her that I even found out she had a boyfriend. She never talked about him. She never talked much at all."

That's when I know I don't need to feel guilty about Nate anymore. He's never been the kind of guy to sit back and not take what he wants. He might have some type of infatuation with her, because yes, she is like a beautiful piece of art, but he wasn't interested enough to have gone after her, even when he thought she was single.

But, just to make sure the air is clear between us, I ask, "Are you pissed at me about this?"

"I was at first, but I'm over it. Then again, I couldn't decide if I was angry at you or at myself. Why are you asking me all these questions anyway?"

"I'm just trying to get a feel for who she is when she hasn't found herself in a life-altering situation."

"Is she doing okay?" He sounds concerned.

As if I don't ask myself this at least fifteen times a day.

"I think so." This makes me pause. Would she tell me if she wasn't okay? I'd like to think she would, but I'll watch her closer to make sure.

"Good, I'm glad to hear that. You two are getting along okay?"

"Of course—who do I not get along well with?" I smirk.

"Why are you always so arrogant? There's no need for that," he scoffs, and I laugh.

"It's not arrogance, it's that Jackson charm. You should know—you've got it too."

"Maybe. So, when do I get to see you again? Mom will be due for a visit soon, too."

"I'm not sure. I need to get through these two months with Camille and into the offseason workout program, then I'll have a better hold on what's happening."

"All right, but . . . Reid, man, I hope you'll allow yourself to let go and have some fun. This little arrangement might work out well if you let it."

Arrangement.

That's exactly what this is, but I find I don't like that word, not at all.

Commotion from the hallway grabs my attention just as Jack sticks his head into the locker room. "Ready to go?" he mouths, attempting to not interrupt my call.

I nod, relieved to not have to respond to Nate's last comment—not the arrangement part, but the part where he hopes I'll allow myself to let go and have fun. I don't know what he's talking about. He said something similar in his speech at the wedding reception.

Standing up, I toss the towel in my bag. "Listen, I've got to run, but thanks for picking up."

"Any time. Remember what I said and call me soon."

"Will do."

Chapter 16

Camille

IT'S BEEN THREE days since Reid and I went to the festival and out to dinner, and we haven't seen any pictures of us emerge on any websites. That's not to say they aren't out there or aren't being saved for later, but for now, life seems to be moving along uninterrupted.

Last night, I dreamed about when Clare and I were kids. It's funny how dreams work. We have a lifetime of memories, but in my dreams I always find us in the same place doing the same thing. We're lying on a blanket in the field behind our parents' home, blowing dandelions and watching the clouds roll over us. Some days I miss the field; other days it's more nightmare than dream.

"What are you doing?"

Reid's deep voice startles me from the memory and I jump. He's leaning against the sliding glass door; I didn't even hear him open it. I also didn't realize how late in the afternoon it is—the sun has already started to drop, and the temperature is cooling off.

Standing up straight, I brush the dust off my shorts as his eyes travel the length of me once before scanning over the mess I've made of his balcony. I'm wearing a pair of cutoff shorts Patrick always hated, but watching Reid's eyes flare slightly, I know he doesn't share the same sentiment. I also realize I don't care if he likes my shorts or not, because I do. I'm not trying to impress him, I'm just being me, and after the incident at the marina restaurant, it feels good knowing I'm taking baby steps. Mentally, I pat myself on the back.

"Don't worry, I'll clean it all up," I say, feeling slightly embarrassed and awkward but smiling on the inside.

"I'm not worried, but what are you doing?"

I look around to see what he sees. The balcony is larger than what you would expect for a condo, stretching the full length from his bedroom down to the living room, which makes it the perfect workspace for me.

"Sanding down any of the finish that might still be left on the frame of the mirror while adding some texture so the new paint will adhere." Earlier, I took the actual mirror out of the frame and placed it against the far wall then pushed his furniture out of the way and laid the frame down on a drop cloth. Around it are rags, two sizes of scrapers, sandpaper, a toothbrush, varnish remover, paint primer, and dust—lots of dust.

"Where did you get all this stuff?" He waves his hand toward my materials.

"Amazon Prime."

"Prime," he mumbles to himself. "Wait . . ." He steps closer to me, frowning. "I never even considered this, but do you need money?"

"Money?" I stand up straight and turn to face him. "No, why?"

"I brought you here, you don't work, and I had this sudden horror that your family cut you off and I wasn't helping you."

This guy is something else, and affection for him blooms in my chest at his thoughtfulness. Isn't it just like him to continue to worry about me and all the details surrounding me too?

"No, I'm not cut off. I have a trust fund that was given to me by my grandfather. It's mine, and my father can't take it from me, but I also do make my own money. The weeks leading up to the wedding, I had a lot of time to work on several pieces. They are in stores throughout Savannah on consignment, and I make money when they sell."

"I see."

I see, too. Reid is wearing a dark gray T-shirt with a worn pair of jeans that sit low on his hips, and he's barefoot. He looks freshly showered, and he looks so good.

Moving over to his furniture, he kicks one chair to face me and sits down in it. "Here, I brought this out for you." He sets down a bottle of beer on the table.

"Thank you, I appreciate it."

Music from inside floats out. Reid kicks his feet up on the balcony railing as I grab a small hand broom I bought and begin to clean up.

"Are you finished with the scraping?" he asks, taking in the frame.

"No, I'll finish it tomorrow." I bend over and start sweeping.

"Then leave the mess. No need to clean two days in a row."

He's being sweet by suggesting this, but there is dust everywhere, and I don't want it to blow over to someone else's balcony during the night.

"That's not really my style," I say, scrunching up my nose while moving around him as he watches me. "Just like I won't leave dishes in the sink overnight either."

"Hmm," he murmurs, not really responding.

Putting the remaining tools in a large bucket, I push it to the corner then take the seat next to him. I try to brush more dust off me, but it's not helping. I'm dirty.

Turning to face him, I prop my feet up next to his. "You're not how I expected you to be."

He chuckles and his brows pop up. "Really? How did you expect me to be?"

"I don't know. The way you carried yourself at the wedding and reception, I think I just thought you would live more of a bachelor lifestyle. You're young, successful, outgoing, and handsome, but here you're so dedicated to what you do, quiet, almost introverted." My voice is almost a whisper as I finish my sentence.

His forehead wrinkles with worry. "You were warned that it was going to be boring here."

"I'm not complaining, not at all. Quite frankly, I have zero interest in any kind of excitement. Being here is exactly what I needed. So, again, thank you."

He lifts his hand and rubs his chin as he thinks about what I've said. His eyes lower as he takes in the dust and the flecks of paint stuck to my skin, and then they slide back to mine. "You're not really what I expected either."

"What did you think I would be like?" I grin at him.

"Snobbier."

A laugh busts out of my mouth, and he smiles along with me.

"Admit it, princess, given what I saw in Savannah, that's a fair assessment."

"Yes, I believe it is."

That wedding was so over the top, the people so pretentious, I would be thinking the same thing. Reaching for the beer, I take a sip and hand it to him. He drinks after me, and I immediately decide his lips on my bottle is sexy.

"Tell me about this music."

"What about it?"

"Why do you like blues music so much? You played it on the car ride down here, and you turn it on nightly. I'm curious."

He leans over and tries to brush the paint flecks off my leg. His hand is warm, and the paint doesn't move. I laugh at his attempt and he just shrugs his shoulders.

"I do like blues—more specifically, soul blues. I grew up listening to it." He reclines more in his chair.

"What is soul blues?"

"It's a combination of soulful music and urban contemporary music. It allows more than just the typical three-chord boundaries found in traditional blues. Think Etta James, Ray Charles, B.B. King."

"I love B. B. King."

"Me too. I saw him once. He was performing in the city, so Mr. Dan bought us three tickets." He breaks eye contact with me and looks out over the city, thinking about the memory. "Instead of going to the concert with his friends, he wanted to take me and Nate. It was my first concert, and to this day, the best."

"Wow, that's amazing." I pull my legs underneath me and curl up in the chair. "Tell me more—who's Mr. Dan?"

He looks at me, reaches over, and picks up my hand. He starts rubbing my fingers, and I have to forcefully keep my eyes from rolling into the back of my head at the sensation.

"After school, while my mother was still working, Nate and I would sometimes go across the hall and visit with Mr.

Dan. He was about ten years older than my mother and played in a blues band at night. This man was born with music in his bones. I asked him once what he loved about it so much and he said, 'Music is the only thing that understands and can respond to all emotions of the heart. When you're happy you hear the melody, when you're angry you focus on the beat, and when you're sad you listen to the lyrics.'"

"Wow, I've never thought about it that way, but I can totally see it."

"He played the piano, the saxophone, and the trumpet. He tried to teach Nate to play the piano for a while, but Nate was never one to sit still for very long. He always had to be moving."

I smile thinking about Nate racing around the tennis court. "I don't think that's changed."

"No, it hasn't." He chuckles. "Music was always floating through the hallways. No one ever complained, and before someone new moved in, they were informed. Griping about the music was not permitted."

"Do you play an instrument?"

He sets my hand down and reaches for the other. "No. Football has always been my thing. For some reason I've always been able to run really fast, and look at my hands— they're huge, better fit to hold a ball than an instrument." He does have really large hands . . . hands I'm certain could do magical things to me.

"Do you have a picture of him?"

"Yep, he's the musician in the photos I have framed and hanging around the condo."

I turn around and look through the sliding glass doors, over to the dining room wall, where there's a black and white image of a three-man band.

"My mother dated a few guys over the years and some stuck around longer than others, but the only male constant I've ever had in my life was him." He chuckles. "He wasn't super friendly, he hated kids, and the only thing he ever talked about was music. He never asked about our day, our friends, or our life . . . it was music or nothing. I suppose we're friends now, but back then he barely tolerated us. We were loud and rambunctious, but he never turned us away when we showed up at his door."

"Where is he now?" I turn back to Reid and see he's fondly looking at the photo.

He takes a deep breath and shifts back to me. "Still living across the hall from my mother."

"Wow. Does he still play in a band?"

"As far as I know."

"Is this him playing now?" I point toward the stereo in the condo.

"No, this is just a playlist I put together a while ago. Hold on, I'll put him on."

Pulling his phone from his pocket, he taps a few times and then the song changes. Soulful piano music reaches us on the patio and is shortly followed by a solo trumpet player. The music is seductive and hypnotic, and as his gaze lands on me, the air around us seems to warm, becoming charged.

"In all the years I've listened to his music, I've never played it purposefully for someone else," he says as he lays his phone on the small table between us and stands.

Strangely, of everything we've shared over the last week and a half, this—his confession about the music—suddenly feels the most personal. There's vulnerability and wariness present in the lines across his forehead and around his eyes, and I can see how his past is colliding with his present.

"Dance with me." His voice is rough as he reaches for my hand and gently pulls me up into him.

My heart starts racing as I step closer and wrap my arms around him. His shirt is so soft and so clean, I worry about getting him dirty, but he doesn't seem to care. His body wash, deodorant, shampoo—all of it swirls around me as I breathe him in. He smells like him, what I've come to associate with him, and it smells so good.

Resting my face against his chest, I feel his steady heartbeat under my cheek. His hands run from my neck to the base of my spine as we sway to the music, and I can't help but close my eyes as I soak in this moment. I know this isn't a forever type of relationship and these moments are fleeting, but standing here in the golden warmth of the setting sun and being wrapped up in his arms, I take as many mental pictures as I can. I want to remember this and him forever.

Too quickly, the song ends and silence falls over us. I pull back and look up at him, but he doesn't let me go. Long eyelashes sweep down as his hooded eyes drop to my lips. The muscles in my stomach clench in anticipation of feeling his mouth on mine, and I lick my lips. A low groan escapes him as he bends forward. His thumb rubs across the wetness of my bottom lip and he pulls it down, but instead of kissing me, he pulls me flush against him and lays his head on top of mine.

Chapter 17

Reid

BILLY'S HOUSE IS on the water, on Davis Islands. It was originally built by a baseball player, but once he retired from playing, he decided to move. Billy, who had just signed a nine-year contract with the Tampa Tarpons, decided to put down some roots.

"Oh, you're here!" Missy squeals as she comes barreling toward us. I knocked on the door, but instead of waiting, we just walked in.

"Hey, Missy." I pull her in for a hug. "Thank you so much for all of this. We really appreciate it." I glance at Camille and narrow my eyes. She's slipped into the role she knows how to play so well, the socialite role . . . and I hate it. Her back is straight, her shoulders are pulled back, and she's smiling at Missy, but her lips are closed. She's perfected that perfect closed-mouth smile you see on actresses and well-known people. They carry it around like it's their permanent facial expression.

"Are you kidding! It's not every day we have newlyweds on the team." She's beaming from ear to ear and her gaze bounces back and forth between the two of us.

Pulling Camille tight up against me, I squeeze her hip and she gives me a confused look then looks back at our host. "Missy, I'd like to introduce you to my wife." My voice catches on the last word, and Camille picks up on it as her eyes shift from Missy to me.

"It's so nice to meet you. Billy and I just adore Reid, and we are so happy for him." She leans forward and gives Camille a quick hug even though my arm is still wrapped around her. "Of course, it would have been nice if he'd told us about you before the wedding so we could have celebrated then." She backhands me in the stomach harder than necessary and I let out an unexpected *oof*.

"Don't blame him." Camille jumps in and places her hand on my chest. "If you've seen any of the press about where I come from, you'll understand why a little bit."

"Girl, no explanations are necessary here. We're just excited to have you. Come on in, I want to introduce you to everyone."

"Okay." Camille goes to pull away, but I clamp down on her.

"Missy, give us five minutes. We'll come find you." I nod reassuringly.

She looks at us, smiles brightly, and then heads off into the house.

Pulling Camille in front of me, I wrap my hands around the sides of her head. "Hey, don't do that." I shake my head and stare down into her face. My thumbs trace underneath the edge of her jaw, pausing to take in the softness of her skin.

"Do what?" she mumbles, my fingers hovering close to her mouth. Her eyebrows slant down.

"Play the part."

"I don't know what you mean." She breaks eye contact with me and looks at something over my shoulder.

"Yes, you do," I say gently, one hand slipping around to the back of her head and tilting it, this time using my thumb to trace her lips just like I did earlier in the week. I swear I could stare at her mouth and her lips indefinitely and never tire of it. The pink gloss she has on smears, and I can't help myself as I bring my thumb to my mouth and suck it off. Her breath hitches as she watches, and my heart rate picks up as silence shortens the distance between us.

I didn't kiss her earlier on my balcony, and for days it's all I've thought about. Don't get me wrong, I sure wanted to, but I wanted to think back on that night after all this is over and just remember dancing with her.

"Camille." Her eyes dart up from my lips and her hands find my waist. "These people are my team, my friends. You may be new, but you're with me, so you're one of us. No one is going to judge you here."

She drops her head and focuses in on my chest. "Everyone judges, Reid. You've just never dealt with the repercussions like I have."

"Not here, and if at any point you feel uncomfortable, we'll leave. Okay?"

Her eyes come back to mine as she nods. Leaning down, I kiss the corner of her mouth, and she lets out a contented sigh.

"Relax, and just be yourself," I mumble against her skin, inhaling the light floral scent of her perfume.

"And who is that?" she whispers.

"The girl who's not afraid to stand up for herself or get dirty." I smirk.

"Dirty?" She pulls back a little.

"Oh, yeah. You working on the mirror all week in those little shorts was quite possibly one of the sexiest things I've ever seen."

Her eyes widen and then she grins. "Hmm, me working on the mirror is sexier than me in this dress?" She takes a step back and spins around. I don't know where she found the garment, but it's classy and so sexy at the same time. It's white, tight, and backless. Kill me.

"Princess, you know you look incredible in that dress—are you trying to drive me crazy?"

Giggling, she steps forward and smiles up at me as her arms wrap around my waist.

"There she is."

Her smile is bright and aimed right at me. I love that I get this smile and others don't, but she shouldn't be wary of sharing it. It's beautiful.

Trailing my fingers down the bareness of her spine to her lower back, I pull her tighter against me. I can feel eyes on us from somewhere in the house, but damn if that's going to stop me from putting my hands on her and having this moment with her.

"Thank you, Reid."

"For what?"

"I don't even know anymore—everything." She pulls back and looks up at me.

Bending down, I lay my lips on hers, and it's the lightest, sweetest kiss I've ever given or experienced, and it feels so right.

"You ready?" I ask her.

"Yes. Just stay with me." She lets go of my waist and threads her fingers through mine.

"Babe, I'm not going anywhere."

The party turns out to be a lot smaller than I expected. At least twice a year, Missy throws a huge party with hundreds of people, but tonight there are less than fifty. Most of them are couples from the team, a few of their close neighbors, and of course the team's PR representative and photographer.

I understand, I really do; the fans love to get glimpses into our lives. It makes us seem more relatable, and in the end, fan loyalty becomes stronger because they feel like they know us.

After about an hour, Camille's nerves settle and she ventures away from me. I keep tabs on where she is, but with Missy always hovering close, I know she's fine.

"She's too pretty for you," Bryan says as he comes to stand next to me. We've moved outside to the lanai; it's too nice out to be inside anymore. He hands me a fresh beer and I scowl at him.

"What the hell?" I already know she's too pretty for me—she's a lot of things better than me—but I don't need it thrown in my face.

He claps me on the shoulder and laughs. "Well, look at her." He waves his other hand her way just as she throws her head back and laughs. Her blonde hair skims across the skin on her back, and I'm wishing it were my hand touching her.

"I am looking at her—I look at her every day."

"Yeah, I bet you do." He gives me a sly grin.

Next to Billy, Bryan is one of the best and kindest guys I know. We go way back to college days, before he became a Heisman contender and then the winner. With everything he does, he strives for perfection, and that makes him such a good quarterback and leader for our team. We all work harder because of him, and that makes us all better.

"Yeah, well, maybe you should get your mind out of the gutter and go get your own wife."

His eyebrows rise as he looks at me then gives me a knowing smile.

Shit.

Just like Jack, Bryan knows me really well. He heard me say plenty of times that I was never getting married, and now here I am getting defensive because he's looking at her, all but beating my chest to declare her mine.

What is happening to me?

Raising the bottle to my mouth, I slam back half of it.

"Nah, I think I'm good." He stares at her a little longer and then says, "She kind of looks like someone I know, at least with the hair and her face."

"Since when do you know people?" I turn and face him. Bryan's reputation is probably the cleanest of anyone I know. He never goes out with women, too busy conditioning and playing football.

He chuckles. "I've known her for a long time, most of my life."

"Hmm. Where is she now?" His smile drops and he starts peeling the label on his bottle.

"Back home."

Bryan also never talks about where he's from. All most of us know is that he's from a small town in central Florida and his best friend is named James. They grew up together and played football together until Bryan went pro.

"And the mystery is solved," I declare, throwing him a smug expression to rile him up.

"What mystery?" He eyes me like I'm about to cross into forbidden territory.

"Why you keep yourself so unattached."

"Hardly." He frowns. "And just because you've now found yourself in marital bliss, that doesn't mean the rest of us need to."

He looks away from me and out toward the water. I study the lines in his face. As his wide receiver, I'm able to read his body language really well, and it's funny how I never saw it before. Some guys like Jack are single because the idea of settling down with one person is unfathomable—too many fish in the sea to taste—but Bryan is a loyal guy, the most loyal I know. He's a one-woman kind of guy, and with all the success he's had, I'm surprised he isn't sharing it with someone . . . or maybe he is and we just don't know it.

"Whatever you say, man. Whatever you say." I end the conversation to lighten the mood.

"Hey, Reid, Camille, come over here and let's have a toast," Jack calls out as he moves around the patio and gathers everyone together under the paper lanterns hanging beyond the pool.

Camille walks straight to me and I can't tear my eyes away. *Damn.* That dress, those heels, relaxed and smiling—if I didn't know any better I would say she's making me nervous by the way my heart is racing right now, and I've never been nervous around girls. She stops right in front of me and the two of us stare at each other, just long enough that someone clears their throat. I wrap my arm around her shoulders, she slides in next to me, and we face my friends.

At the reception, I felt awkward, but mostly indifferent because I didn't know any of those people, but here, in front of my friends and their loved ones as they're all smiling at us, something warm and soft makes its way through my chest.

"If everyone would raise their glass . . ." Jack holds his up in the air and smiles at Camille and me. "I think I speak for all of us when I say congratulations. Sometimes the best surprises are the unexpected ones, and, Camille, you were really unexpected."

The group laughs.

"No, seriously, Reid here is my best friend"—he looks at me fondly and then back at Camille—"and I've never seen him as happy as he's been over the last two weeks. They say the bigger they are, the harder they fall, and I think the earth is still suffering from the shockwaves of this one. Thanks for picking our boy—he's the best there is. Much love to you both, and, Camille, welcome to the Tampa Tarpons!"

Cheers go up and everyone takes a drink of champagne. I follow suit but can't take my eyes off Jack. Seriously, what is with him and Nate? I understand making a toast is expected and nice and all, but they both know what this is—and what it isn't.

Camille squeezes my waist and as I look down into her lovely face, my heart flips over. Have I fallen? For the first time since all this started, I allow myself to briefly wonder, *What if it is real?* And then I mentally shake my head, reality washing away this fictitious moment we've found ourselves in.

"Speech, speech, speech!" comes from someone in the crowd, and heat climbs into my cheeks. Camille's eyes widen, telling me I have to do it.

Severing my gaze from hers, I look out at everyone staring at us and take a deep breath.

"Ah, first off, a huge thank you to Billy and Missy for having us all over tonight. Your continued generosity to the team means a lot to us, and tonight, especially to Camille and me." I look down at her and see the anxiety in her eyes. I know this is hard for her, and it's hard for me too, knowing we're lying to all of them. Chuckling, I look over at Jack and shrug my shoulders because I've clammed up. "I don't really know what more to say."

"Tell us how you met," Missy says, encouraging us with a smile.

"I guess that would be a good place to start. My brother, Nate, plays tennis at Columbia University, and he and Camille have mutual friends, so they run in the same circles. I met her last fall when I was up visiting him and my mother."

"Was it love at first sight?" another player's wife asks.

I pause and look down at Camille. "It was something."

We smile at each other.

"But you were engaged to someone else?"

Ah, here it comes. People want to hear the juicy story. I can't say I blame them; I'd be curious too.

"I was," she says softly, turning her gaze to the girl who asked the question.

"If Reid had not been at the wedding, do you think you would have married him?"

She looks at me, gives me a sad frown, and nods.

"Really? Why?" Missy chimes in. She didn't like that answer.

Camille lets out a sigh. "Reid and I have talked about this a lot, so it's no great secret."

I reach over and take her hand, not sure where she's going with this but wanting to show support.

"And y'all might think I'm crazy, but this is the only way I know how to explain it: I was on a path to marry Patrick. Our families have been friends for a very long time, and eventually it became expected. It wasn't just me—we were both thrown onto that path, that course for our lives, and why does anyone do what they do? For years this was the plan, and we worked toward it. Deviating seemed incomprehensible. I wanted to do my part, believed I was doing the right thing even though

I knew I wasn't in love with him, and he didn't love me either. Sometimes I feel like when we're on a path, whether it's with sports, an education, or a relationship, and we stick to it because we need to see it through. We need to see it to the end. Things like failure, disappointment, and regret lurk in the background, and no one wants to fail or be considered a quitter, especially when other people are involved and it impacts how much they're committed as well." She shrugs her shoulders.

I think more than anything, everyone in this room understands what she is talking about—the commitment, the sacrifice. Each of us has worked our entire life to get on the path of playing in the NFL, and no matter what, we were all going to see it through to the end. Hell, we still are. We're going to play until we can't play anymore.

"What made you do it? What made you change your mind?" Bryan asks, looking at her.

She gives him a little smile then turns to me. "When you know, you know, and I just knew. It was time to make that move, and our story needed a chance."

Blood rushes through me at an exponentially increasing pace. More and more, I'm warming up to the idea of us being a possibility, and deep down, I want to pull her close and say, *Yes, I think we should give our story a chance.*

Man, am I in trouble.

Shuttering these emotions, I grin at her and break the silence. "Tell them what you did at the wedding."

"What did I do?" Her eyes flare.

Looking up, I glance around at the guys and end on Jack— he'll think this is the best. "After I objected and walked up to the altar, she turned around, saw me, and laughed. Stopping that wedding was the craziest thing I've ever done, and she laughed at me."

The entire group starts laughing, and Jack slaps me on the back.

"No, no, no! It wasn't like that at all!" Camille protests.

"Yes, it was, princess, but don't worry about it. In the end, I still got the girl."

Somewhere in the crowd, someone clinks their glass. One by one, the clinking gets louder, and a blush creeps up into her cheeks. Feeling the need to put on a show, I swing her into my arms, dip her backward, and kiss her—really kiss her. To me, this kiss is long overdue.

Chapter 18

Camille

I HAD THE best night tonight. The last time I even came close to this feeling was with Ali, Drew, Nate, and friends in New York City, but even then, the pressure of getting married to Patrick was always there. Tonight, all of that is gone.

The thing about growing up the way I did—old money, socialite, upper class—is that I wasn't given the opportunity to ever mingle with people who were different. Friendships were fake, and yes, even though I lived in New York City, I didn't really have a lot of friends, nor did I mingle with very many people. My circle was kept small, and I focused on dancing.

Several times tonight, I've thought back to when Reid confronted me about 'playing the part.' I understand what he's saying, but that's the only part I've ever played. In fact, as little girls, we were forced to go to etiquette classes, and it was drilled into us how to present ourselves as ladies. Him again mentioning he doesn't like the proper version of me reassures me that maybe it's okay to not be that girl. I don't want to be that girl; I just need to find out how to be me and where the balance is—me at home, me with my family, and me out with friends.

For so long, I've been trying to protect my rose-colored glasses. I know my view of the world has been tinted, but over the last week, I've been trying really hard to shake it off. Tonight I feel like that started to happen. There's nothing wrong with relaxing and being me, and I shouldn't have been worried that I was being fed to the wolves. These are Reid's friends, not my father's, and not Patrick's. They respect him and love him, so of course they were going to give that to me, too.

Reid is from New York. Billy and Missy are from Utah, and they are quite possibly the most down-to-earth couple I've ever met. Jack is an army brat, so he's lived all over, and Bryan is from a middle-of-nowhere farm town in Florida. The diversity in this group of people doesn't make any of them feel uncomfortable or out of place. It's like Reid said: character. They're all unique, they're all wonderful, and they all have the same goal—to live their best life. I feel more welcome here than I ever did at home.

The sound of the sliding glass door opening has me turning around, and I watch as Reid walks out onto the balcony. The party ended around midnight and we're back at his place, but neither of us were ready to call it a night.

"You really like it out here, don't you?" he asks as he heads straight toward me. Our eyes connect, and the weight of his stare has me stepping back against the railing. Tonight he wore a black suit with a pale green shirt; he's dropped the jacket somewhere inside and rolled up his sleeves. The man knows how to wear his clothes better than anyone I've ever seen. It's like he should come with a warning label: *Be prepared to stare.*

"I do." I turn around and look out into the night sky. "What I miss about New York is the city life, and what I miss about Savannah is the proximity to water. Here I feel like I'm getting the best of both worlds: city but small town, Southern, there's the water, and up here there's a breeze. I like being able to see so much. It makes me feel free, like anything is possible."

"Anything is possible."

"Now it is." And it's because of him I can feel this way.

Stepping up behind me, he wraps his arms around my waist. My hair blows in the breeze and I tuck it down to keep it out of his face.

"Did you have a good time tonight?" he asks, resting his chin on top of my head.

"I did. Your friends are really nice."

"Thank you. I think so, too. They're your friends now, too, for as long as you want them," he says softly.

John Mayer filters out from the speakers, and I lean back into Reid, resting my head on his shoulder as we listen to the lyrics of the music. Off in the distance, lights from the boats moving into the port are twinkling at us. Below us, cars seem to be racing to get to their next destination, but here, next to him, everything seems to be standing still. It's like time has stopped and the world is giving us this tiny moment to just be together, to just breathe.

"Did you feel like we were lying to them tonight? I was worried about you."

He seemed fine for the most part, but every now and then I would catch him looking at me, his expression clouded with what looked like wariness, uncertainty.

His hands shift so they can run up and down my arms.

"No, I didn't feel like I was lying. We are married, and no matter how short or indefinite this is, it's like you said: this is our story, and we're just giving it a chance."

Is he saying he wants to give this a chance—to give me a chance? My palms start sweating and I grip the railing. I don't ask him. I can't. It would ruin the moment, and I think back to all the times he's made it clear how he feels about relationships. Plus, whatever I end up deciding to do next, I need to do it for me without influence from someone else. In the meantime, I think about what Clare said. He is hot, and he's been so sincere to me, it is kind of hard to not get wrapped up in his spell, at least while I still have him.

"Camille . . ."

"Yeah?"

"Turn around, princess." His voice is stern, almost insistent as he lets go of me and takes a few steps back.

Slowly, I twist so I'm facing him and leaning back against the railing. His eyes flare at how close I am to the edge, my dress and my hair whipping out into open space. I arch back a little farther, tilting my head, taunting him, feeling brave, and his hands curl into fists. All the emotions of the past two weeks have caught up to him and are evident on his face. His body is tense; there's a strain in his muscles pulling his shirt across his chest, a tightness in his jaw as he swallows, and an intensity burning in his eyes.

"Come here," he says, enjoying the spark between us.

As I close the small gap, the wind blows, picking up my short skirt and swirling it around the tops of my legs. His eyes drop to the new flash of skin, and a shiver runs through me in anticipation of what's to come.

Gently, his fingers reach for my elbow, and I willingly allow him to pull me flush against his hard, solid body. His scent flows over me.

"Have I told you how beautiful you are tonight?" His face is half covered with shadows, the other half illuminated by the light of the moon. Longing is radiating off him, the green in his eyes so bright it's rolling like hot lava.

"Yes, but you can tell me again," I tease, leaning forward and enveloping myself in the heat his body is giving off.

His mouth twitches with a small smile as one hand slides around me and settles on my skin, just above the tiny zipper of my dress, and the other splays out underneath my shoulder blades. His hands are so large and so warm, goose bumps break out as pressure from his fingers draws me even closer. He bends down, placing his mouth next to my ear.

"I have never seen anyone more beautiful than you. You take my breath away."

With that I exhale, stop breathing, and mumble, "You're not so bad yourself."

He smiles as the music from inside changes to a slower song, and unhurriedly, Reid begins to sway, taking the lead. As he rests his head next to my cheek, the stubble accumulated over the course of the long day grazes my skin, one of his thighs moves between mine, and I feel completely consumed by him. Up and down his hands roam on my back, slipping under the edges of my dress. I'm shaking. Can he feel me shaking? Because I sure do.

"Are you going to kiss me?" I ask, moving my head so my mouth flutters against his jaw.

Pulling back a little, his lids lower over his eyes as they slowly drag down my face to my lips. "Do you want me to?" His voice is rough; it sounds like every dream come true.

I nod. "Yes." If he doesn't kiss me soon, I just might combust and die.

Every kiss we've shared up until this point has had a purpose. At the wedding, all the ones at the reception, even the one in the library, and earlier tonight—they were meant to help make this appear real. They were meant to calm us and communicate that we're in this together, and they were from one friend to another. This, however—this kiss is about to be something entirely different.

Drawing his hands away from my back, he runs them up my sides, over my collarbone, and up my neck to wrap around my head. He leans forward, and I arch back to look into his eyes—eyes filled with a yearning so close to my own, it feels tangible. He's so close, and with every breath he lets go, I breathe it in. We both breathe faster.

Back and forth, his eyes bounce between mine, and then they drop to my lips. My tongue slips out and wets the bottom one; his does the same. God, his mouth is so perfect.

Drifting forward, his lips land on the corner of mine, and my eyes slip shut.

One kiss on the left, one on the right, and then one fully in the middle. With a sigh of relief, my lips part, and our mouths fuse together like two pieces of a puzzle. I love his lips. I love how they feel against mine and how they know exactly what to do. He leads the way, and I follow. I would follow him anywhere.

Eventually, I make a move to lightly bite down on the fullest part of his bottom lip, and he growls, bends me backward, and finally takes what he wants.

The stars are shining out past the balcony, the music is playing directly to my heart, and Reid is annihilating all of my senses: his size, his smell, his touch, his sounds, and oh, his taste—so delicious. Over and over his tongue dips in and tangles with mine. I feel devoured and whole, wrecked and cherished. I feel wanted by this man, and that's the best feeling of all.

Rising up on my toes, I wrap my arms around his shoulders and flatten myself against him. He drops one arm, wraps it around my back, and pulls me up higher. We separate to breathe, but his eyes are locked in on mine.

"Stay with me tonight." His voice is so hoarse, the sound brushes over places deep within me, and I shiver.

"Okay." There's nothing in this world that could keep me away from him.

He smiles then leans forward, sucks my lip in between his, and picks up right where he left off.

Chapter 19

Camille

THIS IS THE second time I've woken up next to Reid, but today things feel entirely different. His bed is large, the sheets are so soft I feel like I'm sliding against butter, and everything is warm. I can't help but smile to myself.

Opening my eyes, I see I'm facing him and he's dead asleep. The muscles in his face are relaxed, leaving his skin smooth except for the now day-old stubble across his jaw and cheeks, and his lips are slightly open.

Sure, I've looked at him a lot over the last two weeks, but never like this. I'm in his space, and I feel giddy and lucky that I get to see him this way.

Last night, as we finally made our way into his room, my dress landed on the floor next to his shirt and his pants, and I felt what it was like to truly want another person.

Reid groaned as I stood before him in a white lace demi bra and a white lace thong. After his eyes devoured me, his hands grabbed ahold of my butt, pulling me flush against him in his boxer briefs as his mouth took over. He ran his hands all over me, exploring me, feeling me, and as much as I wanted his fingers to find every secret place of mine, he maintained his restraint, though mine was rapidly breaking down.

Of course I could tell he was just a little bit more than excited, but that didn't stop me from making out with him, nor him with me. We climbed into his bed and he kissed me for hours.

It was glorious.

Last weekend, before we went to the festival, he took me to the coffee shop across the street. He ordered a plain almond milk latte and Cuban bread toasted with butter, so, deciding to surprise him with a break from eggs and vegetables, I slip out of bed and off to my room to get dressed. Instead of grabbing socially acceptable society attire, I pull on a pair of cutoff denim shorts that have stains on them from my workshop, a T-shirt, and some flip-flops. I pull my hair into a knot, grab my sunglasses, and sneak out the door.

The weather outside is absolutely gorgeous. Immediately, my eyes look at the sky. There are no clouds, just an immaculate shade of blue, not that I want to chase them today—I'm perfectly content and happy right where I am. Spring comes earlier and lasts a little longer here than it does in Savannah, and as I take in the bright blue skies, the river, and the surrounding buildings, I can't help but think I could live here permanently.

Traffic is light as I run across the street and into the coffee shop. It's a local place, not part of a large chain, and all week I've been stopping in for their orange cold brew and biscuits. They are delicious.

"Morning, Camille," says the barista behind the counter. She's smiling from ear to ear and my mood elevates even more.

"Morning, Katie." Five mornings a week, Katie opens the shop, and in the afternoons she takes classes for a master's degree. Over this past week, we've talked a lot, and I'm pretty sure I've made my first friend in Tampa.

"How was the party?" she asks, smoothing down her apron.

"Amazing. Reid's friends are so nice." I pull my phone out and show her a picture Missy texted to me. That's the other thing about Katie—football doesn't interest her in the slightest, so she's unimpressed by Reid and his friends.

"That's great! You look so beautiful, but then again, I knew you would. I'm glad you had a good time." She knew I was worried about meeting so many people.

"Me too." I grin at her.

"Want to try something different, or do you want the usual?" she asks, looking over at her pastry case.

"The usual, thank you." I wander to the end of the bar and sit down. Looking at the notifications on my phone, I see I've been tagged in a ton of photos showing up on Twitter and Instagram. I scroll through them and smile. There are so many great ones of Reid and me that the team photographer took, as well as some of me with the other wives and friends.

I look relaxed, happy, and so does he. We really do make a striking couple. He's so much larger than I am, and his dark features compliment my lighter ones. I wonder if he can get us copies of these so I can look back and remember this night later on.

"All right. You're all set." She hands me the bag and the two drinks. A line has formed, so there'll be no chatting today.

"Same time same place tomorrow?" I ask.

"I'll be here." She smiles and heads back to take the next order.

Shuffling out the door, I wait for the light to change then cross the street to Reid's building. I can't stop smiling and I'm sure I look like a goof, but I don't care. It won't be long before my cheeks start hurting, but how can I not smile knowing what's waiting for me upstairs?

"Camille."

My smile immediately drops and my feet freeze on the sidewalk outside the entrance.

No. No. No. This cannot be happening. My eyes have widened, although I'm looking at nothing, and I'm blinking as fast as I can. Dread like ice-cold water slips straight down my spine as I take in a deep breath and slowly turn around to come face-to-face with Patrick.

Silence hangs between us as we stare at each other, the tension thickening so much it could be sliced.

"What are you doing here?" I ask him, feeling like my privacy has somehow been breached.

"Actually, I think that's a better question for you. What are you doing here?" he all but spits out. Patrick is wearing navy chino pants with a Vineyard Vines pullover. He doesn't look out of place per se, but at the same time, he does. He doesn't belong here.

"How did you find me?" I ask, my voice shaking. I hate that he's making me feel this way. Our relationship was never a bad one; we just never should have been an us. We weren't meant to be, and secretly—well, maybe not so secretly— everyone knew it.

He presses his lips together and looks away, not giving me an answer. The keys he's holding in his hands jingle as he crosses his arms over his chest. I spot his BMW keychain, which tells me he drove here instead of flying. How long is he planning on staying?

"You shouldn't be here. You have no right to come here and bother me." Whether he believes my marriage to Reid is real or not, this is Reid's home, and technically we are on our honeymoon. He's so in the wrong for tracking me down—how does he not see that?

"I wouldn't have to if you'd pick up your damn phone and talk to me!" he yells, and a few passersby glance our way.

He's so angry—angrier than I think I've ever seen him.

My nose stings. I hate confrontation more than anything, and he knows this. It makes me incredibly uncomfortable, and my go-to mode is to shut down, not engage.

"I don't want to talk to you—did you ever consider that?"

His eyes narrow like they're trying to bore a hole in me. We're in a face-off, and it's clear to anyone watching. Eventually, his gaze flicks down my body and he scowls. He doesn't like what I'm wearing and is making his opinion known, but I don't care. I don't respond, defend, or move until finally Patrick loses his patience, takes a step toward me, and reaches for my arm. The only person I want touching me is Reid and I suck in air out of shock, quickly shuffle backward, and trip, dropping Reid's coffee. The lid flies off on impact and hot liquid splashes all over me. Gasping at the burn, I instinctively bend over to try to wipe it off and rub my skin.

"Camille—" Patrick bends down too.

"Ma'am, are you okay?" a voice comes from behind me. I turn around to find the lobby security guy glaring at Patrick. Over the last two weeks, this guy hasn't spoken one word to me. He nods as I come and go, knows I'm here with Reid, and right now, I'm so grateful for him.

Locking eyes with Patrick, I stand up and tell him the truth, "No, I'm not."

I frown, and Patrick does too. I'm not sure how he thought this little scenario was going to go, but it's not going his way.

"Camille, don't do this. Please . . ." He puts his hands on his hips. "I'll buy you another coffee, just come with me. You at least owe me a conversation."

"No, I don't," I whisper, thinking of the things I saw in the library, the things he said. Respect earns respect, and he hasn't given me any in quite some time. Besides, I want to tell him I don't owe anyone anything. The only person I owe anything to is myself.

"Ma'am, why don't you head on inside, and I'll take care of this," the security guard says, moving to stand closer to me.

Without another word, without another glance, I turn around and walk through the doors of Reid's building. From behind me, I hear Patrick yell, "This is bullshit," and I pick up my pace.

Why? Why is he here? Why can't he leave me alone? With each floor the elevator passes, anxiety climbs and builds in my chest. I can't get away fast enough knowing he's just outside, and I can't get to Reid fast enough, can't have him by my side fast enough. My eyes blur with tears and I squeeze them shut while waiting for the doors to open.

I'll never be free.

Running down the hall, I burst through the door, slam it shut, lock it, and lean back against it. Folding over into myself, I can't catch my breath as silent sobs rack through my body and the tears finally drop from my eyes.

"Hey, hey, hey." Reid rushes over from somewhere nearby and pulls me into him. I'm stiff, I know it, but every muscle is locked tight and I can't unwind them. "What happened?"

He's bare-chested, wearing only a pair of pajama pants, and I press my face into him as hard as I can to breathe in the clean scent of his skin. There's panic in his movements as he runs his hands over me, looking for some type of injury, anything to explain my current state.

"He f-found me," I stutter.

"What do you mean?" He wraps his arms all the way around me and squeezes protectively.

"He was waiting for me outside. I went to get us some coffee and breakfast, and on my way back, there he was."

Reid stands a little taller, every muscle going rock-hard.

Releasing me, he takes me in, quickly scanning me from head to toe, and pauses on the red marks on my skin from the hot coffee, which also splashed all over my clothes. His eyes narrow and his jaw tightens.

"Did he hurt you?" His voice cracks as he asks me this.

"No." I shake my head.

"Did he touch you at all?" His hands tighten on my shoulders.

"No." I shake my head again then tell him exactly what happened outside.

His eyes find mine, and they're blazing green with a mixture of emotions. "Do you think he would ever hurt you?"

I pause and think about the way Patrick was acting.

"I don't know. I'd like to say no, but then again, he's never acted so crazy before. I don't know why he would come here, or why he even thinks it's okay to. When I'm ready to talk to him, I will. I'm not ready yet. Why doesn't he understand that?"

"I don't know," he says, shaking his head, displeasure painted across his handsome face.

My eyes start to water again, and Reid pulls me back into him. I wrap my arms around his waist, and his chin settles on top of my head. My eyes fall shut. He's so warm, and this warmth feels like security, safety. I'm incredibly thankful for him in this moment—hell, every moment.

"Well, let's hang out here for a while to make sure he's gone, and then after lunch we'll pack up and head somewhere else for a few days until we can figure out how to handle this, handle him. How does that sound?"

"You don't have to go with me—this is my mess." I'm giving him an out if he wants to take it. I won't be mad, definitely sad, but it is what it is.

He pulls back to look down into my face and his hands wrap around my biceps. Brown hair falls over his forehead, and his cheeks are still tinged pink from outrage. "Absolutely not. Like it or not, for now you are my wife, and I take care of what's mine."

The edge to his voice lets me know this isn't up for discussion, and I let out a deep sigh. I'm not ready to leave him yet.

"I hate that you're having to do this. It's such an inconvenience for you."

"Don't worry about it." His mouth quirks up on one side, giving me a lopsided smile. "We're offseason right now, so as long as I'm still working out and checking in here and there, it's fine. Do you have any idea where you'd like to go?"

"Actually . . ." I let him go and walk into the kitchen to put the other items on the breakfast bar. He watches as I grab my phone and send off a text to Ali, my best friend from New York. She has a house somewhere near here, and as far as I know, it's empty. I ask if we can stay there for a few days, and immediately three little dots appear. Her response comes in and I smile up at Reid.

"How do you feel about the beach?"

His eyebrows rise. "I like the beach."

Chapter 20

Reid

I FEEL LIKE I've fallen into someone else's life, like the things that are happening can't really be happening to me. One moment I'm sitting in my condo, perfectly content with my team, my new contract, and my life. In the next moment I'm married to a gorgeous Southern girl and now we're headed to Anna Maria Island.

Once we decided we'd hide out at the beach for a while, we both set off to pack our things. It didn't take us long, but I'm not going to lie—I needed a few minutes to collect my thoughts and calm myself down. I can't believe that asshole came here, demanded time with her, and thought that was going to work. If she hadn't been so worked up, it's quite possible I would have grabbed Jack, gone down to the street, chased him down, and beat the shit out of him. I've had it.

On our way out, we stopped and spoke with Blake, the security guard who helped her out. He assured me Patrick was on a watch list and I would be informed immediately if he ever came back. Although that doesn't guarantee he won't bother her, at least I know there are people here in the building looking out for her.

"How do you think he found me?" she asks as we're pulling out of my building in my car.

"That's a really good question." I had been wondering that myself, and I look in my rearview and side mirrors to see if anyone is following us. Nope. Other than the day we went out to the festival and then Billy's party last night, she hasn't gone anywhere to be noticed. A walk here and there, yes, but with her hat and sunglasses, she's kinda hard to recognize and blends in with the other twenty-something girls walking around.

At that exact moment, her phone chimes with an incoming text, and my hands give my poor steering wheel a death grip. Leaning over, I read the message without asking.

Patrick: When are you going to talk to me?

This dude is relentless. I get that rejection sucks, but he had her and it's his own fault he lost her. Enough is enough.

"I think you need to block him. Better yet, let's get you a new phone." I peek a glance at her to see if I can gauge her reaction. She sucks her bottom lip in and looks down at her phone, considering the idea.

"A new phone," she mumbles. "Do you think he tracked me from my phone?"

"I don't know, maybe. Pictures of us being out last weekend have surfaced here and there, plus all the ones from last night. He was motivated to find you, so it was only a matter of time, but switch to airplane mode to be on the safe side, and let's go get you a new phone."

"Okay, I think that sounds like a good idea."

An hour later, we're pulling away from her mobile carrier's storefront with her new phone on and set up with a new number, her old phone powered off, and we're on our way. The drive down takes us less than an hour and a half. It's far enough away that I don't think we'll be found, but close enough that I can run back to a meeting if I need to.

Pulling up to her friend Ali's house, it feels kind of strange to be staying here, but at the same time kind of awesome. Nate's mentioned to me a little bit about Beau's and his brother's past, so I get that this town doesn't evoke the greatest memories for them, but the house is charming, and looking over at Camille with her big excited eyes, I can tell she loves it.

Climbing out of the car, I'm hit with the salty smell of the air and the sound of the water crashing on the shore. The sun has dropped in the sky, we're just in time to see it set, and my feet start moving before my brain even has a chance to catch up.

"Come on, let's go!" I call over to Camille as she climbs out of the car and looks around.

"Go where?"

"To watch the sunset." I shrug my shoulders and grin.

Grabbing her hand, I pull her toward the wooden footpath that leads down to the beach.

"The last time I went to the beach was when I was eighteen," I tell her as we step down into the sand and walk closer to the water's edge.

"Really?" She looks up at me in surprise and I smile down at her.

"Yep. It was right before I left for college, and I wanted to do something fun with Nate. So, we got on the train and went to Coney Island. He was thirteen, and it is one of the best days I remember with him."

Nate laughed so much that day. Mom had given me twenty dollars so we could grab some food and ride a few rides, and then randomly we found twenty-six dollars rolled up on the ground. It had to have fallen out of someone's pocket, and we were over the moon—you would have thought we won the lottery.

"Clare and I always went to Tybee Island. It's just outside of Savannah. There's a pier and a lighthouse, but not much to do there other than play on the beach. It can get a little touristy, but we didn't mind."

As I wrap my arm around her, a quietness descends as we look out over the water. There are a few tiny clouds off in the distance, but it's essentially a clear night as the orange ball of light makes its way toward the horizon.

"Are you hungry?" I ask, tearing my eyes away to look down at Camille. The breeze coming off the gulf is blowing her hair around; it brushes my arm and feels like she's stroking me with a feather.

A giggle escapes her as she looks up at me, those blue eyes owning me, and it makes me happy to hear her laughing considering the terrible morning she had.

"I haven't thought about it much, but I'm not surprised you have—you eat all the time."

"And you don't eat enough." I grin at her. "Besides, I have to. This body is my paycheck. If something happens to it, well, then I'm out."

"I suppose. Have you thought about what you want to do after football?" She pulls a hair band from her pocket and whips her hair up into a knot on top of her head.

"No." I shake my head, reaching over to tuck a few stray pieces behind her ear.

"Really?" Her eyebrows rise in surprise.

"Absolutely not. For me there is no other option at the moment. I can't jinx it, can't allow any other thought of an alternative to enter the picture. I have to keep my eyes on the prize, and that's playing football. This is my job until it isn't. I'll cross that bridge when I get to it."

"That sounds reasonable enough." She smiles, understanding me. Bumping her hip against mine, she grasps my hand and we start walking.

"Where are we going?" I look at the houses that dot the shoreline. None of them are overly large, like you'd find on other beaches in other cities, and that makes me like this place immediately. Each house is different, unique, and I could see myself feeling comfortable living in any of them.

"Dinner."

As if it knows, my stomach growls on cue.

"After I sent Ali my new number, she sent me back some suggestions for food and activities while we're here. There's a restaurant not too far away called The Beachside Cafe."

"Sounds perfect." Just like her hand in mine is perfect, too. Shifting my fingers, I lace mine between hers.

Walking up to the café, we see there's a nice crowd inside and out. It seems a lot of people came out to watch the sunset and made their way here for some type of meal or snack.

A bell rings over the door as we enter, and behind the counter, an older woman's face lights up with a welcoming smile.

"Come on in and grab a seat anywhere you like. I'll be right over with menus."

We pick a table near the window and Camille falls silent as she sits and stares out at the gulf. The sun is at least half an hour away from setting, but the sky is already turning pretty shades of orange and pink.

"What are you thinking about?" I ask her.

Her head turns and her eyes find mine. They're clear, they look content, and they crinkle in the corners a little as a small smile makes its way across her face.

"How this feels like what a honeymoon should feel like," she says softly, her cheeks getting slightly pink.

My heart thumps hard in my chest, and I can't think of anything to say back to her. She blinks twice, her smile wavers a bit, and then she resumes looking out the window, whereas I can't stop looking at her, can't stop feeling an intensity toward her—about us—that I never imagined was possible. Maybe it's because I've spent so much time with her recently, maybe it's where we've now found ourselves, or maybe it's just her—and that's what concerns me the most. I'm not supposed to be falling for my fake wife.

"Evening, y'all," the older woman says as she approaches our table. "I was wondering if you would drop in tonight or one day later in the week."

I look her over from head to toe. She looks like an aunt everyone loves, but that doesn't keep the red flags from rising right and left. "I'm sorry, what do you mean?" There's a warning tone to my voice, and it only makes her smile bigger.

"You're Reid and Camille, right? Ali and Drew's friends."

I glance at Camille, who is staring at the woman and answers for us. "We are."

"Perfect! I'm so glad you're here. I'm Ella. Drew called earlier to tell me you might stop by and to keep an eye out. I just love those kids. Those Hale boys own a piece of my heart, so anything you need while you're visiting, I'm here for you both."

She hands us a couple of menus, recites the daily specials, and walks off before I even have a chance to thank her. Camille is quiet as she reads the menu then puts it down.

"Do you want to talk about what happened this morning?" I ask.

Her eyes widen and she shakes her head. "No. He caught me off guard, but that won't happen again." She looks back out the window and frowns, fingering the menu. "I know you probably don't understand any of this, and I'm sorry, but I do plan on taking care of this situation, and soon. I needed the last couple of weeks to come to terms with how I'm going to handle my life now, what I'm going to do next. Don't get me wrong—I'm really excited. It's what I've secretly dreamed about, but it's been such a sudden change in direction for me, and I'm trying to get my brain to catch up with my movements. Does that make sense?"

"It does, and don't be sorry. Anything I can do to help you?" I ask, leaning forward and picking up her hand to play with her fingers.

"I think you've done enough already, don't you?" Her voice is low, soft, but her eyes lock onto mine and I can't look away.

"I can always do more." I really mean that.

She rolls her bottom lip in between her teeth and bites down. Memories of last night and me doing the same thing to her flash through my mind, and I suddenly have the urge to pull her across the table and kiss her.

"All right you two." Ella is back, and I pull my hand away. She takes our order, drops two glasses of water, and is on her way.

"I think, for however long we're here, I just want this to feel like a vacation—a well-earned one," she states. "How about you?"

Shifting, I lean back and stretch my legs out until my feet bump the legs of her chair. "I'm down for that. I can't remember the last time I took a real vacation, if ever."

"Not even for spring break in college?" She moves and crosses her legs, giving me more room under the tiny table.

"Nope, not even then. I always went home to see my mom and Nate." Looking out the window, I see the sun has started to dip below the water line, and I tell her, "I've never seen a sunset before."

"What? How is that possible?" she asks, looking between me and the sunset.

"Grew up on the East Coast. I've seen plenty of sunrises, but nothing like this."

"You've been in Tampa for how long and you've never watched a sunset?"

"I've only been here for a year. I was drafted out of college to the Washington Wolves, and before you say, 'But they're on the West Coast,' it's just different. We get up so early for practice, and I'm tired at night. It was overcast all the time, and it wasn't something I've ever thought about doing. Not once have I ever said to myself, 'Today I'm going to invite my teammates to take a trip to the beach with me to watch the sunset.'"

She giggles. "You could have invited a girl."

"That's a hard no. Inviting a girl to do that definitely gives them the wrong impression, and I don't have time to deal with that mess."

"I get it. How long were you there?"

"I played with them for three years and then got traded to the Tarpons. I just signed a five-year contract with them." I can't help the smile that overtakes me. I really am proud of that contract. I've worked hard to earn my place on a team.

"Reid, that's great! You must be so excited." Her face lights up, and pride washes through me.

"Yeah, I am excited. I really do like it here in Florida. The team has a vision and goals that align with mine, what I would like for my career, and I don't think I could be at a better place. Knock on wood, right?"

She knocks on the table then we both watch as the sun disappears, leaving behind a faint glow.

After dinner, we make our way back to the house hand in hand. While we're unloading the car, I look around and spot a teenage boy across the street, leaning against his porch railing and eyeing us like we're breaking and entering. His posture is crazy tense, his arms are crossed over his chest, and his glare looks downright vicious. I chuckle to myself, thinking he must be friends with Drew and Beau too.

Chapter 21

Camille

THIS BEACH HOUSE is a vacationer's dream home. In fact, I think it could be anyone's dream home, even if they don't love the beach. As many times as Ali has talked about this place, it never occurred to me that she was leaving this behind. Tall spacious ceilings, large oversized comfortable pieces of furniture, lots of windows, and a kitchen that's open to the living room, creating a great room. On the bottom level there's a guest room, and upstairs there are two bedrooms, one being Drew and Ali's and the other more of an office and storage room.

We decided the guest room downstairs was the best room for us, and that was that. We never talked about sleeping separate, and he never mentioned taking the couch to give me space; we just climbed into bed together like we've been doing it for years instead of since just yesterday. We fell asleep snuggled up next to each other, and I wouldn't want it any other way.

Sunlight has just started to peek its way into the room when he stirs. Slowly, his warm hand slides over my waist, across my stomach, and he pulls me back against his bare chest. He curls around me, wrapping me up tight, and a sigh escapes me. I could get used to this. We stay this way for about ten minutes, and I'm just about to drift back to sleep when he kisses my shoulder, runs his hand over my hip and across my thigh, and then slips out of the bed. My back instantly cools, missing him.

Instead of heading to the bathroom, he grabs his bag, puts it on the edge of the bed, and starts digging through it.

"What are you doing?" I ask, sitting up, knowing I look like a hot mess.

"I need to work out."

My gaze skims over the muscles in his arms, chest, and stomach. His dark hair is sticking up everywhere, and he's standing in front of me in just a pair of boxer briefs. My mouth goes dry as I take all of him in.

"Now?"

He smirks at me. "I'll be back in an hour or two, and then we can make some plans for while we're here. How does that sound?"

"Sounds good, but where are you going?" I lean back against the headboard and fold my legs up in front of me.

"Just outside. I can go for a run and then do some body weight exercises in the back yard. Later today I'll look for a gym to hit up while we're here."

"Can I watch?" I'm teasing him, but his head pops up and he looks at me—like really looks at me.

The sheet is around my waist, and I'm wearing just a tank top and a pair of underwear. His eyes drift over my hair, my face, my shoulders, my chest, and down to my hips. It feels good to have his eyes on me, so I do the same to him. Those boxer briefs hug every muscle and indentation perfectly.

Tearing his gaze away, he groans, "Probably best if you don't, princess."

I smile at his blatant struggle with self-control, and as I slide back under the covers, he slips on a pair of workout shorts, a T-shirt, and his running shoes. He goes into the bathroom but leaves the door cracked. I listen as he brushes his teeth and gets ready to go. I can't help but wonder when we got so comfortable with each other that it's not even a big deal to leave the bathroom door open. Maybe we've been this way from day one and I just didn't realize it. Maybe I like us this way just a little too much.

Walking back into the room, he comes to stand next to the bed.

"You good while I'm out?" He runs his fingers along the length of my arm.

"Yep." I want to beg him to come back quickly—or better yet, stay—but that's ridiculous. We've been spending so much time together as it is, and he probably needs some to himself. So, I just smile, and he smiles back before he's out the bedroom door.

Letting out a deep sigh, my eyes wander over to the clothes he kicked off last night, to his bag, which he's placed on the overstuffed chair in the corner. I feel guilty that we're here; I feel guilty about so many things. He really had no idea what he was signing up for when he agreed to this, and I can't help but wonder what he thinks about it all, if he regrets it.

I can see how most anyone would think we're running from him, from them, and I guess technically we are, but it's hard to explain why to someone who hasn't gone through years of what I have. I'm not afraid of Patrick, and I'm not afraid of my father. They aren't violent people, just manipulative, and whether they like it or not, they're going to have to live with who I am and who I want to be, or they can live without me.

Wandering down to the kitchen, I pause, as right there in the middle of the island is another paper plane. It's different from the first one he gave me, but it looks equally complicated in the way it's folded, and I love it just as much. I'm touched that he wanted to give me something. Picking it up, I cautiously bring it to my chest and hug it. It's so simple, but coming from him, it means the world.

Smelling the coffee Reid thought to brew before he left, I pour myself a cup, retrieve my airplane, and find my way to the deck on the second level. There are two, one off of a loft area between the bedrooms, and one off of Ali's room. From here, I can see over the small dunes and down to the water. The beach is quiet, the water calm and flat. Other than a few people jogging up and down, it's relatively empty, and I really like it. This was the perfect place to come, and I know by the time we leave here, I'll be ready to move on to the next chapter of my life.

About an hour later, the front door opens and Reid calls my name.

"Up here, on the deck."

I hear him banging around in the kitchen and then he thunders up the stairs, taking two at a time. Plopping down in the lounge chair next to me, he guzzles a large glass of water.

"What?" He eyes me over the rim as I stare.

"What do you mean, what? It's not fair that you look like this"—I wave my hand at him—"after working out like you just did." His hair is wet, his skin is all dewy, his shirt is plastered to his chest, and I swear his muscles look bigger than they did before he left. He looks so good I feel awkward sitting next to him.

He shoots me a cocky grin and I roll my eyes.

"I see you found your plane." He eyes it sitting on the little table next to me.

"Yes, thank you."

"Well, I can't really have you calling this a honeymoon without giving you something to remember it by," he says, slightly sheepish.

His thoughtfulness has my heart fluttering. I pick it up and put it on my lap.

"I love it, I really do."

He gives me a closed-mouth smile, green eyes bright, and runs his hand through his hair.

"How about I take a shower, we get dressed, and then we head off the island to a big box store and pick up things we might need?"

"Like food?" I grin at him.

"Always food." He smirks back. "But I was thinking more like sunblock and maybe a new hat for you. I like your skin the way it is. If it turns pink, it needs to be because of me."

A blush burns through my cheeks at his words and he lights up.

"Kind of like that," he states, all pleased with himself as he leans over and runs his finger down the side of my face.

"Well, if I'm getting a hat then so are you—a big one to cover that big head of yours. Also, it'll help to disguise you from all your adoring fans."

"I don't have adoring fans." He looks at me like I'm crazy.

"Seriously? Have you been on social media? There are at least a dozen fan-made Instagram pages dedicated just to you, and your hashtags are out of control."

"Really?"

I raise my eyebrows. "You think I'm making this up?"

A loud laugh bursts out and his eyes crinkle as he smiles. "Fine. Deal."

We arrive at the store midmorning. It's Monday, so it isn't that crowded, which I'm grateful for.

"So, how do you want to do this? Shop together or divide and conquer?" I ask him.

He rubs his chin as he looks around, and then his eyes jump with excitement.

"I think we make a wager." He smirks down at me then moves to get two shopping carts. There's an older lady at the door checking receipts for return items, and her eyes track him. When he nods at her, she smiles hugely. *Can't say I blame you, lady.* I smile at him too.

"On what?" I ask as he pushes one in front of me.

"Who can find the best disguise," he states as if this is the best idea ever.

"You're joking, right?"

"No, it'll be fun." The way his face is lit up at the idea, he looks like a little kid in a grown man's body.

"Okay," I say, placing my hands on my hips. "What do I get when I win?" I tease.

"You mean what do *I* get when *I* win—you'll cook me dinner, of course." He swats me on the butt and takes off. "I'll find you in fifteen." And then he's gone.

Of course he makes this a game; the man lives to play games. It's in his nature to be competitive, and I find this endearing about him—really endearing.

Racing around the store, I zip between the racks and start throwing random things into my cart, like pullover muumuu dresses, big sunglasses, and a beach chair with an umbrella. I'm not really sure how much of a disguise I can find given that we're going to be sitting on the beach, but I grab two more large sun hats, two new bikinis, and some sunblock.

Ten minutes later, I spot him in the men's department, and I can't help but laugh. He's got on a massive straw fisherman hat, a really ugly Hawaiian print shirt, a T-shirt for a rival football team underneath, sunglasses with multicolored tinted lenses, and a large donut floatie around his waist.

"You look ridiculous."

Hearing my voice, he turns and gives me his megawatt smile.

"And you look gorgeous, as always." All my items are in the cart; I'm wearing my normal attire of shorts and a tank top. His eyes linger on my chest before his lips slowly curve up and his eyes climb to mine.

"You know, now that I think about it, I'm not sure you're disguisable. I don't think it matters what you wear—you were born to stand out."

He pulls the sunglasses off and tucks them in the collar of his shirt. The expression on his face is calm, his eyes tender as he looks down at me. Without saying anything, he reaches for my waist, pulls me against him, and dips his head to kiss me on the corner of my mouth. It's just a ghost of a kiss, but it shoots rockets off in my heart and I grab his arms to steady myself.

"What was that for?" I ask him.

"Sometimes I just feel the urge to kiss you, so I've decided I'm going to from now on. That okay with you?" He pulls back, the lines around his eyes and mouth happy.

"Yes." I'm lost in the adoration I feel for him.

"Good." He steps back, looking pleased under that big hat on his head. "How about you move your stuff to my cart and we'll use one?"

"Okay." I move to grab my things and toss them in then freeze. "What's that?" I point at the lone item in his cart.

"Those are for you." He grins, and I think my heart doubles in size. There in the middle of his cart is a giant bag of gummy bears. "Well, don't just stand there—put your things in."

I toss my items in, and he does the same, shedding all the new items he's acquired, and then he looks from me to them to me. "Actually, why don't you get your tiny ass in the cart and let me push you around, too."

Push me around? I don't think I've ever ridden in a cart, not even when I was a kid, and excitement blooms in my chest. It's silly. It's carefree. It's something I would have never done before, and it sounds like lots of fun.

"Okay, but you have to promise to be careful and not tip it over." I move to climb on the end and then swing my leg over. He helps me in so I don't fall, and the cart stays still.

"Camille, I'm not going to race you around the parking lot."

"I didn't say you were. Ugh, whatever." I shift and cross my legs so I'm leaning against the back with all our stuff in the front. Grabbing his hat, I slip it on then look up and catch him taking a photo of me.

"What are you doing?" I'm kind of shocked.

"Documenting our trip. Who knows when I'll have another one?"

"Okay, well, come down here and let's take one together, and then you have to share them with me."

"You know I will." He moves the hat from my head to his then drops down next to me for a selfie, or should I say an us-ie. The body wash from his shower wafts over me, and he smells so good. I smile as he holds out his long arm and takes the photo. I love that he wants photos of us. I want them too.

"Come on, let's go get some groceries and buy Ali and Drew a blender. How they survived without protein shakes, I'll never know."

Chapter 22

Reid

SHE'S RIGHT—THIS feels like what I expect a honeymoon to feel like, and I don't hate it. I don't hate it at all. In fact, I can't remember ever having a better time than I am with her right now.

Something has happened to her while we've been here over the last week. Granted, I think this all goes back to the fact that I didn't really know her before, but if I had to guess, something's changed. Her real smiles are out in full force, no more of the fake ones. Her posture, although still perfect, looks relaxed, and her laughter is even more infectious than it was before. She's still poised and classy in a way that has me constantly staring at her, in a way that couldn't disappear even if she tried, but now she's goofy, outgoing, and more carefree. It's like she was sleeping and now she's awake.

Every day, we spend almost all our time together. We've spent hours down on the beach, whether just lying by the water, collecting shells, or exploring. We've gone on bike rides that stretch from one end of the island to the other.

We've fished off of the pier, cooked dinner, played board games—you name it, we've done it. The only time we are apart is when I head over to a local gym I found to get in a decent workout. Even then, she's all I think of.

What do I think about? I think about the slope of her neck and how dainty her collarbone is. I think about the shape of her lips when she's smiling at me, just for me. I think about the tiny clothes she wears on her tight body, the way she's considerate of my health goals when she cooks for us, and how she thinks me trying to hide in a disguise is the funniest thing ever. I think about so much, and I know for certain, even long after we've said goodbye, I'll think most about what she looks like when she has her headphones in, her eyes are closed, and she's dancing around the house or on the beach.

Yes, she danced on the beach in front of other people.

The first time, I was watching clips Jack had sent over. She was stretching next to me, and then all of a sudden she wasn't. She twisted in some graceful move and was standing. Her arms, her feet, her body—they glided across the sand, and I know I wasn't the only one watching her. She was mesmerizing, and her skill and techniques painted us all a story of how deeply she's classically trained. She cast a spell on all of us, me most of all. For weeks she's had this constant worry about propriety, about how people will react if she's seen doing something less than perfect, but dancing on the beach, it was like she didn't have a care in the world.

And then there are the nights.

Every night I lie next to her, and it gets harder and harder to not lose myself completely in her. I've tried to respect any boundaries that may be in place between us, but we are on vacation, technically we are married, and even though she's not, right now she sure feels like mine—and I really want what's mine.

This morning, when we woke up, she was draped across me and lying on my chest. Her face was buried in my neck, her chest was pressed to mine, and her leg was bent and across my groin. There was no hiding the evidence of what the combination of her on top of me and the early hour was doing to my body, but she didn't shy away. Instead, she rubbed the length of her leg across me as she stretched out slowly. I could have died. On. The. Spot.

I want her, she knows I want her, and I'm certain she wants me too. This slow burn that's been building between us over the last three weeks is on the cusp of igniting into scorching flames.

I lie here for a good thirty minutes to tame the blood roaring through my body.

"Morning," she finally mumbles, the sound of her voice vibrating from her chest into mine.

I don't respond. Instead, I grab her hips, pushing her down to create some friction, and she lets out a small noise as she wraps her hands under my shoulders and hides her face against my chest.

Eventually she looks up at me seductively. "Maybe later," she whispers, taking in every feature of my face, and then her eyes widen with excitement and she sits up, straddling me. "But first, you promised me a boat ride." She squeezes my shoulders, the warmth of her hands imprinting my already overly sensitive skin, shimmies off me, throws the covers back, and hops out of bed.

I continue to lie there unmoving as her eyes slide to my tented boxer briefs.

"That's your fault," I say in a deadpan tone. I'm teasing her and she knows it, but her cheeks down to her chest flush red. Moving to sit on the edge of the bed, I reach for her and pull her between my legs. As I lay my forehead against her stomach, her hands come up to thread through my hair, and I glide mine down over her lower back, butt, and the backs of her legs. She feels so good. "Just so you know, we'll be revisiting that 'maybe later' statement at some point."

"I think we should," she whispers, her fingers tightening in my hair.

Letting out a sigh, I push her away and stand up. I tower over her, and I love it. "I did promise you a boat ride, so let's go out now before it gets too hot. I'll hit the gym afterward."

She squeals a little, smiling, and hugs my arm. "I'm so excited! I haven't been out on a boat in a really long time."

I don't tell her that I've never been on a boat.

Hours later, after a little fumbling and what I feel is a lot of dumb luck on my part, we've taken a rented boat from Anna Maria down past Sarasota and back. I now understand why people love boating so much—there's a sense of freedom in being on the water under an open sky and having the wind blow through your hair.

For lunch, we stopped on a small island Ali told us about. It was deserted and covered with large, undamaged shells. Camille filled an entire bag with unique finds as we walked around the perimeter, claiming she wanted to put them in a jar as a souvenir. I took pictures of her and us instead. Those will be my souvenirs.

"Tell me something I don't know about you," she says, looking over at me from where she's lying stomach down on her towel.

"Like what? I feel like you know most all of it by now."

"Do you have a bucket list?" She kicks her legs up behind her and my eyes trace the curve in her back to her ass.

"Not really." I lie down next to her on my side, propping my head up on my hand.

"That can't be true. Everyone has a list of things they consider to be their dreams and goals in life." Between the hat and her sunglasses, I can't really see her face, but she's shaking her head like she doesn't believe me.

"Okay, dreams and goals," I repeat, thinking about her words and how they apply to me, my life. "Goals I'm on board with. I guess you could put winning the Super Bowl on there for me, but as for dreams, why are the things we most desire to do in life dreams? Dreams are fake, not reality. If something is important enough to me, I'll make it happen. It's as simple as that."

She rolls on her side to mirror me as she contemplates my response. The top of her bikini gaps a little, and I desperately want to push her onto her back and lick from her navel to her throat.

"All right, wise guy. What about someone who wants to visit Italy but doesn't have the money? Wandering through small villages, eating amazing pasta, drinking wine from the vineyards, seeing famous structures from the past like the Colosseum—this is on their list to do in their lifetime, a dream for them."

She has a point. I understand wanting to do things but there being a lack of money. Look at where I'm from and how my mom worked to provide for us, even if we didn't have a lot.

"Okay, I'll give you that, but not everything on everyone's list should be focused around the fact that they don't have enough money. Think about those who want to run a marathon, hike the Appalachian Trail, or write a book. It's free to run, free to hike, and free to write. These would be goals. These things are obtainable, and if they mean enough, a person will make them happen."

"So terrible." She shakes her head. "A bucket list is supposed to be romanticized and admired by the individual creating it. You make it sound like a to-do list—so uninspiring."

"I don't mean to. Like I said, I've never really thought about it. I like setting goals for myself and achieving them."

"Agree to disagree. Now tell me what's on your life to-do list." She smirks, and behind my sunglasses, I roll my eyes.

"Obviously win the Super Bowl at least once during my career. I plan to buy my mom a home and have her accept it. Soon, I'd like to buy myself one, and after having Zeus around, maybe even get a dog."

"That's it?" She frowns. "Isn't there anywhere you'd like to go, something you'd like to see?"

Picking up some sand from the ground between us, I rub it between my fingers and watch as it falls. My answer to her question feels personal; it makes me feel vulnerable, and I'm not sure I like it. If anyone else were to ask me this, I wouldn't answer, but I know sharing thoughts like this, sharing parts of me with her—it's okay.

"There's never been one particular place I wanted to go. I just want to go everywhere. That was the goal growing up—to get out of the Bronx and see the world, the world being anywhere other than New York City. You would call it a childhood dream to play in the NFL, but I saw it as my ticket out, a goal. If I worked hard enough, I could make it happen, and I did. From the moment I stepped onto that first plane ride in college till now, I've been everywhere. Every game in every city was a new adventure. Do I have dreams of going somewhere far away and exotic? Not really. If the opportunity arose, great, I would go in a heartbeat, but it isn't anything I sit around and think about. What about you? Clearly you've thought long and hard about this."

Watching me, she reaches over and swirls her finger in the sand pile I just made. She smashes it down and I shake my head at her silliness. She giggles.

"I want to own my own store. It doesn't even matter where, I just want it to be mine and I'd like to call it Vintage

Soul. I want to see the Northern Lights in their full brilliance. I want to take a hot air balloon ride."

Is it wrong that as she talks about the things on her list, the wheels in my brain start turning as to how I can make all of them happen? That would imply that we are going to be together longer than the two months, though, something neither one of us has talked about.

"A hot air balloon ride—aren't you worried about falling out?"

She laughs. "No! It's a big basket. There's no falling out."

"Hello." I wave my hand over my body. "Big guy here. Basket won't be that big if I get in one."

"Wait." She sits up. "Are you scared of heights?" She's grinning from ear to ear.

I sit up with her and start packing up our things. "No, I'm not afraid of heights. I just don't see the need to put myself in a situation where I could possibly die. Admit it, plunging toward the earth after falling out of a hot air balloon would be a really dumb way to die."

She throws her head back and laughs even louder this time. I love her laugh. "Reid, if you fell out of a hot air balloon, people wouldn't say, 'Wow, what a dumb way to die.' They'd say, 'Wow, that guy is a dumbass for falling out.'"

I can't help but laugh along with her. She's right, and I would be the first person to say that too.

"Speaking of rides, our half-day rental is probably getting close to being up."

She frowns, but her skin is already starting to look pink. I run my finger down her shoulder and she sees it too.

"Come on, princess. Time to go."

Together we wade out to where the boat is anchored. I toss the food and beach bags onto the back then position us so we're right next to the motor. The water comes up to my chest, and she has to hang on to me to prevent herself from going under. We're still close to the island, not out in the open water, but we're mostly concealed from anyone who might see us.

Wrapping my hand around her back, I pull on the string. "You do realize these bikinis are so small, you might as well be naked."

"What?" She laughs, dropping down so her lips lie just above the surface of the water.

"I mean, come on—you have to know." I pull off her sunglasses and hat and toss them onto the boat with mine. "It's only a couple tiny scraps of fabric, and they don't leave much to the imagination."

"That's such a guy thing to say." She splashes me with water, grinning.

"Yeah, but I can't help it—look at you." I drop my gaze slowly down toward her chest and then drag it back up.

She smiles and blinks, drops of water sticking to her lashes. She's so beautiful, sometimes I feel like I can't breathe.

"Come here." I find her arm and pull her closer, warmth from her body layering over me. Her legs automatically wrap around my waist, and her hands slide up my arms and over my shoulders, pushing her flush against me and leaving her mouth only inches away.

She licks her lips and I drop my head forward to lick them too. They taste a little like salt mixed with sunblock; they taste good.

"Reid."

"Yeah?" I mumble.

"Kiss me." Her hand slides up my neck to the back of my head and she pulls to eliminate the distance. Her lips crush against mine, open, and I instantly dip my tongue into her mouth. Now she tastes like cherry gummy bears from our lunch.

Time gets lost as we sway with the water and the incoming wake from passing boats. Back and forth we roll into each other and into the boat, and more than once I ask myself how I got so lucky as to be here.

I kiss her, biting the skin of her neck and listening to her moan as she tilts her head back, giving me permission to slide the fabric of her top to the side and suck on her perfect breasts.

Gripping her ass, my fingertips slide under the edge of her bikini bottoms so I'm palming her skin to skin, and I rub her against me up and down.

"You feel so good," I tell her, staring into the blue of her eyes that matches the cloudless sky.

"You feel even better," she responds, tightening her legs around my hips.

"I need you." My heart is hammering in my chest at my admission.

Without hesitation, she says, "So take me."

No three words could be more perfect for this moment, but not here. There's no way I'm doing this here where it's fumbled, quick, and possibly interrupted. I'm going to take my time, explore every inch of her skin, and I desperately need to hear her call out my name.

"How about I take you home?"

She nods and leans forward to kiss me again. Wet lips and wet skin are such an aphrodisiac as my body melts even farther into hers.

I don't know why we've waited as long as we have, but I wouldn't change a thing. Every shared look, every kiss, and every tender touch has been leading up to this, and I want it more than I've ever wanted anything. There's something about the buildup and the anticipation that's already made this the best experience I've ever had.

Chapter 23

Camille

EVERYTHING BETWEEN US, since day one, has always been so comfortable and so effortless. Nothing needs to be questioned or said; we already know.

The whole ride back to the house, he keeps his hand on the bare skin of my thigh, his thumb rubbing circles, and I breathe in sync with each swipe.

Neither one of us says a word as he pulls into the driveway and parks the car. We climb out, he meets me on my side, and he reaches for my hand as we walk to the front door. Excitement burns through me, and I feel a blush run up my neck as I think about the things we're about to do.

The door closes behind us and he walks straight to our bedroom, pulling me behind him. My eyes trace the muscles across his shoulders and back, and I admire how perfect his body is. He works hard for it, and it shows.

"You sure about this?" he asks, looking back at me, not surprising me at all. Besides the fact that he's been considerate and a complete gentleman our entire time together, he's asked me what I wanted in everything we've done and let me make my own decisions. This makes me feel an array of emotions from powerful to understood. Patrick always made my decisions for me. Granted, I know it was my fault because I wanted to make him happy, I just don't know when I let him take over so much that my happiness suffered and I lost myself.

Smiling, I take a step closer to Reid as he stops in the entryway to our room, and I look up into his heavily lidded eyes. "I've never been more sure in my entire life."

Reaching for the hem of my dress, I pull the little beach cover-up over my head. Reid blinks then drinks me in as I stand there in my bikini.

"All week I've dreamed of untying these four little ties. These here on each hip." His hands brush against them and my skin, causing every nerve ending to light up and sing out loud. "This one on your back." He turns me and trails those long fingers up my lower back, causing me to shiver and be covered in goose bumps. "And this one here around your neck."

He pushes my hair out of the way and warm lips find their way from my shoulder to my neck, over to the tie. My eyes briefly slip shut as his teeth grab a loose end and pull. Slowly, the strings unravel, my top gaping and then falling as he tugs free the knot on my back. The entire piece flutters to the floor, and he hums his approval against my temple.

Large hands wrap around my rib cage and slide up until he's cupping my breasts. My head falls back against his shoulder and I moan as his mouth latches onto my neck, tasting, exploring, learning. I'd like to say I plan on spending just as much time on him, because I do want to know every inch of his body, but at the moment, I can't. I'm spellbound by his touch.

While one hand continues to caress me on the top, the other slides down the front of me, moving from my neck, between my breasts, across my stomach, and under my bikini bottoms, putting him directly over my center. He can feel what he's doing to me, and I want him to do more—so much more.

From behind, he closes the distance between us and his excitement presses into my lower back. I swivel my hips, rolling over him, and he groans, dipping his fingers inside.

"Camille, I want this so bad. I want you so bad. You have no idea . . . weeks," he mumbles against my skin.

I turn my head to look at him; his lips are swollen and just inches away. "Then what are you waiting for?"

He hesitates just for a second, his nostrils flaring at my words, and then I'm spun around in his arms as his mouth slams down on mine. The height difference between us has him bending down and me arching my body up. His large hands cover my entire lower back as he pulls me into him. I don't know what I did to deserve this, to deserve him, but I'd do it over and over again.

Desperate to feel his skin against mine, I grab at his shirt and start pulling. Tearing his lips away, he reaches behind his head and has the shirt up and over and on the floor in one swoop. Heat pours off his skin and soaks into mine like the sun's rays. He smells like vacation, dreams, and forever all rolled into one.

Staring down at me, his eyes lock onto mine, and we're both breathing hard. His cheeks are splotched red and his fingers wiggle with the desire to touch me. Never has it felt like this, and I wonder if it's because of the man in front of me, or if it's because of me. Maybe it's both.

"You are the most gorgeous man I have ever seen." And I mean that, both inside and out.

He blinks, brushing those long eyelashes against his cheeks, and swallows.

Placing my hands on his hips, just where his low-slung swim trunks sit, I begin to slide them across and up his skin. There's the soft tuft of hair under his belly button, each indentation of his stomach muscles that my fingers go up and over, and the size and strength of his pectoral muscles through his shoulders. His skin is smooth, perfectly olive, and rippling under my touch. Leaning forward, I place a single kiss on the center of his chest. His groan at the contact vibrates into my lips, and I blow on the wet stamp they left behind.

Not able to withhold any longer, he slides his hands up my back, hooks them under my armpits, and deadlifts me. I instantly wrap my legs around him and bring my mouth back to his.

Over and over his tongue makes love to mine. His head moves from one side to the other to get deeper, to get more. No one has ever kissed me as thoroughly as he does. It's like he wants a taste of my soul, the very heart of me, and if he doesn't know it already, it's his for the taking.

"I can't get close enough to you," he mumbles against me with soft, full lips. "You taste so good, so perfect, so mine." One hand squeezes my bottom. It's large enough that it can splay almost across both cheeks to hold me up while his other arm wraps around me, hugging tightly.

Hearing I'm his has me smiling, and he takes advantage by biting my lower lip and sucking it into his mouth. I squeeze my legs around his waist, shifting my hips down, and roll across the tip of him.

With a sharp inhalation of air, we're moving. He walks us to the bed and leans over until my back hits it. He uses one hand to hold up his weight, and the other he reaches behind to run up my thigh and to the side tie of my bikini. Emerald green irises focus on me as he slowly pulls the strings on the right and then repeats on the left. Dropping my legs, he pulls his hips back and pulls the material free. It also finds its way to the floor.

It's the first time I've been completely naked in front of him, and there's not one ounce of self-consciousness present anywhere.

Looking down, he runs one finger around my breasts, down my stomach, and then side to side between my hip bones.

"These tan lines are incredibly sexy. I like them . . . a lot." His eyes bounce to mine then back down, his voice more hoarse than I've ever heard it. Responsively, I arch up under his touch.

"I bet you have a tan line too," I taunt, and his lips curl up on one side into a smirk.

Standing between my legs, he inches back, and I prop up on my elbows to get a better look at him. He hesitates with the tie on his swim trunks, and I glance up at him. He's watching me, and the emotions written across his face are real and open. His gaze is tender, the muscles in his jaw are only a little bit tense, and his nostrils flare just slightly when he breathes.

"What's wrong?" I ask him.

"Nothing."

"What are you thinking about?" I shift so I'm sitting up.

He shakes his head; he doesn't want to tell me, and that's fine. After all this time, I understand. This, what we're doing—it's a big deal. It changes us.

I swipe his hands away, and they fall to his sides as he stands there and lets me slip his trunks off.

I'm not sure anyone could ever be prepared for a naked Reid, and my heart rolls over in my chest as I take in every inch of him—and I do mean every inch. He's beautiful, and my thighs tighten with excitement knowing what they're about to receive.

"I was right." I glance up at him through my eyelashes then drag one single finger from right to left over the glorious muscles that make a V. "Tan line."

Not able to contain myself, I lean forward, lick him from root to tip, and then take him in my mouth. He moans and rocks up on his toes as his hand reaches out and his fingers tangle in the hair on the back of my head. A rhythm is set and I feel pride knowing I'm the one who's making him shake— *me*. Even though I know why we waited so long, a tiny part of me is protesting. It feels like lost time, and that just confirms to me that my head and my heart are in this together.

"Princess," he whispers. "You have to stop."

"Are you sure?" My hand wraps around him tighter.

"No." He chuckles, and then slowly backs away. "But, I'd prefer this to end another way, at least this time." He smiles down at me with brown hair sticking up everywhere and gloriously flushed skin.

I scoot back across the bed and he follows, blazing a path up my body with his very wet tongue. I'm certain, had I given him the chance, he would have made a meal of me, but I'm ready to feel him, all of him.

Stopping on my breasts, he takes his time ravishing each one as I grip the sheets underneath us, impatience about to win out as my heart beats a hundred miles an hour.

"Salty," he mumbles. He was salty, too, evidence that we spent half the day on and in the water.

"Reid." I pull him, begging him to make another move, and he does.

His large body aligns and rubs across me in the most erotic way. His mouth latches onto mine, and my arms and legs fold around him, keeping him close. Even if we never went any further than this, I would die a happy woman.

Sliding my hands over his back, I rub them up and down and then lose my fingers in his hair. I want to touch all of him, all at once, and I feel feverish with desperation.

Rolling my hips, the tip slides in, and he freezes and throbs at the contact.

Lifting up, he hovers over me as his clear eyes find mine. They're questioning, brows raised, and I nod. I trust him implicitly with the line we're about to cross, and it's apparent he trusts me too.

Pushing in, his eyes fall shut with pleasure just before he drops his lips back to mine. He's over me, around me, in me. I'm completely consumed by him, and I'm aching for all of it. As the minutes tick by, I feel like we're back in the water, swaying with the waves. Some are gentle, some are rough, but it's exhilarating, and I know I'll keep going back for more.

More. More. More.

Eventually, his hands slide under me and tilt my hips. He goes deeper, finding more, and it's oh so good. Sweat is shining off our skin, hearts are racing, and breaths are harsh and loud. Nothing has ever compared, and as the waves build, peak, and then crash down, I submerge myself in the current and blissfully ride it out until I'm spent and lying on the shore.

Heart pounding, beat by beat, it expands in my chest with an overwhelming sense of love for him. This man, my temporary husband—can he feel it? Does he know?

This moment . . .

Him . . .

All of it . . .

He's just saved me and ruined me at the same time.

Chapter 24

Camille

I COMPLETELY UNDERSTAND now what it means when people say time flies when you're having fun. Three weeks have flown by, and deep down, I know our time here is just about up.

Time.

It's funny how time and separation really can change perception. For five years, I've been in the thick of it with my family and with Patrick. We went from being just a couple of teenagers to young adults, where other people began pushing us in the direction they wanted us to go to better suit their goals and aspirations.

I've thought a lot about Patrick over the last couple of weeks. I've thought about the dynamics of our relationship, his relationship with his family and mine, and all the involuntary subtle tells of his unhappiness that now seem so obvious—the way he'd briefly look down when my father would speak to him, when he chose a northeastern college and shocked us all, how he would strip off his tie and pop the cap off his favorite bottle of beer every chance he got. Patrick doesn't want that life either anymore, but he's just like me in the sense that he wants to make those around him happy and proud. He's probably also lost like I was. If he steps off the path, what does he do next?

I hope he's used this time to think about that. I know he's angry, but there's nothing wrong with me wanting to take a little me time. That's all I did, and I know soon he'll see it was the best thing for both of us.

Although, I still haven't forgiven him for the Brittany fiasco and for tracking me down at Reid's home. Maybe I should have talked to him. If the situation were reversed, I'm certain I would want the same thing.

Reid asked me the other day if I missed him, and I do. He was my friend for a really long time, the one person who understood everything about our lifestyle and the expectations. It's because of this that I feel guilty for leaving him to deal with the fallout.

Guilt.

I also feel guilty because I've dragged Reid into this mess. Granted, he doesn't complain, but he never asked for any of this. He was just offering me an out, one I selfishly took. I am so grateful that I did, in more ways than one.

Thoughts of Reid and earlier this morning float through my mind, and I close my eyes. We took a shower together after his workout, and the water wasn't the only thing that was hot. His body is like a work of art. He has almost zero fat, more muscles than I knew the body actually contained, and his strength and endurance are off-the-charts impressive. Steam, water, soap, his hands, his tongue between my legs— all of it is imprinted so deep in my pores, I'm certain I will feel him on me indefinitely.

I'm sitting here on the beach, just down from the dock pathway. My knees are pulled up, my arms are wrapped around them, and my chin is resting on top. I've been here for a while, and the tide is on its way in. Seagulls have circled a few times, looking for food, and I wish I had thought to bring down a loaf of bread. I've heard people call them beach pigeons or rats with wings, but I think they're beautiful, just like this beach.

Before Ali, I had never heard of Anna Maria Island, and I don't know if that's a bad thing or good. It's bad because, of all the beaches I've been to in my lifetime, this one is by far the most beautiful, and it's quite possible I never would have found it without her. It's good, though, too, because it's like the best-kept secret ever. There are no large chain hotels, no big attractions, just a simple little sleepy beach town filled with eclectic shops, some amazing restaurants, and the blue-greenest water I've ever seen.

In New York, the air smells dirty. In Savannah, the air smells like the paper mills. In Tampa, the air smelled humid, but here on the island, it smells of salt water. It's head clearing and soul cleansing.

On Fridays during our stay, Reid drove back up to Tampa to attend the weekly team offseason meeting, and I used that time to plan out what is going to happen next. I've done my research, from the business name and how to file for an LLC to website design companies and launching social media pages to promote the work I've already done. I have given thought to a storefront, but that part of my vision is still fuzzy. I can better decide after scouting locations once I'm back in Savannah. So, for right now, I'll continue to consign pieces and advertise to restore and make custom pieces. Because of all this, I feel more excited than I do anxious about what is awaiting my return, and that's how I know it's time to go.

We can't stay here forever, and I don't even want to. I do love my family, I love my workshop, and I love how Reid gave me this. I still catch myself wondering why he did it; maybe one day he'll tell me.

The sand shifts next to me as Reid sits down. I don't take my eyes off the horizon, because if I do, if I look into his handsome face, I'll change my mind. It's silent around and between us except for the water lapping on the shore and the hum of the wind dancing through the sea oats surrounding us.

"Hey," he says, looking at me. My hair blows in the breeze, and he reaches up to tuck it behind my ear.

"Hey," I say back, my eyes slipping shut at the touch of his fingers.

I've been living in a fairy tale, and I know it's time to face reality.

When I first got to Reid's, I asked myself two questions: who am I, and what's important to me? I may still be figuring out who I am, but at the end of the day, I know what's important is living my life for myself. Those who truly know me and love me have all said it, especially Clare, and it wasn't that I couldn't make my own decisions before; I just thought I was being kind and selfless. But, even though my intentions were always meant to be good, truth is, no one cared. I wasn't appreciated or valued; I was being used. Well, no more.

"You okay?" he asks, his voice low and rumbly.

"I will be." I know that's the truth. People can't hurt you if you don't allow them to.

Stretching his legs out and crossing his ankles, he puts his hands behind him in the sand and leans back casually.

Glancing over, I let my eyes drift up from his bare feet to his unshaven face. He's wearing a gray T-shirt and navy blue athletic shorts, his hair is sticking up everywhere in the breeze, and he looks perfect—so perfect my stomach clenches with how much I wish this were real . . . that in the end, we were real.

"What are you thinking about?"

My eyes jump to his face; his brows are lowered and he's frowning.

"At the moment, sunsets," I tell him, looking back out toward the water to hide what I'm feeling. "They're so pretty and feel so calm. Sunrises always make me excited for a new day, make me want to get up and conquer the world. Sunsets make me want to slow down to enjoy the moment as it winks good night. Honestly, I don't know which I like more. They're both beautiful."

He chuckles. "You do know you don't have to pick one over the other. You can love them both."

I smile with him. "Yeah, I guess. I think it's just ingrained that we have to choose. Did you ever play this or that as a kid? Winter or summer? Beach or mountains? Blue or green? Hamburger or hotdog? You always had to pick one, it could never be both."

He doesn't say anything, just watches me, his long eyelashes sweeping down over the soft skin under his eyes when he blinks. He's so beautiful.

"Sunrise or sunset? I think you're right—I do love them both."

"I usually am right." There's humor in his voice as he bumps his shoulder against mine.

"Reid, why did you do all this for me?" I must have asked at least a dozen times.

He doesn't answer, just shrugs his shoulders.

I lean in, and he bends his head to let me kiss him. His lips are soft, warm, and so familiar, and now it's just natural to be affectionate with him. He doesn't seem to mind, either; since the day of the boat ride, we've both been pretty insatiable.

Pulling back, he takes his time and studies my face. Whatever he finds, it causes him to look away and let out a deep sigh.

"So, it's time to go home?" He bends his knees so he can bury his toes.

"Can't stay here forever." I shift a little to face him and cross my legs under me.

"No, I suppose not." He sounds resigned, sad.

"Although, if I had to pick a place for forever, this would be it."

He nods then tilts his head to look at me, brown wisps of hair fluttering on his forehead.

"Are you ready?" His concern is so genuine, his green eyes so seeking, my throat tightens with emotion.

"I am." I reach over and lay my hand on his leg.

"Are you happy?" he asks me, his vulnerability sneaking out just a tiny bit.

"Happier than I've ever been." My eyes lock onto his and they don't waver. I want him to see how I feel, and what he's given me—all of it.

Slowly, he smiles, and the last piece of my heart begs to go to him. I gladly give it over.

"Come on, let's go for a walk." Standing up, he brushes the sand off his palms then holds out a hand to help me up. Sliding my fingers into his, I squeeze, wishing I never had to let go.

"Why are you looking at me like that?" I ask. His expression is adoring, but also filled with mischief.

"Because you're so tiny and cute, sometimes I want to manhandle you."

"Manhandle me? What does that mean?" I ask, brushing the sand off of me.

Bending over, he grabs my arm with one hand while the other slides around my legs, and the next thing I know, I'm thrown over his shoulder in a fireman's carry.

"Reid! Put me down!" I laugh, and the seagulls near us scurry away.

He starts jogging and laughs. "You're so light. I should have been using you for my workouts these last few weeks—but then again, maybe not. My exercises would have shifted to a different kind." He slaps me on the butt then swings me around so I'm in front of him and my legs are wrapped around his waist. "I want you to know I had a really good time here with you. Every minute exceeded what I could have ever imagined. No regrets."

His thoughtful words ease a little of the guilty tension in my chest. He did have a good time; I know he did—we both did.

"No regrets." I echo his words and lean in to hug him. He hugs me back. It's the best hug I've ever had.

"One more picture?" he murmurs next to my ear.

"Yes." I smile at him as I wiggle out of his hold and drop down. I love that he's taken so many photos of us.

Pulling out his phone, he turns us so our backs are to the water and he can get us in the frame along with the sunset. Standing up on my tiptoes, I get as close to him as I can. The scruff on his cheek brushes my face as he drops down to be closer. We smile, he takes the photo, and I think life can't get much better than this.

Chapter 25

Reid

WE KNEW THIS day was coming—it just got here a lot faster than I was expecting.

We're a couple weeks shy of the agreed upon two months together, but heading back to Savannah now is not an unreasonable move. After all, we went on a honeymoon, and now it's over. Clearly, she has to get back to her life and I have to get back to mine, and if we are being watched, it is what it is.

The drive up from Florida is mostly quiet. Repeatedly she mentioned just catching a flight home, but I insisted on driving her. That is something a new husband would do—and, well, something a decent human being would do, too. There is no way I'm not returning her to her doorstep, pretty much exactly where I found her.

Looking over at Camille, my heart squeezes in my chest. Her feet are propped up on the dashboard and she's flipping through the photos of our time together on my phone. I had to have all those pictures. I don't know why—I'm not that sentimental of a guy—but I couldn't get enough of them, her, or us. A few I sent to my mother, which made her happy, and then a few we posted on our social media accounts. That's what a real couple does, right?

A real couple . . . my mind trips over this, because we may have started out strangers, but too much has happened for us not to be a real couple, at least not now. I've never felt this way for another person. Somehow, she quickly became someone who means more to me than anyone else, and maybe that's the difference. She was never some girl I was just going to hook up with; she's always been so much more. Yes, the chemistry between us is off the charts, but I wasn't looking to make that the only thing between us, and because of that, we became friends.

"I think we should send this one to Drew and Beau and caption it *Matt's new love*." She grins as she shows me the picture of little Matt leaping into the air to catch a football.

Turns out, Drew and Beau, Camille's friends from New York, grew up across the street from Ali's house. She moved in, met Drew, and the rest is history. The boy we saw glaring at us the night we arrived is their younger brother. There are three of them, the Hale brothers. He must be around fourteen. I remember when Nate was that age. Hormones, attitude, and in general, he just wanted to be older than he was. This kid wasn't that different. Once we introduced ourselves, he came over a bit here and there, mainly to hang out with me and toss the ball around.

"You know them better than I do. If you think it's funny, send it."

Drew swims and is headed to the Olympics, Beau plays tennis, and this kid Matt wants nothing to do with either of those things. I get it, though; Nate always wanted his own thing, which is why he gravitated toward tennis.

"Okay, I just airdropped all these photos to my phone." She smiles at me and lays my phone on her leg.

"What's your favorite thing we did?" I ask as light blues music plays in the background.

"Oh, that's a hard one. I don't think I can pick just one." She frowns and traces the edge of my phone with her finger. I don't know why, but my insides are reacting to this. It feels like she's touching me, but she's not. It's a stupid electronic device. I'm losing my mind.

I laugh to myself and at her, eyeing her smugly. "Did you just say you aren't choosing? No this or that?"

She grins back. "I guess I did. You're rubbing off on me."

My lips press into a thin line as my eyebrows rise.

Her eyes widen as she follows my train of thought, giggles, and then shakes her head and slaps me on the thigh.

"You're incorrigible!"

"Maybe, but that's only because of you. It's your fault, princess," I accuse, smirking and enjoying the playful banter.

"Fine. If random comments have your mind immediately slipping into the gutter, I'm not complaining. You can join me—I frequent it often."

"What?" My jaw drops open.

"You heard me." Her cheeks blush pink, and *damn* she's adorable.

A few hours later, I pull up to the curb in front of her house. My heart sinks in my chest knowing I'm going to be leaving her here and heading back home alone. As I kill the engine, we eye each other briefly, silently, before I let out a deep sigh and get out of the car.

Together, we haul all her things into the foyer, and she leaves them at the base of the stairs. I watch as she digs through her recently purchased beach bag and pulls out the large vase of shells she collected, along with the paper airplane. Walking into her living room, she places them both on the table next to the window where the first plane I gave her sits. She arranges them then turns to me and smiles.

"There, perfect!"

This girl is something else. She has so much, yet it's the things that cost nothing that she keeps beaming over.

"This really is a great house," I tell her as we walk through the rooms and back to the stairs. I pick up most of her bags and we move to take them upstairs.

"Thank you, I think so." She looks around, down over the railing. She pauses briefly and then looks at me, a tiny frown marring her perfect lips.

After spending the last couple of weeks together and knowing I'm not staying, this house suddenly feels too large, too empty. Just her, here all alone . . . I'm not sure I like this—not at all.

"I've actually done a lot of work on it over the last couple of years. I didn't stay in New York for the summers. I came home because this is where they wanted me to be, and it gave me something to do other than fundraisers and lunch at the clubhouse."

"Having my fingernails pried off sounds like more fun than that."

She giggles. I love the sounds she makes.

Leaving her stuff in her room, I wander around the different floors and the different rooms with fresh eyes while she settles in and flips through her mail in the kitchen. When I was here before, I was more or less in shock, but now as each minute passes, I begin to feel more and more uncomfortable. At the beach, and even a little bit toward the end of our time at my condo, I felt like an equal to Camille, like she and I as a pair was natural and we belonged together. Here, I'm starting to not feel like that at all, even after everything we've shared. This house is so far removed from anything I've ever seen or even been in, and I've been to a lot of well-to-do football players' homes, but here I feel out of place. I don't want to; this is Camille and her fingerprints are all over the details, but the evident wealth is a reminder that we were never supposed to be, and suddenly I begin doubting the idea of us being a couple. I'm hesitant, and I'm never hesitant.

My chest aches as I think someone like Patrick is probably much better suited for her than me.

"Are you hungry? I can make us some dinner," she asks, walking into the library, where I'm standing. I'm unconsciously sliding the wooden ladder used to retrieve books from the top shelf back and forth. My hands drop and I turn to face her. She's smiling, and even after five weeks, the impact it has on me is still like a punch in the stomach.

"I'm getting there. I'd love dinner." We left first thing this morning and stopped for lunch on the way, but now it's four o'clock.

"More like you love my cooking," she says, spinning around and walking out of the room.

"That I do, princess, but I'm thinking we need to order in. You'll need to replace the food in your refrigerator." I follow her into the kitchen and grin.

"Ordering in sounds good to me." She stops next to the center island, and her face dips with a strange emotion. It seems I'm not the only one who's lost in thought. Then she's moving toward me, into my arms. Immediately, I hug her back and drop my head to the top of hers.

She calms the storm in me, and I wonder, *This can't be wrong, can it?*

The uneasiness I felt a few minutes ago is overtaken by longing, and not just the physical kind, but the emotional kind, too. I'm not ready to leave her yet. In fact, I don't know if I'll ever be ready. Maybe she feels the same way, and maybe that's why we're clinging to each other like it's a permanent goodbye.

"Can I stay tonight?" I ask, my head bent down, my lips in her hair.

"Of course." She squeezes me tighter as some of the tension dissolves out of her shoulders.

"When do you think you'll talk to your family?" I run one hand up and down her back as she leans back and looks up at me with eyes so blue, and now so familiar.

"I don't know." She frowns. "Sooner than I want to. I'm sure they already know I'm back. Here in Savannah, nothing is a secret, yet everything is, if you know what I mean."

"Do you need me to stay?" I ask, narrowing my gaze and looking for any clue that she does. I would in a heartbeat if she wanted me to.

"No, but thank you. They'll never stop unless I make them. It didn't use to be this way—I didn't use to be this way." She shakes her head and pulls away from me. "It's important to me that you know that."

"Okay." I agree with her, because it does seem important to her, but I have no idea what she's talking about. How has her life ever been any different?

"It's because of my past, and the things I have to say to them . . . it won't be a shock."

I nod; she seems so certain. "Well, you know I'm only a phone call away."

"I do." She inches closer and rubs a soothing hand up my chest. Giving me a grateful smile, she adds, "And I appreciate that more than you will ever know."

She grabs her phone off the counter and we move back into the living room.

"Do you know what you want me to order?" she asks as I flip on her television and select a music channel.

"No, I'm indifferent. It doesn't matter."

Sitting down on the couch, I reach for her hand and pull her to straddle me. Her legs fall beside my hips as she settles on my thighs, and she stills.

Instantly, the music playing in the background is lost. My senses are overloaded, sight winning out, consuming my attention. Neither one of us moves, just staring at each other.

"You are so beautiful," I whisper, taking in so many details of her face. Pale blonde hair, heart-shaped face, perfect eyebrows, freckles across her nose, and a bottom lip slightly fuller than the top. Reaching up, I tuck a few loose strands of her hair behind her ear. My fingers tremble, but she doesn't seem to notice.

Her eyes widen just a little, and she takes in a long, slow breath before releasing it in a rush.

Tossing her phone on the couch next to us, her hands run up my arms and wrap around the sides of my face, her thumbs brushing the stubble across my cheekbones.

"Reid . . ." She pauses, her eyes imploring me to already know what she wants to say, but I don't, and that makes me afraid, because it might not be something I'm ready to hear. Sucking her bottom lip between her teeth, she blinks, and little wrinkles form between her brows.

With my hands on her hips and a slight shake of my head to keep her silent, I pull her closer until her chest brushes mine and my lips seal onto hers.

Hours and hours I've spent kissing her over the last few weeks, but this kiss feels different, more. It's unhurried, deeper, more sentimental and tragic at the same time. Her fingers run across my scalp and tangle in my hair. I mimic her, gripping her silky strands and tilting her head to taste even more. She feels me harden beneath her and rolls her hips, letting out a small moan.

God, what her sounds do to me.

Piece by piece, our clothes vanish. We take our time exploring and memorizing in the late afternoon light, until finally, rising up, she positions herself over me then sinks down. My eyes roll back in my head and the tendons strain in my neck. This is the purest kind of torture—knowing how out of this world this feels, how she feels, and that I can't have it every day.

"Reid," she whispers, her eyes closed. Her head tilts back, and her hair tickles my hands as I begin to guide her hips to move with mine. Her face is a mixture of pure pleasure and pain—pleasure because the two of us together is complete ecstasy, pain because this is devastating her heart like it is mine, and I completely understand.

Time passes.

There's no frenzy, no rush, only a gentle tenderness to our cadence that creates and builds something so intense, it leaves us both shaking in the end.

I pull her as close as I can, her chest flattens against mine, and she tucks her face into my neck.

Somewhere in the deepest part of me, I hear a whisper like strokes of a feather. It cherishes her and calls her my wife, and in this moment, she is, by every definition of the word. She's my wife, I'm her husband, and what we just shared was real and true. I made love to my wife.

Warm wetness rolls over my collarbone and onto my chest.

"Hey." I tip her chin so she looks at me. There are sad, watery tears in her big blue eyes, a pout on her swollen lips. She blinks a few times as I study her, and my heart damn near bursts. I can't allow this to be because of me. I need her smiling, not crying. "This isn't over. We aren't over—you know that, right? I'm not going to disappear, and neither are you."

"I'm not ready to say goodbye to you," she says quietly, like she's not supposed to admit it out loud.

"Then don't." It's as simple as that.

She lets out a sigh, the muscles in her face relax, and after a few blinks, the sorrow recedes.

"Like we've said since the beginning, nothing has to be decided today, okay?" I trail my fingers over her face, erasing the tracks of the few escaped tears.

She stays quiet but gives me a small smile, crinkling the corners of her eyes.

"We'll figure this out, together." I nod, willing her to agree, but she folds herself into me, hugging me tight.

Right this moment, I'm ready to throw in the towel and say let's do this, but I know I can be impulsive and we're both caught up in this whirlwind of emotions. For once, I know I need to slow down and take a step back. I can't just think of myself here, which is why I'm certain we can't make any decisions today. We've just spent five weeks together, essentially isolated from everyone, and I need some time to think about this, to be sure, for both of us.

"I'm going to miss you," she mumbles against the skin on my neck.

"I'm going to miss you, too." I'm still in her; we haven't moved, my arms are wrapped around her, and my eyes slip shut.

How do people survive these emotions? I don't understand. I feel raw, vulnerable, exposed, and then to top it off, she slays me as she whispers, "My favorite thing we did was everything, because I got to be with you."

Chapter 26

Camille

"I CAN'T BELIEVE you let him go," Clare says from the entrance to my workshop. I was wondering when she was going to show up. I thought it would be yesterday, but she's waited two whole days.

I put down my paintbrush and turn to her. She's wearing a long light pink dress. It's loose and has spaghetti straps, showing off her perfect, flawless skin. Her hair is long and wavy, floating down her back, and my insides clench at the sight of her. She's so beautiful. She's also glaring at me.

Two mornings ago, I knew when I woke up he would be gone, and he was. I slid my hand across the sheets wondering if they would still be a little warm, but nope, they were cool and smooth like they had been unoccupied for quite a while. What I did find, though, was another paper airplane. He sure knows a bunch of different patterns for planes. Instead of picking it up, I decided to leave there, on his pillow, his side of the bed, his plane. I know it's dumb, and it's just a piece of paper, but it makes me feel closer to him.

"How do you know he's not here?"

She cocks her arm on her hip and frowns. "Because he's not."

Letting out a sigh, I take my brushes over to the sink and begin to rinse them out. As usual, there's no *hey* or *nice to see you*; it's just straight into arguing. That's one of her go-to moves: judge, argue, or evade. She hasn't had an actual heartfelt conversation with me in years, and I don't consider the five-minute *you're making the biggest mistake of life* speech before my wedding one either.

"What did you want me to do, tie him down?" Maybe I should have tied him down; the thought of him still being here and up in the house has me smiling. Then my thoughts turn in a different direction and my smile widens. Yes, we've been creative over the last couple of weeks, but never in a million years could I see Reid restrained. Poor guy couldn't sit still to save his life. Even his job involves him running, and it's like it goes down to the core. Plus, he's a very *very* involved participant. I feel my cheeks redden at the thought.

"If necessary, yes!" Clare yells, pulling me back to the present.

"Clare, he has a job to get back to, remember?" I move back to the project I was working on and start cleaning up. "I don't think he even wants to be with me. This was only supposed to be a temporary deal—two months, that's it, and then we separate." We might have become friends—even more than friends—but he's never talked about what would happen after our two months, and even when we returned to Savannah, there were no reassurances or plans made for us to even see each other again. If he wanted to be with me, he would have told me, right?

"Are you kidding me? That's a lie and you know it." She paces around the room.

"Do I? He's been pretty up front from day one that he never wanted to get married, he has zero time for relationships, and this was just a means to an end for me."

I turn away from her and walk to the little refrigerator sitting in the small makeshift kitchen space. I grab a bottle of water and take a few swigs. I don't want her to see how the thought of Reid and me ending, just like that, really kind of devastates me.

"Did you tell him you wanted to see him again? Give you guys a real shot?"

"No. It can't come from me. He knows I like him—that much is blatantly obvious—and he has to be the one to decide if we're more or not."

"Why? Why are you again letting someone else make the decision for you?"

Her words are like an arrow. She points her bow, aims, and takes her shot, right at my heart. I feel pierced, like I'm bleeding out on the floor. How can she say that to me? For weeks my backbone has been hardening to where I feel my spine is made of steel. I make my own choices. I determine what happens next in my life, and I'm not bowing down to anyone anymore.

"He didn't make the decision for me—I made it for him! I feel bad enough that he's already had to give me so much of his time. I've inconvenienced him in so many ways, from his family to his personal life and his professional life. I feel guilty enough, and I am not about to lay myself at his feet and beg him to stay. After all of this, it has to come from him. I deserve that. Don't you think I deserve a guy who will fight for me because he wants me, not because he needs me in order to advance his career? Well, I do."

"I still think you're wrong," she says in a much softer but still confident tone. "I think if you had asked him, things might have turned out different."

As much as I want to be wrong, too, I don't think I am.

Reid did text me when he got home, and I received five more yesterday and three so far today. The messages are pretty basic, surface level. He asks about my day, what furniture I'm working on, if I've talked to my family, that kind of stuff. In return, he tells me about Jack's latest shenanigans and things going on with other teammates, basically giving me a play-by-play of his day. I think it's sweet of him to reach out, I'm just not sure why he's doing it. He hasn't once mentioned missing me.

"And why would you think that? I haven't talked to you in weeks. You know nothing about us, and quite frankly, I don't think you know anything about me—not anymore."

Anger I've been trying to suppress bubbles to the surface. What is with people always assuming they know me and what's best for me? Just like everyone else in my family, Clare has never, not once asked me what I want. Maybe a few weeks ago I would have had a hard time articulating it, but I know now, and with that thought, the anger recedes and I'm left feeling detached from anyone, everyone . . . alone.

Before Reid, I was lonely, even though I was still a part of the family, the social scene, but now, after him, this is a whole new type of empty. I know I should be powering strong through my new wave of freedom and independence, but that doesn't change how I was shown what a great life looks like with a great partner who lifts you up instead of tearing you down, and then it was snatched away, as if someone's in the background laughing while saying, *Just kidding*. It feels like a punishment. Maybe it is.

"Camille," she says, approaching me. Her eyes are large, and there's a distant sadness in them that's unavoidable. I don't see her as much as I used to, and the older we get, the less often it happens.

"No, don't you 'Camille' me. You left me at eighteen. I'm twenty-three years old, twenty-four next month—what do you really know about me anymore? Five years is a long time, Clare. People change. I've changed. You should know that, but you don't."

My eyes shimmer with unshed tears, but I refuse to let them drop. That steel spine of mine has me lifting my chin just the slightest, daring her to disagree with me, and I watch her chest expand as she takes in a big gulp of air.

From across the yard, we hear the doorbell ring.

"Who's that?" she asks, her head turning toward the house.

"Our father." I roll my eyes. "I swear he has spies. It's like he knew I was back in town before I even did. He"—I raise my hands and sign quotation marks—"put me on his calendar and scheduled us an appointment."

"What does he want?" she asks, spinning back to look at me.

"You know what he wants—what he always does: control."

Clare doesn't say anything, just tilts her head a little and studies me.

Silence falls over us and my heart starts beating harder in my chest. I hate confrontation. I hate making people unhappy, and I hate that this is how we're ending things.

"Will you be here later?"

She shrugs her shoulders and I feel mine collapse. It's such a losing battle with her, with everyone, and I'm over it—I'm over it all. I just spent the last five weeks repairing parts of me I allowed others to damage, and no more. For so long I've suppressed my voice, and that ends today—with her, with my father, and even with Reid. If they don't like who I am, that's their loss.

Standing a little taller, I tighten my ponytail, brush the dust off my clothes, and pin her with a glower. "I'll see you when I see you." With that I turn and walk out the door.

Shaking my head, I stomp through the back yard. I mean, why even come here? All she ever does is scold me and tell me I'm making the wrong choices, choices that were originally because of her and for her. Well, I'm done waiting around for her, too. I keep clinging to these moments because she's my sister and I love her, but they are so few and far between lately, what's the point? What did I get today, five, maybe ten minutes?

I slam the kitchen door as I enter the house. I find my father in the living room, staring out the window toward the carriage house. Was he watching me? Us? Can he see she is here? He turns to face me, wearing his typical suit of armor—a suit and tie—and I spot several manila folders tucked under his arm. I am so not in the mood to deal with him or his crap today. His gaze sweeps over me from head to toe and he frowns. Interestingly, I feel numb to his apparent disapproval, and this fuels me with even more strength to do what I have to do.

Bring it on, Father. It's time to get this over with, once and for all.

Chapter 27

Reid

COMING OUT OF the locker room, I'm surprised to see the skies have turned dark. This morning on my way in to the training facility, they were bright blue, but now they're filled with low-hanging clouds. Florida thunderstorms still amaze me. They roll in and roll out in barely the blink of an eye, but in the moment, they can be ferocious.

It's been two weeks since I've seen her, and man do I want to, I just don't know where we go from here. This weekend coming up will be the end of our two-month arrangement, and I have no idea how she feels about this, nor have I asked her. I've texted her, she's messaged me back, and we've spoken a few times, but neither one of us has initiated much substantial conversation. I don't know what to say to her, and maybe I'm a little bit afraid she'll say something I don't want to hear. I know this was never supposed to be permanent, but I can't seem to let it go. I don't want to let it go. This is a new feeling for me, and I'm in uncharted waters, but I have this spark of hope that maybe, just maybe, she and I will work out.

"You gonna wait it out?" Bryan asks as we stand near the doors. It's funny, because my mind immediately drifts to Camille. Am I waiting it out to see how she wants to proceed? That seems kind of dumb. I've always been a take-charge kind of guy, and waiting isn't my forte.

Looking over at him, I see he's watching me, knowing my mind has gone somewhere else. He quirks an eyebrow, and I chuckle.

"Nope, I'm going for it." And I am. There's nothing planned for this weekend, so it's the perfect time for me to drive up and finally have that talk. She has to know by now; either she's in or she's out, and I'm ready to find out.

"All right. Be careful out there." He slaps me on the shoulder and I take off.

One by one the raindrops start to fall, slicing through the air and landing on my overheated skin. I've been pushing myself harder and exhausting my muscles, trying to find a way to not be consumed by her, but nothing is working. Jack has given me a few strange looks, and the guys are steering clear. They all think I'm surly because she's back in Savannah and I'm here, and that is part of it, but it's not that. It's that she's everywhere. Her coffee creamer is in my refrigerator, there's a book she left on the end table, and I even found a pair of her socks on the patio. There are little things all over that I can't escape. Even my clothes smell like her because she changed the dryer sheets.

Then again, I'm not trying to eliminate her either. I haven't moved any of her stuff or thrown one thing away. I like them there mixing and mingling with mine. I want them there.

It's time I tell her as much.

The speed of the rain quickly escalates and I drop my head as I move through the parking lot. Heat from the asphalt swirls around my legs as I weave in and out between the rows. My shoulders are getting damp and my hair is already wet, but the rain fuels me. Technically I don't even need to wait until this weekend. There's nothing really keeping me here, and the more I think about it, the more excited I get to see her. Suddenly, I can't wait to get home to pack, and I pick up my speed. I came in later this morning, which only left the spots toward the back open, and halfway there, I stop short as someone steps in my way and stands right in front of me.

"*Patrick.*" His name hisses through my teeth.

What the hell is he doing here?

Is he following me?

Tension starts in my toes and climbs straight up my body. The rain, the parking lot, everything around us disappears, and I have to subdue my immediate reaction of fight or flight, because I want to kick this guy's ass. I'm so focused on him and the rage pumping into my muscles I forget where we are.

"Do you have a death wish?" I ask him, blinking as I try to clear the haze of red between him and me.

His eyes widen briefly and then he smirks.

What. The. Hell.

Looking him over, I see he's wearing his typical uniform of business attire, but he's got on a black zip-up jacket with a hood pulled up over his head to keep him dry.

"Camille asked me to come here and have you sign these." He attempts to shove a folder at my chest, but my arms remain by my sides. I don't want anything from him, nothing at all.

He waves it in front of me, but I keep my eyes locked on him. Rain quickly begins to soak it, and he drops his hand with an exasperated sigh.

"What is it?" I growl at him.

"Divorce papers." The smirk is back and I narrow my eyes.

"No, she didn't." I cross my arms over my chest and glare down at him like he's lost his mind. "She didn't ask you to come here." Camille wouldn't have sent these without letting me know . . . right? We texted last night before bed and she never mentioned it, just said she's been trying to get different affairs in order. I just assumed she was talking about dealing with her father and the logistics of getting Vintage Soul up and running.

"Yes, she did!" he shouts at me.

I glance around the parking lot to see if anyone has noticed us, but they haven't. Those leaving are sprinting through the rain, oblivious to the fact that I'm about to end this guy once and for all.

"You know, for a smart guy, you're quite possibly the dumbest person I have ever met."

His eyes flare, a little wild, a lot crazy. I mean, what's his angle? Does he think she's going to go running back to him, because I know for a fact she's not. No matter what happens between her and me, this guy is out for good.

"You've officially pissed me off past the point of no return." I take a step toward him and he moves back. "If you come near me one more time, or if Camille tells me you're still sniffing around her, I will have my lawyer file a restraining order, and I'm certain you don't want that highlighted in your next campaign."

His face blanches as he takes another step back, and then he tilts his head to the side with his eyes widening like he's just solved the world's most complicated puzzle.

"You really have no idea what you've gotten yourself into, do you?" He laughs and shakes his head. "Look, we've all let you bide your time, have your fun with her, but now it's time to say goodbye. You were a short-lived rebellion on her part, and now it's over. We know how to handle Camille. We know what's best for her, and it isn't you."

He's making her sound like a child, like she's not stable. That's not the girl I saw, and even if she wasn't, that's fine by me. I liked her just as she was. I don't need her to be anyone else but herself, and there's nothing we couldn't deal with together.

"Maybe not." I shrug my shoulders. "But it damn well isn't you either. Camille doesn't need to be *handled*. She can take care of herself, and this just proves you don't know her at all."

His gaze zeroes in on me, and it's sharp, focused. I don't like it. I understand that he's known her for a really long time, and obviously their history together means something, but if they were meant to be, he wouldn't have cheated, and she wouldn't have married a stranger.

Thunder rolls over us and the deluge of rain intensifies. This entire scene is ominous, and somewhere close by, lightning cracks. We both flinch at the sound that follows, but neither one of us moves. Slowly, his lips turn up into a menacing sneer, and I brace myself for what he's about to say. I can tell I'm not going to like it.

"What I know is you've been playing house with a murderer."

Murderer?

What is he talking about?

My silence pleases him as I study his face, my nostrils flare as I breathe in, and that sneer of his turns into a condescending smile.

"What, you didn't know?" He takes a step closer to me, but I stand my ground, giving nothing away and looking down my nose at him.

"Know what?" I cross my arms over my chest.

"That she killed her sister."

He says this so plainly, like it's everyday conversation, I have to replay his words to make sure I heard him correctly.

"I don't believe you."

"Oh, let me guess—she didn't tell you. Tsk tsk. Shame on her." He shakes his head, clearly not really meaning it. "Go ahead, Google Clare Whitley—you'll see."

Dropping my bag to the wet ground, I pull my phone from my pocket and search for Clare. Sure enough, headline after headline fills the page: *Senator Whitley's daughter dies a tragic death. Savannah loses a beloved Whitley daughter. Clare Whitley dies. A life taken too soon, too young.*

It makes no sense to me, and my heart rate increases with anxiety and disbelief. We talked about Clare at least once a day, and Camille told me she was at the wedding. I know she's spoken to her based on conversations we've had, and I once heard her talking to her on the phone from another room.

Didn't I?

Stepping back, I scrub my hand over my face, pushing the water away. I suddenly no longer feel like I have the upper hand, and this leaves me uncertain of everything. I feel wet, and I feel confused, but taking a moment to think back to other comments she's made, I can see how this is a possibility.

Fuck. This entire situation is so messed up.

I look back at Patrick and our eyes lock. His face is blank, and I don't know what he's thinking, but he's watching me closely.

Moving away, I start pacing back and forth. The rain is steady enough that my clothes are now soaked through, but I barely feel them.

Was it all a lie? It couldn't have been.

But, if she didn't tell me about this, what else didn't she tell me? I didn't keep anything from her. I was up front from the beginning, about everything, and I allowed myself to trust her.

I let her in.

Closing my eyes, I inhale deeply and allow the sadness and embarrassment to wash over me. I fell for this girl hook, line, and sinker, and I have no one to blame but myself. How I'm feeling right now—this is my fault. I let this happen to me. I should have known it was too good to be true.

Patrick clears his throat and I glance up at him. It's kind of poetic that she sent him here to be her henchman; these people have no heart. He's done standing here, and so am I. I'm done with all of it. This was never supposed to last anyway.

I mean, really, what was I thinking? I'd save the princess and we'd ride off into the sunset together? That's not real life; this is—people lying and people leaving.

Walking back over, I rip the folder from Patrick's hand and bend over to keep everything dry. A pen slides out along with two sets of the same papers. Flipping through each one, I see she's already signed them, so I do the same. With each swipe of the pen, cracks rupture my heart. Just as quickly as we started, we've now ended. Dropping the pen on the ground, I hand him his set and keep mine along with the folder. Knowing her family has connections, I'm certain this will be expedited, which means I'm officially divorced.

Divorced.

"You know, I almost feel bad for you—almost," he says with victory in his eyes. "But then I remember you actually thought a girl like her was going to end up with someone like you."

He starts laughing as if I'm suddenly the idiot, and I swear the sound is amplified by the rain. Here and now, I officially concede and think to myself, *You win, asshole.*

Turning around, I grab my bag and effectively remove him from my line of sight. I hope to never *ever* see him again, and I place one foot in front of the other to keep myself moving forward as my heart bleeds out into my chest. Every emotion is slamming into me, and I can't grasp any single one long enough to ride it out. I'm bombarded and overwhelmed, pissed off and dumbfounded. Someone please tell me—how did I get here?

From the very first moment I pulled up to her parents' wrought iron gate, I knew they were not my kind of people. I should have walked away—why didn't I walk away? Two months of lies. Two months of manipulation, perfectly executed by a privileged upbringing. Two months easily dismissed with the ultimate rejection.

My fingers grip the damp folder, wrinkling it as thunder rolls through the sky.

Thank God I didn't ask for longer.

Spotting my car one row over, I quickly slip between two vehicles and walk out into the row. Tilting my head up, I pause to let the water run down my face. It's warm and cool; it's soft and it stings. I want it to rinse away the evidence of my damaged heart. I need it to absolve me of the shame I feel inside. Just ten minutes ago I was ready to give her my all, but all along she's known it was never going to be me.

Needing to get home, I open my eyes and my head snaps to the bright lights that flip on directly to my right. They flicker through the gray rain and fear races down my spine at the sudden onslaught of sliding tires desperately trying to grip the wet ground. I lurch forward, determined to move out of the way.

One breath.
Two.
Everything happens so fast.
Everything explodes with pain.
Everything goes black.

Chapter 28

Camille

I MISS REID.

It's crazy how I went from not knowing him at all two months ago to now feeling like part of me is missing. I know this is for the best, know he had a life to get back to, but still, I wish I were more a part of it than I am. I wish he wanted me to be.

I want to say life sucks, but I know in the grand scheme of things, it doesn't. Despite not being on speaking terms with my father—which, quite frankly, I don't see as a negative—things have transitioned pretty smoothly, and it makes me regret losing years of my life. I should have put my foot down sooner. I never should have let them guilt me, and I never should have let them steamroll me into a life that wasn't meant for me. I wish they'd understand, but they don't.

Finally having that conversation with my father went about as well as I expected. He demanded things of me, and I directly told him no. Although we talked ad nauseam about my marriage to Reid, I was adamant in my decision regarding him. By the end, I left us in his hands. I simply reminded him that he'd already lost one daughter, and whether or not he lost the other one too was up to him. He told me he'd be in touch, but I haven't heard from him since.

This morning I needed to get out of my house, so I grabbed a coffee and wandered the streets, walked through a few squares and down to River Street. Clare and I used to love coming here as little girls. With no one watching and no one caring, it was exciting to be part of a normal crowd filled with tourists. We could eat all the candy we wanted and laugh at the street performers, and no one was there to take our picture and splash it across page six of the local papers.

Today, it's quiet. People pass me on their way to work, food delivery trucks are unloading at the many restaurants, and boats pass by heading to and from the mouth of the river. It's beautiful out, but early April in Georgia always is. I look for a potential commercial space, but nothing I find feels right, so I head home.

Home.

Does this even feel like home anymore? It used to, but that was before, before I felt like I had a choice, and now I do. Nothing is keeping me here, so do I really want to stay? If I don't, where do I want to go? Definitely not back to New York—I'm too much of a Southern girl at heart—so maybe up to Charleston, or even back down to Tampa.

Tampa . . . my heart frowns. I can't think of Tampa and not think of Reid. There's been no communication from him today, and I realize I might have to accept the possibility that he's in the process of letting me go. You can't make someone want to be with you, no matter how you feel about them.

The rest of the day I spend in my workshop. It's cathartic in that I can focus on me and organize my thoughts, but at the same time I can lose myself in the work and just zone out.

From the back pocket of my shorts, my phone rings. I don't recognize the number but answer it anyway.

"Hello." I tuck the phone between my ear and my shoulder as I move to the sink to quickly rinse off my hands.

"Hey, Camille," a male's voice drags out. "It's Jack."

It takes me a second to place the name, and when I do, adrenaline shoots straight down my spine. His voice is dark and foreboding.

"Hey, Jack. Is everything okay?" I dry my hands and press the phone harder against my ear in anticipation of what he's going to say. The only reason he would be calling me is if something bad happened.

"Reid is in the hospital." He blurts it out so matter-of-factly, and I grip the counter to keep from falling over.

"What? Why?" My heart rate picks up while I try to control my breathing. So many things could have happened to him and life can change so fast—I know this better than anyone. Although I have to know what happened to him, the fear of the outcome almost has me wanting to hang up. If I don't know, it hasn't happened.

"He got hit by a car."

My heart stops and I process his words.

"Hit by a car?"

"Yep."

A thousand thoughts start running through my mind, and of course I'm immediately thinking something terrible. For the past five years, it's been my default to automatically assume the worst, and tears prick my eyes.

"Where?" I lean over the counter and place my forehead on my arm.

"In the parking lot of our main training facility."

"How? When?"

"It was raining pretty hard and the driver didn't see him in time. Slid right into him, earlier today."

"Oh my God." I squeeze my eyes shut and ask the question I'm most fearful to know the answer to. "Please tell me he's going to be okay?"

Jack lets out a long sigh. "He'll be fine, but he's banged up pretty bad and I think you should come stay with him."

I jerk up and start walking toward the house. "Absolutely. Where is he?" I would go anywhere and do anything for him.

"St. Joseph's Hospital."

"I'm on my way."

"Great. This is my number, call me when you get here."

"I will. Thank you, Jack."

"Drive safe."

It takes five hours and fifteen minutes between walking out my door and into the automatic doors of the hospital. I pushed the limit on how fast I should've been driving, but I couldn't help it. All I could think about was getting to him and seeing that he's okay.

The first thing I'm hit with is the smell. I hate the smell. There's this funky mixture to it of disinfectant and sickness that permeates everything it touches. It reminds you that hospitals are full of death, and I can't help but wonder how many people have already died here today.

Died . . . hospital . . . Clare.

I haven't been back in a hospital since Clare died, and hate isn't a strong enough word for how I feel about being here. Plus, I'm going to have to tell Reid soon. He deserves to know, and know it all.

Jack meets me at the elevators, wraps his arm around me, and smiles as we climb in to make our way to his room. Jack is a little bit taller than Reid, and wider. Being this close to him, although slightly comforting, is weird, and I can't wait to be in Reid's arms instead.

"I'm glad you're here." He squeezes my shoulder.

"Me too. How did you get my number?" I ask as the doors open and we step out into the hall.

"The team has it on file."

"Oh."

He nods at the two nurses at the central station then stops in front of Reid's door.

"He looks worse than he is, just remember that," he says in a low voice.

"What exactly happened to him?"

"Stepped out from between two parked cars crossing the parking lot, not paying attention, and he got hit."

"Oh, no." My hand flies to cover my mouth.

"He broke his left wrist and his left collarbone, and he has a concussion."

"Is the concussion why he was admitted?"

"Yeah. For the first couple of hours he was sick a lot and kept repeating the same things over and over again, but the CT scan showed no fracture or bleeding, and neither one of his breaks required surgery, so that's good."

I'm certain my face shows exactly how I feel: relieved and then panicked. "Football?"

"Doctor says the breaks are clean and he'll be as good as new in six to eight weeks with some rehab on his wrist. The silver lining here is it wasn't his knee, leg, or ankle. Those require more time, and some never fully recover."

"Well, that's good then."

"Yeah, it is." He pats me on the back and then opens the door.

As we walk in, I see there are two beds. It's a shared room, and I'm incredibly grateful that the first bed is empty. I know Reid is just sleeping, but he looks dead, and I can't help the anxiety this causes or the tears that come.

His face is scratched up on the left side with what looks like road rash, and his head is wrapped where he must have landed on it. His wrist is bandaged, and they've wrapped an elastic bandage over his arm and around his body to keep it immobile and pressed against him.

Jack was right, he does look terrible, and my heart aches for him. No one wants to see someone they love in this situation.

Love.

Yep, there's no more denying to myself what I feel for him. I do love him, and even if it's not reciprocated, at least for a short time I was the lucky one who got to show him that love, a love he so deserves.

Jack briefly touches my elbow to draw my attention, and it takes everything in me to tear my eyes away from Reid.

"Hey," he whispers. "Now that you're here, I'm going to head out. I need to get some sleep before my workout in the morning. If you need anything, you have my number, and don't hesitate use it."

"Okay, I will. Thanks again for calling me, Jack. I really appreciate it."

He gives me a closed-mouth smile, glances once more at Reid, squeezes my arm, and then leaves.

Silence fills the room. It's a little after ten at night and other than a small light that illuminates the whiteboard, it's dark. On the board, it shows he was just checked on, so I know we'll be alone for a while.

Dragging a chair next to his bed, I sit down and look over every inch of him. He's so handsome, and I'm so overwhelmed with emotions at seeing him after the hours it took to get here, I give in to the tears that have been trying desperately to fall as I silently sob.

What would I do if something had really happened to him? If he had died? I try not to think morbidly like that, but after losing Clare, it's something I think about constantly—

losing someone I love. The pain from the first time was beyond anything I could have ever imagined, and I don't think I could survive it twice.

Running my fingertips down his arm, I notice his skin is cool from not being tucked under the blanket, but it's still warm. I tangle my fingers with his and lay my face on top of his hand. I listen to him breathe, listen to me breathe, and chant to myself on repeat that everything is okay.

"Stop crying, I'm fine," he mumbles.

His voice startles me and my head shoots up to look at him. His eyes are still closed—he looks exactly the same.

"I can't help it," I tell him, quietly as to not add to the headache he probably has.

"Well, try." He scrunches up his face with pain.

His voice is deep and raspy. It sounds angry, but then again, I probably would be too if I was hit by a car.

"You didn't have to come here. I'm fine. I'll be fine." He takes his hand out from under mine and lays it on his stomach. Watching him pull away from me pings my heart and leaves me slightly confused.

"Yes, I did," I tell him.

"No, you didn't," he practically growls, and this has me feeling uncomfortable, out of place. Never in my mind did this scenario play out—that he genuinely wouldn't want me here. I mean, I already missed him and was hoping I'd get to see him sometime soon, obviously not like this, but was he not thinking about seeing me?

"I did."

"Why?"

"Because you would have come for me . . . wouldn't you?"

He doesn't say anything as his eyes crack open and find mine. They're slightly glazed, and I don't know if that's from the medicine or because of me. I really don't understand why he's so angry that I'm here. We didn't leave things badly, at least I didn't think so, and I've done everything the way he wanted us to.

Feeling uncomfortable, I lean back in my chair and away from him. He watches me, those green orbs glaring, the only movements him blinking and licking his dry lips. Minutes pass, and eventually his eyelids droop then he falls back to sleep.

Throughout the night, the nurses come in and wake him up. He doesn't get sick again, but it's clear he has one wicked headache. He also doesn't speak to me again. He looks for me the minute he's awake then proceeds to glare until he falls asleep once again. I don't sleep at all, just sit there and wonder what I've done wrong.

Shortly after eight, the door opens and the doctor walks in with his nurse following. She smiles a little too brightly at Reid then narrows her eyes as she sees me next to him.

"Hello. I'm Dr. Armstrong." He holds out his hand for me to shake. I stand and do so.

"Nice to meet you. I'm Camille, Reid's wife." The words slip out so effortlessly I don't even realize I'm saying them. Next to me, Reid grunts, and all three of us turn to look at him. He's scowling at me, and that's when I notice he isn't wearing his wedding ring. I don't know why I thought he might still be. Maybe the hospital took it off because of the swelling? I know our arrangement is over and we haven't talked as much as I would have liked over the last couple of weeks, but I find I am disappointed. Glancing back at his face, I get the impression he's mad I said that, and now along with uncomfortable, I feel stupid, too.

Sensing the tension quickly escalating between the two of us, the doctor clears his throat. "All right then. Reid, do you want to speak privately, or is in front of your wife okay?"

"I'll wait outside," I answer for him, quickly heading for the door.

Both the nurse and the doctor look at me with surprise and then skepticism. Heat climbs into my cheeks as a wave of embarrassment takes over. It really didn't occur to me that Reid wouldn't want me here, and I'm starting to wonder how wrongly I might have perceived our time together. That last night, in Savannah, I was certain he felt something greater, just like I did. His body language, his facial expressions, how he made me feel like I was the only person in his world . . . I don't understand.

I lean back against the wall and look down at my grandmother's ring. I run my thumb over it, and a lump forms in my throat as I begrudgingly accept the fact that it's time to take it off, too. It wasn't a real marriage. The two months are essentially over, and so are we.

The door opens and they both exit. The nurse wrinkles her nose at me as she walks away, and the doctor only makes brief eye contact after he's done signing a bunch of papers.

"We're discharging him. He knows what needs to happen next, just make sure you wake him up every two hours for the next twenty-four hours, okay?"

"I will," I tell him.

He nods and then wanders off.

Chapter 29

Reid

I DON'T KNOW why she's here.

I mean, I do—Jack called her—but why she came and is sticking around, I don't know.

For the last three days, she's been waiting on me hand and foot, and I haven't said one word to her. What is there to say?

Mostly, I've been sleeping. The doctor said I probably would the first week, which is fine with me. Keeps me from moving, and keeps her off my mind.

The concussion, although not severe, was enough to jar my timeline of events a bit. It's made it hard for me to focus on anything for too long of a period, and I've had a difficult time with balance, which means every time I go to get up, she jumps to help me, and I hate it.

I also hate how she keeps looking at me. At first it was with pity, and I get that I look terrible, but she needed to knock it off with the doe eyes. As of this morning, she's shifted to annoyed. I understand I'm not being very nice to her, but I didn't ask for this or her, and she certainly doesn't deserve pleasantness.

Wrinkling my forehead, I feel the skin pull, and it hurts. I have six staples in my head just past my hairline, road rash covers the side of my face, shoulder, and left arm, and then there are these damn breaks. If I'm lying flat on my back, I don't feel any pain, but the second I breathe too deep or try to move my upper body or arm, it all burns and stings, hurting like hell. Breaking a collarbone is no joke.

Needing to get out of my bed, I've wandered to the couch, and I've been glaring at Camille as she moves around my condo, trying to keep herself busy. I don't want her here, but that doesn't change the fact that she is. Currently, she's in the kitchen making me a protein shake, and the blender is so loud I feel like a knife is being rammed into my head.

I've never broken a bone before, not even a stress fracture. I take very good care of my body, and now I feel completely out of control. All I'm thinking about is how I need to work out, but I can hardly move. My muscles are revolting from the need to be used, exercised, and it's put me even more on edge than I already am.

The blender cuts off and Camille pours the shake into a cup. I track her with me eyes as she walks over and hands it to me. She's wearing low-slung pajama pants with donuts on them and a tank top that matches. She looks comfortable— too comfortable for my liking.

I take a sip of the shake, peering at her over the rim of the glass, and then place it on the end table to my right.

She glances at the cup, then at me, and her lips press into a thin line. Crossing her arms over her chest, she turns her head and looks out the large sliding glass doors leading to the balcony.

"Can I get you anything else?" She's attempting to pull off politeness, but she's straight-up irritated. *Well, that makes two of us, sweetheart.*

"Camille, just go home. I'm fine, and I can take care of myself." My voice is thick and rough due to a terrible combination of medication, pain, and nonuse.

Her eyes come back to mine and she frowns.

"Oh, so he *can* speak. I was starting to wonder if you'd lost your voice along with your manners."

"Excuse me?" I narrow my eyes at her and both of my hands—the one in the sling and the one resting on the couch—ball up into fists.

"You heard me." She leans forward into my space. "For days, you've ignored me, not once have you said thank you, and quite frankly, I don't understand. What is wrong with you? Why are you acting this way?"

Is she joking? She must be, because otherwise, along with being a liar, she's become narcissistic—or maybe she always was.

Using my good hand as leverage, I scoot to the edge of the couch, forcing her to move back. "What's wrong with me is that I want to be alone. I don't want you here." My voice is loud. I sound like a dick, and I don't care.

"Why not?" She drops her arms and starts pacing back and forth in front of me. "You didn't mind me here before. I mean, forgive me for being confused, but you aren't telling me anything."

"That's because I don't want to talk to you. Why is that so hard to understand?"

She takes another step back and props her hands on her hips. Her blonde hair is piled up on top of her head, and pieces of it have fallen loose. She blows one off her face and frowns again.

"Are you trying to pick a fight with me? Is that what you need right now? Because I don't want to fight with you." She shakes her head and stands her ground.

"What I need is for you to *leave*." I slowly stand up without flinching or swaying and glare down at her. Her head tips back as she stares up at me and her cheeks turn pink.

I have to admit, I'm surprised she's still standing here. I've already told her several times that I basically want nothing to do with her, and instead of withdrawing and leaving like she would have when I first met her, she's calling me out on my bad behavior.

"Leave," she mumbles to herself, the initial annoyance slipping, leaving something like bewilderment and hurt in its place. Whatever—she's hurt me more than anyone ever has. This is why I don't do relationships. None of this is worth it.

"Reid." She squeezes her eyes shut and takes a deep breath. The pink in her cheeks runs down her neck and flushes the top of her chest. She drops her head, runs a hand over the messy pile of her hair, and then looks back at me with discontentment in her eyes. "You've strung me along for weeks since you left Savannah, and now after these last couple of days, you're just going to blow me off? I think . . ." She looks around the condo like she's looking for an answer, and then she finds her way back to me. "I think it's time we had that conversation." She crosses her arms once again. It's a protective move, and it's confrontational.

"What conversation?"

"You know, the one where you tell me nothing has to be decided today. Well, I think it does. Not to put you on the spot after all you've been through, but apparently you've already made up your mind, and I need to hear you say it. So, time's up. Go ahead." She throws her hand up in the air in front of me in a *the floor's all yours* gesture then tucks it back in. "Tell me what happens next between us."

What happens next? She lied to me for months and divorced me without talking to me first. I had no say then, so asking me now is irrelevant. It's pretty safe to say there will never be a *next* after all this.

"Between us? Camille, you can't be so naive as to think we were going to work out."

She doesn't say anything, doesn't confirm or deny; she just stares at me, waiting for me to say more.

I look past her shoulder and around my condo. In three days, she's infiltrated it even more than when she was here for two weeks. There are yellow pillows on the couch, yellow flowers in the kitchen, and bits and pieces of her everywhere: magazines, her Kindle, shoes, a coffee cup from the shop across the street on the island, a hat hanging off a kitchen chair, the blanket from the guest bedroom draped across the loveseat. So many things are out of order and out of place.

Looking back down at her, my eyes bounce back and forth between hers as I provide her with the only explanation I can give. "I don't love this life, nor do I want to. This, you and me"—I wave a finger between us—"it was a means to an end for you, nothing more. It ended. We've ended."

Little wrinkles form between her brows. "You don't love this life? What does that mean? You don't love sharing a life with me?" she says incredulously.

With my lips sealed shut, I shake my head, and she exhales sharply while taking a step away from me.

"Wow, I guess I was wrong." She places her hand over her chest and rubs it like it's aching. "I thought all those weeks together were amazing. I thought you and I together were amazing . . . weren't we?"

The dejected and confused look on her face has my brain stuttering. She's blinking faster and breathing harder. Her physical reaction to my rejection of her is causing a visceral response, and all my muscles are coiling tight. I didn't think this conversation would go this way; I thought this was what she wanted. I certainly didn't expect her to come off so wounded.

"Look, don't go acting like a stage-five clinger. Yes, we had a good time together, but this was never going to last. You knew that, and I told you time and time again. Besides, not only is my season going to be starting soon, now I have to deal with all of this. I won't be distracted—not by you, not by anyone."

I've never had to break up with a girl before. They've always known we were just having a good time together until things ran their course. I've never had to deal with any of this, and it confirms to me that I chose the right path— the one that includes none of this bullshit. Incidentally, she already ended it with those divorce papers, so the fact that she's making me do this right now pisses me off even more.

"So that's it?" She shrugs her shoulders. "You're just going to pretend like we never happened?"

"We didn't happen. Yes, we had a good time, but it was fake and only situation induced. I barely even know you, and you certainly don't know me since we're having this conversation."

I mean, how did she think I was going to react to being served divorce papers at my place of employment? I deserve better than that.

"That's not true and you know it." Her eyes have widened and they're slightly glassy. This fuels my animosity, and I step closer to her.

"Do I? 'Cause with what I've seen and heard, I'm quite certain I don't know who you are either."

Her lips part and she shakes her head in confusion.

"What are you talking about?" She throws her hands out. "You're making no sense, and why—*why* are you so angry with me?"

"Because I wouldn't even be in this situation if it wasn't for you!" I yell at her, my voice echoing around the condo.

"What situation?" she yells back, not flinching or hesitating at my outburst.

"Oh, for the love of God." I walk around her and toward the hallway to my bedroom. I'm done with this conversation. It's making my headache unbearable, and I'm done with the drama of her. Facing her one more time, with a sincerity in my tone that breaks even my own heart, I tell her, "Camille, it's over. It's all over. I signed the divorce papers. There's no reason to drag this thing out any longer. It's time for you to go."

She wraps her arms around her middle and as her chin quivers, she takes an involuntary step back, like I somehow pushed her. "But . . ."

"Answer me this one question: did you or did you not kill your sister?"

Her skin pales, her eyes widen as she stares at me, and her jaw drops open. Her extended silence is more telling than any words, and the air between us seems to shift. It's no longer filled with tension, but guilt and grief are pouring off her. Whatever, not my problem anymore—not that it ever really was. How she could have looked me in the eyes for weeks and not told me this, I'll never know, but then again, she liked not telling me things.

"I did," she finally whispers, a single tear falling. "How did—"

I don't even let her finish. "Go home."

The finality of those two words is so on point, even she knows there's nothing left to say.

God, I was such a fool, blinded by so many things. When did I become that guy where a pretty face had me losing sight of what's important to me—character? I could never be with someone who, after all the time we spent together, lies to me—and yes, omission on that large of a scale is lying. I don't know how she did it or why, but it doesn't even matter. I don't want to know. At this point, I know enough, and it's that I'm done.

Her shoulders slump as she looks at the ground, her chest rising and falling forcefully with each breath. A dozen emotions flash across her downturned face. I know she doesn't want me to see them, but I do. I'm not sure why she's so surprised; this is what she wanted. She set all of this in motion, and now I'm the one who has to pick up the pieces—literally. I have to deal with the broken pieces of my body, my heart, and my pride.

Licking her lips, she wipes her face then brings a shaky hand to her mouth and holds it there while she thinks. Is she trying to find a way out of this mess? Is she hoping to come up with some excuse that'll cause me to change my mind? Because it's not happening. There's nothing she can say or do to dig herself out of this one. From the papers to Patrick and the accident to the lies, one man can only take so much.

Finally, she lifts her head and pins me with a cool, detached stare. I've seen this expression on her before, and I'm appalled as I watch her go through the motions in front of me, to me. Reaching up, she tucks a few strands of loose hair behind her ear, clasps her hands in front of her, and pulls her shoulders back. My eyes narrow and my nose flares as I take in her stance. She's shifted back into her socialite persona, and nothing in this world could infuriate me more.

"Reid." She glances to the side, her eyes roaming and stopping on her tools outside.

"What, Camille?" My tone expresses my impatience for this to be over and done.

Her eyes slide back to mine and the sharp disinterest they radiated just a few moments ago has now thawed, leaving them dull and gray—thundercloud gray. Not once have I ever seen them this color, and my breath catches in my throat. She appears so calm, poised on the outside; it's what she's mastered, but her eyes are telling me she's raining on the inside. Adrenaline sends waves of tiny sparks under my skin, and I brace myself for what's to come.

She licks her lips, tips her chin up, and takes a deep breath. "Thank you, Reid. Thank you for all you did for me, and for all the time you spent with me." Her words are slow, soft, but so heavy with meaning my heart rate picks up and pounds forcefully against my chest. "I want you to know you were the best thing that's ever happened to me, and . . ." She pauses, swallows, and blinks, forcing the desolation to disappear from her eyes. "I will remember you for the rest of my life."

Turning, she stoically makes her way to the kitchen, grabs her purse where she left it on the end of the counter, and walks to the front door, not stopping to pick up any of her things along the way. She slips on her shoes, and without looking back, she's gone.

I'm not sure I even take one breath, but the second the door clicks shut, my heart splinters right down the middle, leaving me gasping for air.

Chapter 30

Camille

DIVORCE PAPERS.

I didn't think it would all happen this fast. Actually, I was hoping it wouldn't happen at all, but I guess it did. He said he signed them, and now I'm just waiting.

It's been two and a half weeks since I last spoke to or saw Reid, and every day my heart hurts exactly the same. I wish it wouldn't, especially after the way he treated me, but it does. I've tried to think of him less and find a new normal for life now, but I haven't succeeded yet. I get that he's angry—I was angry for him. Football is his life and he came really close to losing it, but the way he talked to me seemed to go above and beyond that.

I regret not telling him about Clare. I should have, and it was wrong of me. Somehow he still found out, and his reaction was exactly what I was expecting—terrible. I would've liked to talk to him about her, but he'd made up his mind and I guess now I'll never have that chance.

I know relationships come and go; that's the nature of life. If we're lucky we find someone who brings out the best in us, who understands us when we're at our worst, and we get to spend an indefinite amount of time with them. That isn't always the case, though—the time part—but for a brief period, with Reid, it sure felt like it, and I felt like the luckiest girl in the world.

At this point, I can't go back and change anything, and as heartbroken as I am about losing him, I'm trying to look on the bright side. After all, I did put myself out there, even after the last five years, and I'm proud of myself for that.

Hearing the back gate swing open, I look up and find Patrick walking toward the doorway to my workshop. It's the first time I've seen him since he showed up outside Reid's building, and I'm over fighting with him. Based on the defeated lines on his face, he looks over it with me too.

Turning away from him, I lower the volume of the music, and I take this moment to pull myself together and prepare for whatever it is he has to say. I mean, haven't we been through enough? I know I sure have.

"Do you care if I come in and sit down?" he asks, waiting for me to invite him in.

"Nope." I look at him over my shoulder. "Not at all."

Quietly he walks in and drops down in one of the two lounge chairs I keep for company here in the coach house. I can only think of one other time he's visited me here long enough to sit, stay, and watch, and he wasn't himself that night; something was off. It was one of the most casual and easy nights we've ever had. He never said what was wrong, but he wanted to be near me, and that made me feel important. It made me feel like more than the arm candy I usually felt I was. It was a night like that one that had me thinking we could do this marriage thing, but it wasn't enough.

Tonight, Patrick is wearing a white button-down with the sleeves rolled up, navy blue slacks, a brown belt, and brown dress shoes. He looks every bit the part he was groomed for. Actually, he looks every bit like the man he wants to be.

Only, today he looks tired. There are deep purple shadows under his eyes, his skin is ashen, and his hair looks like he's been running his hands through it all day. His perfect composure isn't so perfect, and that has me feeling uneasy.

Putting the lid back on the can of dark wood stain I was working with, I walk to the sink to rinse and clean the brushes. He watches.

"Do you want something to drink?" I glance at him over my shoulder.

He hesitates and then says, "Beer."

Patrick loves beer. Local craft IPAs are his favorite, but not a lot of people know that. In social settings, he reverts to scotch. After all, appearances are everything.

Pulling two from the refrigerator, I pass one over and take the chair across from him.

"You look like you," he says, and a small smile tips my lips up. "Not that you didn't before, uh . . ." His cheeks turn red and he looks away. "I just mean you look like the you you used to be, before everything changed. You look good."

I think this is the first time in five years he's complimented me for being me instead of scolding me for not being who he thinks I should be: Clare. Part of me wants to point this out, but watching him play with the label on his bottle, I can tell he already knows.

Birds from outside are chirping, and somewhere in the distance, church bells are ringing. The air between us is calm, exhausted, and I watch as he leans forward to rest his elbows on his knees. His hair falls over his forehead and he lets out a deep sigh.

"Patrick, what happened to us?" I pull my legs up into the chair with me.

"I don't know." He shakes his head then lifts it to look at me. "I've thought about this so much over the last couple of weeks, and I can't pinpoint when things changed, when they started to go wrong, how I changed . . . I am so sorry, Camille, I really am—for all of it."

His eyes are pleading for me to believe him, so I do. In all the years I've known him, Patrick was never a bad guy. He was loyal, kind, and he cherished my sister. I think maybe deep down he knew we weren't supposed to be together, and the pressure of it all finally got to him. That doesn't excuse his behavior, but where he lashed out, I ran away. We each dealt with the situation differently.

"Me too," I tell him, and I mean this. I hate how bad things got and how they ended. Patrick and I have been through so much together, and I think maybe that's why I was hanging on for so long—hanging on to the memory, memories of our childhood, memories of Clare that only he and I can share, and memories of what our friendship used to be.

Taking a swallow of his beer, he turns his head away from me and looks out the window. I have nothing to say to him. He came here to talk, so when he's ready, he will. In the meantime, I drink my beer and watch him sink even farther into himself.

"I miss her, every day, and I think I just got so caught up in the life she and I had planned, and then you so seamlessly stepped into the role, I just didn't see how bad things had gotten." He looks back and his eyes trail over me. "And of course it doesn't help that you look like her. I mean, I know you aren't her, but the vision I had . . . it was always her face, and I tried to make you her. I'm sorry."

I understand what he's saying. After Clare died, I went out of my way to look like her, talk like her, and be like her, so everyone around me would suffer less. They always wanted her more, loved her more. She was the perfect daughter, girlfriend, and sister, and it was my fault she was gone, so giving them what they wanted seemed less like a penance and more like a reprieve.

"I accept your apology, Patrick, I really do, but there are so many things I'm angry at you for, things I don't see myself letting go of for a long time."

"I know, and I don't deserve your forgiveness, not yet at least, but I'm hoping to get it one day."

"Maybe. One day," I answer earnestly.

He leans back in his chair, running a hand over his face and around to the back of his neck. "I miss you, too."

"And I've missed you, but I don't miss who you've been the last couple of years. You were my best friend for a long time. I gave you way more allowances than you deserved, and well, now you're not. It's hard, too, because we navigated this life together and now I'm alone. That's okay—it is what it is—but everything is so off and so unsure. You know what these people are like, so you know what life is like for me now. My father won't speak to me, the people here in this town . . . well, let's just say the invitations aren't exactly rolling in. I don't want to go back to New York, but I feel out of place here, and then there's Reid."

My voice catches on his name and I look away toward the window of the main house where his paper airplanes sit. It hurts, but I'm not talking about Reid with Patrick. Of all the things sitting foremost on my heart, he is front and center, and he would not like me discussing him with Patrick of all people.

Letting out a deep sigh, I look back at Patrick and watch as he pulls a piece of paper from his suit pants, opens it, and lays it on the small table between us. It's a printed out photo of Reid and me on the beach.

With shaky fingers, I pick up the piece of paper and stare at it. The people in this photo are not the people we are today, and my heart cries out from the loss.

"Why do you have this?" I ask, searching his suddenly tortured face.

"I hired a private investigator and he found you at the beach. This was the day before you left—"

"I know when it was—I was there!"

"Right." He looks down at the photo and frowns. "I didn't know where you went after you left Tampa. He found you then reported to me where you were. Before I could decide what to do next, you were home. At the time, all I cared about was where you were, not what you were doing, and then you were here, where I needed you. He emailed me your file and all the images, which I'll forward to you when I leave, but I didn't look at them until last week. I kept thinking you'd reach out once you got back, but you didn't."

"You had me followed?" My eyes narrow. This feels like such a breach of my privacy, of my life, and my ears start ringing at his audacity. I'm shocked, hurt, outraged.

"I wasn't following you and I wasn't trying to spy on you, I promise. I just wanted to know where you were." His words are rushed, his voice distressed. He gets up and starts pacing. "Camille, you walked out on me. I know that doesn't make this right, but I had Clare, and then she was gone. Then I had you, and you were gone. Part of me was panicking, and the other part of me had your father barking orders in my ear."

"Patrick, this is not okay!" I stand up and move behind the chair, away from him.

"I know that!" he yells back.

From his other pocket, he pulls out another paper with a photo of him and me at the rehearsal dinner. He walks over, snatches the photo of Reid and me out of my hands, and places the two side by side on the table.

"What being with me does to you"—he points at our photo—"and what being with him does to you." He places his hands on his hips and drops his head. He's breathing hard, pausing so I can take in the two images. "I see it now, Camille. I really do." His voice is low, crestfallen.

I see it too. The girl in these two photos looks completely different.

At the dinner, I'm pale, thin, and impeccably polished. There are dark circles under my eyes, and I look so withdrawn. We're standing next to each other and his arm is around my waist, but my arms are down with my hands clasped in front of me. We're supposed to look together and happy, but we both look stiff, like strangers.

On the beach, my skin is golden and glowing, my hair is wild and wavy, and my eyes are bright. I'm laughing and looking at Reid as he gazes down at me adoringly and grins from ear to ear. We're walking and his arm is thrown over my shoulders, keeping me tucked in close, and both of my arms are wrapped around his middle. We look relaxed. We look happy. We look in love.

We were in love.

No, I am in love. I still love him, no matter what.

Picking up the photo again, I look at myself. I don't even remember laughing with Patrick, at least not since Clare died. A knot forms in my throat and I try to swallow it down.

"At the wedding, and even right after, I was so mad at you," he says quietly.

I hug the picture to my chest and look up at him. He's watching me, frowning as he shoves his hands into his pockets.

"I didn't understand why you would just leave me the way you did, knowing everything that was at stake. I needed to change your mind. But, the more time that passed, the more I began to see just how wrong things were. You wouldn't take my calls, wouldn't return my texts, and then when I approached you on the street, your reaction to me wasn't one of avoidance, but of fear. You genuinely looked afraid of me, and that made me take a step back and pause. For the first time in a long time, I started questioning what the hell I was doing—not even just to you, but to me too.

"And then, to make things worse, there was your dad breathing down my neck all day, every day, and I just felt stuck. You know how he is. It's easier to go along with him than to fight it, so that's why I did it."

"Did what?" I clutch the photo closer to me, afraid to hear what he's about to say.

His forehead wrinkles with confusion and he tilts his head like I should already know.

"Issued Reid the divorce papers on your behalf."

"You did what?" I yell, thinking back to those last couple of days when he was so angry with me. Of course he was—I would have been destroyed to receive those without any warning.

"I never should have done it." He shakes his head. "I knew it was wrong, and I'm sorry. I just wanted you to be mine again, but I didn't expect him to react the way he did—"

"Wait." I hold up my hand. "You saw him?"

His expression drops and suddenly he looks sick. "I hand-delivered them—don't you already know this?"

"No." I shake my head, eyes wide with horror. "Oh my God . . . when was this?"

He lets out a sigh and pulls one hand from his pocket to rub the back of his neck. "Shit," he mumbles. Slowly, his eyes move over my face to find mine, and they're sad, haunted. "A few minutes before he was hit by that car in the parking lot. It's my fault. I ambushed him and basically forced him to sign them. He was distracted and not paying attention, and it was raining really hard. I didn't see it happen, but I heard the impact of the car hitting him. I knew it was him, and then his teammate was yelling for help as he ran over from his car. I'll never forget it."

"Did you stay to help him?" I know my eyes are begging for the answer I want to hear. I so badly want him to tell me he stayed to help, that he wouldn't leave this person who obviously means something to me lying on the wet concrete.

"No. His teammates came running and I overheard one of them calling 911, so I left."

My mouth falls open. Who is this person standing in front me? How could he do that?

"Patrick, how could you?" Tears flood my eyes as my heart beats wildly. Reid said this was all my fault, and now I know why.

"Don't worry, Camille, I have more guilt about this than you can imagine, and I have to live every day with the choices I've made. There's nothing you can say that will make me feel worse than I already do." He frowns and his gaze droops with the weight he's now carrying.

"Why didn't he say anything to me about this?" I ask, more to myself than to Patrick, but he answers anyway.

"I don't know."

Oh God—no wonder his hatred toward me was off the charts. I'm surprised he even allowed me to take him home.

I would have had him removed from my room at the hospital had it been me. And after everything he did for me, too . . .

Slowly, tears begin to fall from my eyes. Unbeknownst to me, it seems I hurt the one person who has come to mean more to me than anyone else, and this has me dying on the inside.

Reaching into his back pocket, he pulls out a set of papers that are stapled and folded in half lengthwise.

"What's this?" I ask as he hands them to me.

"A copy for your records."

Opening them, I see on top is a form titled *Final judgment and decree of divorce incorporating settlement agreement.* It's dated two weeks ago and is signed and notarized by a judge who is a friend of my father's, along with Reid, and . . . me.

"I didn't sign this!" I shake the papers in front of him.

He gives me a look that tells me everything. *Of course.* This has my father's dirty fingerprints all over it.

"And Reid saw this? With my *fake* signature on it?"

"Yes," he answers solemnly.

I don't respond. There's nothing I can say to change this or make it better. I'm so disappointed in Patrick, so heartbroken over what's happened to Reid.

Poor Reid.

All he's ever done is be there for me, and look what that got him—a broken heart and broken bones. Despite what he said a few weeks ago, I know he cared for me, very much. You don't do the things we did or act the way we did if you don't care deeply, and knowing this hurts me the worst.

Picking up the two photos, I stack them on top of the papers then walk past Patrick and straight out the coach house door. Behind me, Patrick calls out, but I'm done. I don't want to see him anymore. He was supposed to be my friend, but he was instrumental in hurting not only me, but now Reid, too. This time, the choices are mine. Patrick mentioned he has to live with his, and well, I have to live with mine, too, including who I allow in my life and who I don't.

As the kitchen door closes behind me, I lock it and close the chapter of my life that is Patrick.

No more.

No more manipulation, no more control, and no more of me giving everyone the benefit of the doubt. They've all shown their true colors one too many times, and I finally see it all for what it's worth—nothing. Reid talked about character, how it's the most important to him, and I fully agree. It may have taken me a while, but I finally got here.

Moving through the house, I make my way upstairs and to my room. There sitting on the pillow, right where I left it, is Reid's paper airplane. It's not the fanciest of the three, but it's simple and perfectly folded.

Laying the papers and the photos down, I climb into my bed, under the covers, and stare at the plane. Of all the gifts in the world, it's true what they say about how the ones from the heart mean the most. He didn't have to give them to me, which is how I know all three came from the heart—his heart.

Reaching over, I run my fingers along the wings, the center unfolds, and I see the markings of ink. My breath catches as I sit up, pick up the plane, and gently unfold it. There, written across the top in all caps, are three words: *I love you.* Underneath it says, *You asked me why I did all this, and the answer is simple: it was love at first sight. I might not have recognized these feelings in the beginning, but they made themselves very clear, very quickly, and I would do anything for you, any time. I'll always be here for you.*

Heat rushes through me as my fingers tremble and I read the words over and over again.

He loves me?

Why didn't he just tell me?

But I already know—he's not a words guy; he's all action. On and off the field, he takes care of others the only way he knows how: by doing. He's decisive, protective, and strong. He's attentive, generous, and so very thoughtful. I should have known then, because it's so easy to recognize now.

Jumping off the bed, I race down to the table in the living room that holds the other two airplanes. I pick up the first one he gave me over two months ago on our wedding day, flip it over, and carefully pull out the tail. There, scrawled across the white page in black ink is: *I never thought a girl like you would ever marry a guy like me. Thank you for saying yes.*

My chin involuntarily quivers, tears roll down, and I start to shake. I don't know how to feel. I'm elated to know he loves me like I love him but destroyed at the same time because I might have inadvertently ruined it all just by being born as who I was and because of who I know. No one would blame him for walking away and saying enough is enough. Love isn't always enough.

Reaching for the second, I delicately unfold it, and inside it says: *This is already the best honeymoon I'll ever have.* And it was—the best honeymoon I would ever have. For a man who never wanted to get married or be tied to someone else, this gesture, his words . . . they're so kind and so true. They've given me hope, but they've shattered my heart, too.

Clutching them to my chest, my eyes catch on the jar of shells I placed next to the planes. Some are broken and some are whole, but together they are all beautiful, just like Reid and me, and now, knowing he feels this way, I can't give up. I won't give up, at least not until I've given it my all.

Chapter 31

Reid

THERE'S A KNOCK on the door that has my head swinging toward it. No one ever knocks on my door. Jack just walks in, and we have security downstairs. Making my way over, I crack it and find the last person I ever expected to be standing on the other side: Camille's grandfather.

I'm openly staring at him, and he's staring at me. It's not awkward; it's confusing.

"Sir." I feel my brows pull down as I open the door wider.

"Son." I watch as his eyes drop and look over every injury visible, not seeing the one that hurts the most, the one inside my chest.

"Please come in." I step out of the way as an invitation.

He smiles, walks in, and makes his way toward the windows on the far back wall. Following, I move into the living room, turn off the television, and then stop, leaving the full length of the room between us.

"Can I get you anything?" I offer. I may not be happy with how everything worked out between Camille and me, but being rude to someone for no real reason isn't the right way to go about things either.

He turns and looks around the condo before making his way to the couch. "No, thanks. Nice place you have here." He sits right in the middle.

"Thanks, I like it. My friend Jack lives across the hall, so that keeps things interesting."

He chuckles. "I bet it does. I also bet Camille liked it here." His gaze travels and stops on a piece of wall art I found in Camille's room once I returned from Savannah. It's just like her, too, to have hidden a present for me. I hung it right away so anyone who comes in will see it, and I can't bring myself to take it down now.

Sometime during her stay here, she found an old four-paned window, stripped the paint off the wood, and repainted it a distressed white. She popped the glass out, covered it with chalkboard paint, and wrote the lyrics of the choruses from four of my favorite jazz songs by Mr. Dan, in cursive, in white chalk. The black and white matches the color scheme of my living room, and it looks perfect on the wall.

"She said she did, but I think she preferred sitting on the balcony the most."

His gaze drifts over and he sees the mini workshop she set up outside with the drop cloth, makeshift wooden workbench, and tools. I should have gotten rid of them by now, but I haven't.

"She always did love the outside the most," he says, thinking about something unrelated to being here.

It's funny, when I first met her, I would have never guessed she loved being outside. Her appearance and apparent upper-class upbringing gave off the impression that she would be more high-maintenance than laid back. But, he's right—as I got to know her and she relaxed some, she did transition and spent a lot of time outside. Deep down, though, I loved both sides of her, because they're part of who she is.

"My Camille," he says gently, interrupting my thoughts. "She's always had this inner strength her sister never had. Clare loved this life, our life, because it was easy and it was handed to her. She was that child who was always content just sitting inside and playing with one of her toys, because that was what she was expected to do. Don't get me wrong, she had her own ambitions, but they revolved around making those around her happier than she made herself. Not Camille, though. She never needed approval from someone else to be happy, because she found happiness within. From the moment she was born, everything was an adventure, and everything became a challenge. Recipes were meant to be created, not followed. Music was best loved by making it, loudly, not listening to it. She couldn't just climb a tree, it was how high can I go? And don't get me started when it comes to her free will versus my son's determination to break her."

Images of Camille losing herself while working on the mirror, dancing on the beach, and cooking me dinner with food smudged on her clothes flash through my mind. When she wasn't feeling pressured or confined, she was adventurous and spread her wings. She surprised me, but in the best way. Of course, she also surprised me in the worst.

"Please, come sit with an old man." He gestures to the chair perpendicular to him.

I sit, he stares at me, and then he lets out a deep sigh while frowning.

"Patrick told me what he did."

My brows furrow with displeasure at his name and I cross my arms over my chest.

"I'm really sorry you were injured because of it." His gaze travels over my face. The road rash has faded, the stitches are gone, and I've taken my sling off. The only thing visibly remaining is the cast on my lower arm.

"He didn't do anything. I walked in front of the car—the accident is all on me."

"I don't think he sees it that way."

Turning my head, I look away as my jaw tightens. "With all due respect, sir, I don't care how he sees it."

"Patrick isn't a bad guy." He throws one arm out across the back of my couch. I look back at him and raise one eyebrow in question, and he chuckles.

"Please tell me you didn't drive down here just to tell me that."

"I didn't drive here, I flew, and my plane is waiting for me when we're done."

Of course he has his own plane. Then it hits me why he's here, and my heart falls into my stomach. I knew eventually I'd have to give it back, know it's not mine to keep, but for some stupid reason, I still wanted to.

Getting up, I go retrieve his wedding ring from the top drawer of my nightstand.

For weeks, this ring was stuck on my finger. I was certain I'd need the Jaws of Life to remove it, but the day after Camille left, I was in the shower and it slid right off. I was so surprised I dropped it on the floor. Even now, just holding it, it feels warm and familiar, and it hurts to know it's no longer going to be mine, just another piece of me that's about to walk out that door.

"Here, I think this is what you're looking for." I hand him the ring and he frowns as he looks at it in the palm of his hand.

"No, son. This is yours now." He pinches it between his thumb and forefinger, raising it to hand it back to me, but I take a step back, away from him. Reality is, it was never truly mine.

"We're divorced. It's yours, and it should go back to you." I sit back in my chair, and we both wordlessly eye each other. He's impeccably dressed in a suit and tie, and I'm wearing a Tarpons T-shirt and pajama pants.

"Yeah, about that," he says, placing the ring on the coffee table in front of him, sliding it toward me and then shifting uncomfortably on the couch.

My hands ball up in my lap as I feel my face dip into a scowl.

His gaze finds mine. There's zero expression on his face, and the only hint of remorse evident is in the way the muscles twitch around his eyes. "She doesn't know you're divorced."

"Yes, she does. She signed the papers," I immediately respond.

"No, she didn't." He lets out a long, embarrassed sigh. "My son—her father—had the papers drawn up, and Camille's mother forged her signature."

What?

Sitting up straight, I pause and take a minute to gather myself.

Anger slowly builds and begins coursing through me, and not even for myself, but for Camille. She may not be my favorite person right now, but my immediate response is to lash out in her defense.

"She can't do that. That's illegal." My voice is raised, but he doesn't flinch.

"Well, she did, and in his typical controlling way, he convinced Patrick he had to deliver them and persuade you to sign them, aggressively if necessary. You should know, the papers have been filed. You and Camille are divorced."

The way he speaks, there's no inflection in his tone; he almost sounds bored. I get that stuff like this is probably commonplace in his world, but it's not for me, and I'm appalled by the audacity of his family members.

"Who are you people?" I lean back to move a few more inches away from him and grip the fabric of the chair's arms.

"I can assure you we are not all bad. I apologize for my son, and Patrick has been dealt with, but Camille, that poor girl—she's innocent in all their scheming. None of this is her fault."

I try to let this sink in. My original gut reaction was that there was no way she'd sign those papers, and I was right. The Camille I left in Savannah would have never had those papers drawn up and sent. Guilt digs in a little as I realize I didn't give her the benefit of the doubt when I should have. I should've taken a moment to call her, to hear it straight from her, but then again, Patrick gave an impressive performance with some very important details purposefully left out.

"Reid, I've spent some time with Camille over the last couple of weeks, and I have to say, she's completely transformed from the girl she was not too long ago. I don't know what you two did during your time together, how you treated her, or the things that were said, but she came home so different than when she left. Pieces of the old Camille—the younger Camille—were shining through, and I can't thank you enough. She's always been the light of my world, and I just want to see her happy. You did that."

"A murderer is the light of your world?"

His eyes widen just a bit before he narrows them. The words taste wrong on my tongue, and I didn't mean to blurt it out that way. I realize I'm being disrespectful, but I don't care.

"Who told you she was a murderer?" he asks, tilting his head.

"He did. She did." I shrug my shoulders as if this is common knowledge, and I start jiggling my leg with pent-up energy.

He leans forward and adjusts his tie so it's sitting straight. "Oh, that girl. What happened to Clare was an accident. They were in the wrong place at the wrong time. It's not her fault."

"So, what happened?" I ask, wanting him to tell me the truth—the truth no one has bothered to mention to me yet.

"If she didn't tell you and you haven't looked it up, I think that's a story for her to share—that is, if you really want to know. Remember, Reid, things aren't always as they seem. All of us have been dealing with Clare's death the only way we know how: one day at a time. Admittedly, we all know Camille took it the hardest. I can't imagine what being a twin and losing that person would be like, would feel like. So, show her a little grace. If anyone deserves it, she does."

He stands and fastens the top button of his three-button suit jacket. I follow, feeling bereft. He can't be leaving; so much more needs to be said.

"She lied to me," I state, clinging to the anger I've used as fuel for the past couple of weeks.

He pauses, studies me, and asks, "Are you sure about that?"

Just like that, I'm not.

"I will take this." He picks up the ring and slides it into his pants pocket. "Although, I still feel like it's yours. I guess if you want it, this time you'll have to earn it. If you decide to pursue Camille, be prepared to have your socks knocked off. You haven't seen her light yet, but when you do, you'll be in awe."

With that he gently claps me on my good shoulder, gives me a small squeeze, and then he's gone.

Sitting back down in the chair, I let the silence of the condo surround me while an eerie feeling settles over me. I think about the fake divorce papers—well, not entirely fake—and how they were used to once again make Camille a pawn in their game. When will it stop for her? I mean, this is just ridiculous, but I can't help but wonder, does she know now? Someone had to have told her, right? Wouldn't she have reached out to tell me? I'd like to think so, but with sharp clarity, I know the answer is no—not after the way I talked to her. I wouldn't want to communicate with me either.

Oh God. I rub my chest as it's started to ache.

Then I think about how I might have misjudged her based on Patrick's claim of her being a murderer. Granted, she didn't argue with me when confronted, but I never should have taken her word for face value. She started closing in on herself the minute I mentioned her sister, something she kind of did every time the subject was brought up during our time together. Clare was spoken of in passing, but we never talked about her, not really.

Her grandfather's wrong—I have seen her light. In those rare moments, I was awed, and I went out of my way to see if I could get her to shine again and again.

Leaning forward, my elbows land on my knees and my head drops down. A heavy remorse capsizes my heart.

What have I done?

For so long, I've had this mentality that I had to be in charge—in charge of my family, in charge of my career, and in charge of me. No one controls me; I make my own decisions based on what I think is best, and I determine my own destiny.

What I don't do is leave things to trial and error. I don't expose any vulnerability or weakness in myself, and I don't allow myself to be in situations where I could get hurt. These things come from being unprepared or entering an unknown, like a relationship, and look where I am now: on my ass at home, brokenhearted and miserable.

All of this mess is because I let Camille in. I let down walls that have been erect for so long, I thought they were impenetrable, but apparently they weren't. Those walls were there for the sole purpose of protecting my heart—my seven, ten, and thirteen-year-old heart.

I always firmly believed marriage was not for me. I never wanted to get married, never had the desire to become so attached to someone. My mother, on the other hand, chased, revered, and wanted love so badly. She's a hopeless romantic who's never stopped believing her person is out there, and I always ended up the casualty as someone new would come and then eventually go. No one stayed.

As her son, I've never considered her life beyond being a mother. That was her role, and looking back now, I see a woman who was trying to enjoy her life and get through it the best way she could.

Mothers aren't supposed to have a lot of boyfriends coming and going. In traditional families, there's supposed to be a husband, a dad, and for us, there wasn't, but the terrible thing I realize now is, as much as I hated what felt like her revolving door of men in our life, I've never thought about exactly how many that was. No, I don't remember my father—he left after he found out she was pregnant with Nate—but all through my childhood, she only dated three guys.

Three.

As a boy, I looked up to each and every one of them. In the same way my mother wanted love, so did I, and with wide eyes, I fell hard for each of them. As a child, it feels like three role models—four if you include my father—who, in the end, walked away. Ultimately, it was about them not being compatible; I get that now, but back then, I didn't. It felt like a rejection of me, who I was. To have someone present for years, to love them and then have them leave with no looking back . . . it does something to you that's irreparable. It all made me who I am today.

Now, though, I can see it wasn't really like that. She was a woman in her late twenties and thirties, the same age I am now, and three is nothing. I have friends who go through three a weekend, and all of this suddenly makes me question everything.

My thoughts drift back to Nate's speech at our wedding. At the time I didn't understand why he said it would be okay to be vulnerable, said I didn't always have to distance and numb myself because those who truly loved me would stick by me, but now I do. I stopped letting people in, because subconsciously I thought they would eventually leave, but Camille didn't. I forced her out.

Damn.

Maybe Camille isn't the only one who deserves a little grace; maybe I deserve to give some to myself, too. After all, not once have I ever thought I was one who needed to be saved, but maybe I was wrong.

Maybe I was wrong about a lot of things.

Chapter 32

Camille

HEARING THE DOORBELL ring, I race down the stairs with my bag in hand and scowl at whoever could be here. It's rude to show up somewhere unannounced, especially this early in the morning.

All night I lay awake and replayed the conversations Reid and I had over the last two months. They were real, and the moments were real; people can't fake those kinds of emotions. He has to be lying to himself about me, because what other reason could there be?

Dropping my bag by my feet, I fling the door open, and there on the other side is Reid. He's standing with his hands in the pockets of his favorite jeans—yes, I know they are his favorite because he told me so—a navy blue pullover from his athletic wear endorsement deal, a white shirt underneath, and flip-flops. His hair is all over the place, there's stubble across his jaw, and he looks tired—so good, but tired.

I should say something, but I can't. He's here, at my home, and I think I might burst from the inside out.

"Hi," he finally says, breaking the silence. His voice is low, hesitant, and my heart soars at the sound.

My eyes snap to his and I feel frozen—frozen with fear, frozen with hope . . . just frozen.

"You took your sling off," I nearly shout at him. "It's not time to take it off."

His mouth twitches on one side. "The doctor said it was okay. The bones need to work their way back together through movement to heal." His eyes fall to my bag. "Going somewhere?"

"Yes," I reply, but I don't tell him where. Instead, I just stand there, staring at him like he might disappear if I blink too many times.

Rubbing his hand across the back of his neck, he looks at our feet, frowns, and then back at me. "Okay, well, I don't want to keep you, I was just hoping we could talk."

"Of course! Come in!" I fling the door open. It's quite possible that once he enters, I'll lock the door and never let him leave.

He looks over my shoulder into the foyer and nods. I take a step out of the way and he walks in past me. Sunshine, sage, and fabric softener drift by. My eyes briefly flutter shut as I'm overwhelmed by the smell of him. I've missed his smell; I've missed him, so much.

"You drove all the way up here just so we could talk?" I close the door and follow him.

He nods.

"Did you drive all night?" I ask.

He looks over his shoulder and his light green eyes penetrate straight through to the core of me. "I couldn't sleep."

Moving into the living room, I stand behind him and watch as his gaze travels to the table, the place I put his paper airplanes on display. The spot is empty and the muscles in his throat move as he swallows but says nothing.

"Can I get you something to drink?" I ask, barely able to fumble out the words. My heart is racing and I'm incredibly nervous to have him here. I thought I'd have time to form coherent thoughts before I saw him, but he beat me to it.

Bringing his attention to me, he takes a good long look, blinks, and says, "Okay."

Racing into the kitchen, I lean on the breakfast bar and squeeze my eyes shut. He's here. I'm so happy he's here. I don't know why yet, but it can't be terrible if he drove all this way, right? Plus, he doesn't realize I know this, but he did tell me he loved me, and love doesn't just go away.

I fill a glass with ice water and take it to him. His eyes immediately find mine and stay on me. That nervousness grows and flutters in my chest as I sit down on one end of the couch; he's already sitting on the other. I angle my body so I'm facing him. I know what I'd like to talk about, but I'm not sure about him, so I wait for him to lead.

"Camille . . ." he starts off, but he says nothing more. Leaning forward, he places the glass on the coffee table. The sleeve of his pullover slides up, and the cast on his arm peeks out. Instantly my eyes burn, because I now know the real reason he was injured, and he was right: it was all my fault.

"Reid," I say quietly, watching every move he makes.

Letting out a deep sigh, he scrubs his uninjured hand over his face and sits back farther into the couch. "I owe you an apology."

What? He doesn't owe me an apology; I owe him one— no, I owe him a thousand apologies. He did nothing wrong. This is all on me. I shake my head, because truly, I don't want it. I just want him, and I'm so happy he's here.

"Yes. I shouldn't have said the things I said to you. I shouldn't have jumped to conclusions, and I should have taken the time to listen to you." His eyes are so remorseful it nearly rips my heart out. "I know I'm an in-your-face type of person and have a tendency to be overbearing, but that doesn't excuse it. I took things too far, which resulted in you completely shutting down on me. Who could blame you? I don't. You deserved better, and I'm sorry."

"I was on my way to you," I blurt out.

"You what?" His brows rise up his forehead and his fingers curl into his palms.

"Yeah, see, the thing is . . ." I scoot closer to the edge of the couch and a little closer to him. "I'm not done fighting for you."

Surprise flashes through his eyes. It's only there for a split second, but I see it.

"Fighting for me?" he questions, his lips twitching as he tries not to smile.

"Yes." I want to tell him everything, need to tell him everything. No secrets, no more. "Patrick came here yesterday and told me what he did."

Reid's lips press into a flat line and he looks away. I understand why the mention of Patrick would make him react this way, but I need him to believe I wasn't part of it.

"I swear, I didn't know about the papers, and when you said it was my fault, I should have pushed you harder for an explanation."

His eyes slide back to mine and I twist my fingers in my lap. I'm apprehensive. He makes me jittery. I don't want to say anything that might upset him and make him want to leave.

"It wasn't your fault, and your grandfather paid me a visit yesterday, too." His voice is deep, smooth, forbearing.

"He did?" I sit up a little straighter.

He nods.

That means Reid knows, and relief trickles in. He knows I wasn't being deceitful, knows I wasn't being dismissive of our time together and am still in this, more than ever. But, he still needs to understand that I'm always going to fight for him, too.

"I'm glad to hear that and I hope he was able to ease your mind about a few things, but even if he hadn't, I was still coming for you."

He doesn't say anything, just chews on the inside of his cheek.

"The thing is, I hate conflict and confrontation. It's always been in my nature to bow out, whether I just decide to go with the flow or remove myself completely. But, I do realize that by forfeiting, I'm not allowing my voice to be heard, and for too long, I've had to accept that. Not today, though—not about this. You aren't just important to me, Reid, you are everything. When it comes to you, I will never be quiet, never again, because I get it. I get you, and I know who you are, inside and out. You're the rock for everyone in your life. You're protective, and you give and give and give. I want to be that for you if you'll let me."

The grandfather clock from the formal living room chimes as Reid stares at me. His body has gone tight, his chest rising and falling at a faster rate, but instead of responding, he just swallows. Heat suffuses my body. It starts in my toes and rises inch by inch until I'm covered with a full body flush. I thought it would be harder to put myself out there, but it wasn't, not with him. He's worth it, even if I do feel like every emotion, thought, and part of me is enlarged and exposed.

"Also, I'm sorry, too—for so many things." I glance away and my eyes find the water glass. Condensation has built up on the outside and is slowly rolling down to the table. "I know I was wrong to mislead you about Clare. From the start, I should have told you about her."

Mentioning the loss of Clare in combination with the anguish of how Reid and I ended two weeks ago, how desperately I missed him, and having him here to pour my heart out to, I've reached the pinnacle of my emotional stability, and it teeters. Feeling as bare as I do to the one person I feel the safest with, tears fill my eyes and begin to fall. I can't help it; there's no stopping them.

Leaning forward, his large hand covers both of mine. It feels so comforting to be touched by him, and I want to climb into his lap and melt into his body. His fingers brush over the wedding band I'm still wearing, and he lightly gasps as he looks down and sees it. I don't feel bad for wearing it, and I won't. He pauses before he looks back up at me.

"I would have liked to have heard about her from you," he says, being the support he's always been to me. I don't want this to be about me; I want it all to be about him because I love him, but I know he needs to know this last part of me before we can even consider moving forward. It's too big. It's too much a part of who I am and why.

Taking a deep breath, I look back at Reid and see the sadness I feel reflected in his eyes. He hurts for me, and that nearly brings me to my knees.

"It's so complicated. All of it is, and that makes it hard." I roll my lips between my teeth.

"Why don't you start by telling me what happened."

"You don't know?" I ask him, surprised.

He shakes his head. "My stubborn personality had me convinced I didn't need to know. I thought I knew enough, and since we were done, I chose not to look it up."

"Oh."

I look down at our hands. Part of me feels disappointment in his reasoning, but another part of me feels grateful because I can tell him the story without there being prior prejudices.

At my pause, Reid releases me then wraps his uninjured arm around my hips to drag me up next to him. Leaning my head against his shoulder, I breathe in the scent of him and close my eyes in remembrance.

"We were supposed to be heading to my father's country club for breakfast. It was the end of the school year, a late start day, and I was feeling selfish. I just wanted some time with her, so I convinced her to skip school and spend the day with me. They were expecting us, all of them, but I didn't want us to go. I swear, she spent every minute she could with Patrick, and it was like I got pushed aside. The realistic part of me knows this wasn't true, but with the way things seemed in my head and felt in my heart, I was crazy jealous."

"Patrick?" he asks, confused.

"He was her boyfriend."

"I see," he says, and nothing more.

"While she was getting ready, I flopped down on her bed and watched her. She tried to ignore me, but she was a people pleaser, hated when people were unhappy with her. Turning around, she put her hands on her hips and asked me, 'What?' I'll never forget her in that moment. Her room was on the east side of the house and the sun streaked in, lighting her up like a spotlight. Her hair was so blonde, her posture so perfect from years of dance, and the dress she'd chosen to wear that day made her look like royalty. I remember thinking she was so beautiful and everything I wasn't. Sure, I danced too, but at the time, my hair was dyed bright pink and I had a large henna tattoo covering one hand."

"Pink hair? You?" he asks, looking at me skeptically.

A small smile emerges as I think about the reactions I got after I dyed it. I loved it. "Yes. My father was not happy, but he never had the expectations for me that he did for Clare. I guess you could say I was the black sheep of our family. He had given up on me a long time ago. Somehow I convinced her to spend the day with me, for old times' sake. We packed up a picnic, grabbed a few other things, and headed to our spot behind the house at the very end of the field. Not a lot was said—not much ever was. I think for us it was just about being near each other.

"'Do you think you and Patrick will get married?' I taunted her, lying in shorts and a bikini top my father never would have approved of, hoping to get a bit of a tan. I already knew the answer. Even I saw that those two had something rare, something real. 'Absolutely,' she said. 'I'm surprised you're even asking.'

"She hated it when I talked about Patrick, thought I wasn't supportive of them, but I really was. I was the most supportive of anyone, but when someone is as perfect as she was, you have to have something to tease them about, and he was it. She climbed up off the blanket, tossed her hair over one shoulder, and wandered over to pick a few dandelions. Behind the lenses of my sunglasses, I watched as, one by one, she made a wish, blew on them, and watched the seeds float through the sky. She was eternally superstitious and would do anything and everything to not tempt fate.

"I told her, 'I just think you should spread your wings and get a taste of what's out there.' She turned and looked at me like I was crazy. 'Guys are not like ice cream—you can't go out there and taste thirty-one different flavors.' 'Sure you can! And that sounds fantastic to me,' I replied. We were eighteen, and the world was supposed to be our oyster. She said, 'Sounds terrible to me. I love him, Cam, I really do.'"

I'd forgotten until just now that she used to call me Cam.

"I told her, 'I know you do, but what kind of sister would I be if I didn't try to dissuade you at least a little? I mean, you're about to move to New York City! The largest city in

America. The possibilities are endless. Just think: no more fake Southern charm, and no more Father.' Clare just giggled, and deep down, I knew that was the life she wanted."

"Honestly, I can't see how anyone would want that life," Reid says, interrupting me. "Or Patrick," he growls.

"He was different then, just like I was—not that that's an excuse for his behavior lately, but it's the truth." I run my hand down Reid's thigh. Warmth permeates through his jeans.

"What did she say next?" he asks, reaching over with his casted hand to run his fingertips over my arm.

"She said, 'I happen to like all that Southern charm, and you're getting your wish. I think Father is as pleased as you are about you heading to Providence. You two are too much alike.' Of course I was appalled by this, and I said, 'I am not.'

"She loved saying this. It was her one go-to when she needed to get under my skin, just like Patrick was mine with her. 'You are. Both of you are stubborn and strong-headed.' I remember my head whipping over to look at her, and her eyes were sparkling and laughing at me. It was the last time I ever saw her like that."

Sometimes I see her like this in my dreams, laughing and happy. It's always this scene, and I'm always so relieved—until the scene plays out. It never changes, no matter how hard I try.

"Pause." Reid twists a little to get a better look at me. "You were going to go to college in Providence?"

"Yep, Rhode Island School of Design. Furniture design."

"Wow, I can see that now, and I know you said dancing was your sister's thing, but I guess I just assumed you loved it too. You had to put in a lot of work to get as far as you did."

"I did." I frown, thinking back to the hours and hours I spent in the studio after she died. I was clinging to anything and everything that made me feel close to her, and dance was in her soul. She loved every second of it. "Clare got into Juilliard. I was so lost after she died, I deferred all major life decisions to my father, and he thought it best I went in Clare's place, to fulfill her dreams."

Reid tenses beside me. "What about your dreams?"

"That summer, without Clare, I didn't have any. Life felt over, and the only thing I wanted was her. He pulled some strings, sent a donation, and one year later the admission was transferred. I spent that entire extra year here, dancing eight to ten hours a day, trying to be the best—the best for her, for them . . . everyone but me."

"Huh," Reid mumbles.

Leaning forward, I pick up his water and take a sip. I know what's coming, and I know I have to tell him, but I've never told anyone. Everyone in our world already knew, and I never talked about Clare in New York. I just didn't see the point, and it was all still so fresh.

Putting the glass down, I curl back into his side.

"I jumped to my feet and threw my shirt on. 'Take that back,' I yelled at her, and she just laughed, screaming, 'No way.' It was common knowledge how much I hated being compared to him while Clare was compared to our mother. Of course, even though I love her, she's not any better. She folds like a deck of cards when it comes to my father.

"So, I picked up a handful of dirt and held it high so she could see I was about to fling it at her. Squealing, she started running. Our house sat at the western northernmost part of the property, and we were at the south end. Clare started running east. There were trees on the perimeter of the property, which would be easy enough for her to duck into and hide behind. We'd run through those trees more times than I could count, and I took off after her. 'Yeah, you better run fast!' I hollered.

"I chased after her, we ran through the field, and at that moment, I was the happiest I had been in so long. It was just me and her, my sister, my best friend. I knew after that day things would change—they already had, really. Time was flying by, and our days together were almost up. I was embracing every second of our time in that field.

"As I started running, I realized we'd been out longer than planned. The sun had dropped behind the tree line, we were in that golden hour phase of light, and soon it'd start getting dark. It crossed my mind that we needed to head back. I was certain by then they were looking for us, but instead of calling her in, I chased her harder. We'd spent so many hours running through every inch of the field . . . but when Clare looked back at me, laughing, and then her face distorted with such acute agony and fear, time immediately went into slow motion. I watched as she fell to the ground, grabbed her leg, and let out the most horrific, pain-filled scream. I thought maybe she just tripped or stepped in a hole, but nope. I landed on the ground next to her, and there in the middle of her calf were two large puncture wounds. She'd been bitten by a snake."

Chapter 33

Reid

"HOLY SHIT," I say, fully entranced by her story.

"Yeah. There are thirty-nine nonvenomous snakes in Georgia and six venomous. Speculation is that the snake was sleeping. It should have woken up from the vibrations on the ground headed its way, but that's not always the case, especially when it's from a small female and not a large heavy animal. There was no warning, or if there was, I guess Clare wasn't paying enough attention to hear it. She stepped right on an Eastern Diamondback Rattlesnake, the most venomous of them all. We heard the rattle of the tail as it retreated away, and I will never forget that sound."

I've never heard that sound, except for what they play for sound bites in movies. I can't imagine lying in bed at night and hearing it. I'm certain I would never forget it either.

"We were a good mile away from the house and neither one of us had our phone. Once we got her to calm down and then up and moving, her leg started to swell, badly. That's when we knew we were in trouble. She wanted me to run ahead and get help, but I didn't want to leave her, and I forced her to keep going. Night was coming fast and I was afraid."

"I would have been afraid, too. I have zero experience when it comes to snakes and no idea what to do in that situation."

"Things I learned after the fact that you shouldn't do when bitten: move, because it increases the blood flow to the heart, or get anxious and worked up, because it increases your heart rate—both of which we were doing. I had ripped off my shirt and tied it just above the bite to hopefully slow down the dissemination of the venom, but she kept swelling and I kept having to loosen it. It was all happening so fast. You're supposed to receive medical attention for a snakebite within thirty minutes. It had been well over that before I finally left her in the field and ran ahead for help—well, ran is an exaggeration. I was hyperventilating and pretty much hysterical, and I couldn't go very fast.

"By the time the paramedics got to our house and we drove through the field to get to her, she had already started vomiting, lost function of her arms and legs, and had difficulty breathing. Her heart failed on the way to the hospital and she was pronounced dead immediately after arriving."

"I don't know what to say." I shake my head. The entire situation sounds utterly horrendous, and I can't even imagine what it was like for her to witness it.

Camille turns to look at me. Her eyes are so despondent and hollow, intensifying the sheer need I have to erase all of this for her.

"They say the chance of a person dying from a snakebite is so low, it's nine times more likely you'll die from a lightning strike. There are only five or six fatalities on average per year. It's because of this—well, this and other things—that

I've always felt responsible. Time was in our favor. I didn't move fast enough, soon enough."

I run my hands down her arms and shake my head, willing her to somehow agree with me. "Camille—"

"No. Whatever you're going to say, don't." She readjusts so one of her legs tucks up under her, the other hooking over my shin, then she reaches out and squeezes my waist. "There's nothing you can say that will change how I feel. This is what I live with every day. I was the reason she was in the field. She died because of me, and they're right to call me a murderer."

Anger toward myself because I once thought that disgusts me, and animosity toward those who've called her that charges through me. I want to strangle anyone, everyone who's ever made her feel like it was her fault.

"It was an accident. You are not a murderer—I know you know this," I grit out, trying my hardest to contain the anger I feel for her.

She shrugs her shoulders and drops her eyes to her hands. Her fingers flex in the fabric of the pullover, and one by one, I feel them push into my skin.

"People don't understand what it's like. Yes, losing a sibling is devastating, I'm not trying to take that away from anyone, but losing your identical twin . . . it's incomparable. She wasn't just my best friend—she was me. I lost myself, and I lost all the good parts of me."

"That's not true. I may not have known you before, but I see so many good things in you, so many that sometimes I wish I were more like you."

She leans back in surprise and her eyes find mine. "Really? Like what?"

"Camille, you are so kind." I reach up and tuck a piece of her hair behind her ear. "You say you like to keep the peace, and I know you do, but you genuinely want those you care for to be happy. You always look for the best in others, giving them the benefit of the doubt even if they don't deserve it. With me, you've been loving, creative, and happy. You've made me want to be a better person, because you deserve the best from me."

Her bottom lip quivers as she studies the details of my face. She's so beautiful, inside and out, and I deeply want her to see it, too.

"Thank you." She blinks slowly, her long eyelashes sweeping down and up like they're waving at me.

"Can I ask you a question?" I ask her.

"Of course."

"How did you and Patrick happen?"

"He sat next to me at the funeral. It wasn't intentional on his part—my parents called him up—but after that day, we sort of gravitated toward each other at school, social events, graduation. He understood more than anyone else how badly I was hurting, and in return, I understood him, too. I needed him and he needed me. Later that summer, Patrick was required to take a date to a political fundraiser, and he asked me if I would go. Of course I said yes since we were friends, but one event turned into many, and before I knew it, people had declared us a couple. I didn't care, though—being with him made it feel like my sister was still here, and I'm certain he felt the same way. Numb with emotion, I molded myself to be what he needed, what everyone needed. After all, all of it was my fault. My parents were thrilled, and for the first time in a long time, it felt like they were proud of me."

"Did you love him?" I hate asking her this, but given everything between them, I perversely need to know. My heart starts racing.

"No. I *missed* her," she says, clearly hoping I'll understand her meaning, and I do. "I still miss her, every day."

"Tell me more," I encourage, running my hand across her thigh.

"In normal life, when someone dies, we grieve them and move on, but for me, every time I look in the mirror, I see her. I don't see me. I feel like a living breathing memorial, and it's really hard to differentiate between her and myself when we are one and the same. People mourned her to me. I became a living ghost of her, and I lost myself even more.

"Since before we were even born, we were a 'we' or 'the girls.' I was never just me, and when she died, it's like I stopped breathing because life as I knew it was over. I had to learn to breathe on my own, and it was really hard, but thankfully I did have my grandfather, and I had Patrick."

At the mention of his name, I involuntarily pull my hand away. She catches the movement and stops me. Retuning my hand to her leg, she holds it in place.

"Patrick helped me the most." She frowns. "While others just assumed I was grieving, he knew what I was dealing with was on a whole different level. He took me to the doctor, found me a therapist, joined me at support groups for those who had lost a twin—he was really there for me when I needed someone. But, looking back, as grateful as I am for him, I feel like he was using me as a way to not deal with his own heartache. I gave him a purpose, a distraction."

"I get that. It also helps me understand why you were so loyal to him."

"He was my friend," she says sadly. "I thought letting go of him would be like losing her all over again, if that makes sense."

"It does." They were all a package deal, a life together full of memories. Of course I can see how it would feel like losing her all over again. It's like effectively closing the door on so much of her life.

"But surprisingly, it didn't, and yesterday, when I walked away, I was just done. I didn't feel bad at all. In fact, I felt relief."

"I'm not going to lie, I don't like that he was here." I tilt my chin a little higher. "I'll never tell you who you can and cannot be friends with, but I feel very strongly about him not being around you."

She gives me an endearing smile and runs her hand from my waist up to the middle of my chest. I'm certain she can feel my heartbeat, and I hope she does. In so many ways, it beats just for her. "He's not coming back. You don't have to think about him ever again."

"Good."

"I meant it when I said I was going to fight for you. I may have had to work myself up to it, but I was almost there, and then yesterday, all the remaining puzzle pieces fell into place. Nothing was going to stop me from going to you."

Hearing that she wasn't giving up on us, on me—it's a balm that soothes the part of me that's been empty without her.

Leaning down, I touch my lips to hers, and from the inside out, my soul weeps in relief. Neither one of us moves, remaining still as the gravity of the moment settles around us, until she exhales. It's long, slow, and filled with a relief so tangible I reach out and embrace it through her lips, her face, her hands, her body. She slides onto my lap, flattens herself against me, and although I hug her gently due to that damn collarbone, I hug her thoroughly so she knows she's mine.

"I'm sorry, Reid, for everything," she quietly says into the skin of my neck.

Wrapping my hands around her face, I move us so we're nose to nose and she's looking me in the eyes. "Don't be.

Don't ever be sorry, because I would do it all over again if it meant bringing me here to you."

Warm tears slip out of the corners of her eyes and roll across my fingers. I abhor that all of this has moved her to tears, but from now on, if anyone is going to be the one to dry them, it's me.

"I'm sorry for how I behaved back in Tampa. I hate how I spoke to you." I really do. Never again will I be so quick to judge; there's always more to the story.

"You have nothing to be sorry about." She shakes her head lightly and her sweet breath washes over my face.

Inching forward, she closes the distance between us and kisses me with abandon. There's a desperation to our movements that's slow and hard, forgiving and freeing. I can't get close enough.

Almost three months ago, she breathed life into a need I didn't know I had, a simple spark that turned into a flame and spread like a wildfire, burning me up from the inside out. I welcome the heat, never want to temper it, and with her, I'm certain I never will. She's the catalyst, the oxygen needed, and because of her, I'm transformed.

Reclining back, I grab the pullover behind my head and yank it off. My T-shirt comes with it and I drop both on the floor next to us. Her warm hands roam over me, drifting lightly over the bump of the break and then up into my hair.

"Your hair is so long." She smiles, running her fingers through it, making it stand straight up.

"I know." I chuckle. "Whereas yours is just as gorgeous as always."

I run my hand over the back of her head, cradling it reverently. Her cheeks flush and she leans forward to place her forehead against mine.

"I missed you so much," she whispers, her swollen lips just inches from mine.

"I missed you more."

Starting at the top, I make my way down as I unfasten each button of her shirt. Sliding my hand back up between her breasts, I peel the fabric away, leaving her in beige lace. A pang of longing pulls the breath from me as I admire every inch of her skin—so pale, so smooth, and so perfect.

Leaning forward, I run my nose across the length of her shoulder, and goose bumps chase behind. Tangling one hand in her hair, I pull her bra strap down with the other and admire how her skin smells like peaches. If I didn't have these injuries, there's no doubt I'd tackle her to the floor, but as it is, I end up taking my time.

Her hands run over my back as mine cup and take in the weight of her breasts and my mouth sucks in her nipple. She gasps and arches underneath me.

A man could die just from yearning to hear the sounds she makes.

I want to tell her to sit still, that if she keeps moving this will be over before it begins, but I don't. I can't say a word. Instead, I take off every stitch of our clothing and worship her the best way I can.

The warmth of her skin as it caresses mine makes me feverish. The taste of her lips has me intoxicated, and the feeling of her heart beating with mine leaves me delirious. How one person can cause so many different visceral reactions is beyond me, but I want it. I want it all.

Us, together, moving, breathing, enraptured as one— there is nothing greater than this expression of love, a love I intend to hold onto for forever.

Sometime later, we make ourselves some lunch then head upstairs to her bed. Both of us are exhausted and quickly fall asleep. Hours pass as we nap curled around each other, until I'm finally awoken by the twilight sun. Everything is warm—

her room, her bed, her—and I feel more content than I have in my entire life. How I went all those weeks without this—hell, all those years—I'll never know.

Slipping out of her bed, I'm on my way to the bathroom when I spot the original photo I saw of her and Clare. I bring it with me, crack the door, and turn on the light. Of course, now when I look at it, it's plain as day that the girl smiling at the person taking the photo is not Camille, and the girl with her head thrown back laughing is—the girl with the pink hair. Yes, they are identical twins, but the differences between them aren't that subtle. Clare's face is rounder, her eyes are farther apart, and the energy that's present in Camille just isn't there. Clare is beautiful, but she looks colder, stiffer, and from all they've said, perfect for Patrick.

Patrick and I will never be friends, but I do feel sympathetic for his loss. Loving someone for so long and so completely, and then to have her tragically taken away . . . I can't imagine the pain and hope I'm lucky enough never to experience it firsthand, but then I change my mind. At the end of our life, one of us will have to die first, and it hurts to say this, but I hope it's her, not me. I don't want her to go through great loss twice. Once is enough.

Sliding back in the bed, I pull her up next to me, and her arm drapes across my chest.

"Where did you go?" she mumbles against my skin.

"Nowhere," I tell her, and deep down, I mean it. For weeks, even though we weren't physically together, I've been with her and only her. She consumed all my thoughts and heavily filled my heart.

My wife.

Well, technically she's not, but that's not from our doing and wasn't our choice. If I have anything to say about this, the paperwork will be resubmitted and our status will be remedied somewhat quickly.

"Camille," I whisper, my lips in her soft hair as my hand runs down the bare length of her spine.

"Hmm," she murmurs, half asleep.

"I love you."

Starting at her foot, her skin ripples all the way up to her hand on my chest, where her fingers curl into her palm.

"I do. I love you, and I just thought you should know."

"Reid." She pulls back, looks at my face, and then cups my cheek. Her thumb slides back and forth, making me feel treasured. With a small smile, her eyes are happy as she says, "I know you do."

"How do you know?" I question, returning her adorable smile.

Sitting up, she leans over to her nightstand, opens the drawer, and pulls out three wrinkled pieces of paper. I immediately know they were the airplanes I made. That's why they weren't downstairs—she found my notes.

Laying them on my lap, she crosses her legs as she sits close, and I wait for an uncomfortable shyness to take over, but it never does. I have nothing to hide from her, nor she from me, and for the first time in my life, I want to share every part.

"It was the ink on the third one—I saw it first, and, well, of course I had to go read your other hidden messages. These mean more than you will ever know, Reid. Tomorrow you have to refold them so I can keep them forever."

"Were you surprised?" I ask, a little sheepish but a lot more curious.

"Surprised isn't a big enough word. I was many things, but mostly so happy because I love you, too."

"Yeah?" I ask, hope healing all the little broken cracks in me.

"Oh yeah," she says, grinning from ear to ear. "I love you very much."

Chapter 34

Camille

EIGHT WEEKS HAVE passed since that day Reid showed up on my doorstep.

Eventually, I told him all my biggest secrets, burdens, and sources of guilt, and being the man he is, he absorbed it all and in return exuded a strength I found complimentary to my own. I don't need him, can do this life on my own, but with him, I feel like I can take on the world, two being greater than one.

"So what do you think?" I ask as I join him out on the back veranda of my parents' plantation home.

"I think it's beautiful, and all so incredibly different from how I grew up."

"It is pretty, isn't it?" My eyes trail over the vast landscape in front of us and I smile. Memories, minutes, moments— they never leave us, and as much as we try to shake free, they're like cobwebs. You can feel them, but you can't quite find them. They cling, and there's no escaping, the good or the bad. Today, with the hint of humidity in the air and a sky full of endless clouds, I'm reminded more of the good, and being here, I'm at ease.

"It's quiet," he says.

"Wait till night time. The cicadas, toads—you name it, they all come out, and it's so loud. I thought living in the city was quiet."

After Grandfather visited Reid, his next stop was at my parents' home. I'm not sure what all was said—really, I don't even care—but it was my mother who came begging for forgiveness. Of course, I gave it to her.

My mother used to be stronger, but once my sister died, the light in her eyes died too. She was vibrant, always the perfect host, dazzling any room she entered. But, after that night, she slipped into the back of the crowd and politely remained just barely seen and not heard at all. I know this happened to me, too, but I'm not that girl anymore, and it seems she doesn't want to be either.

I know as well as anyone what life is like under my father's thumb and how hard it is to go against him. It turns out me taking a stand and Patrick taking a stand by outing my father's secrets to me then heading back to Boston gave her the strength to finally put her foot down as well. She'd had enough, just like the rest of us, and today we're here because she invited us to brunch before we head back to Tampa.

To our home.

No, we're not selling my house here, but it's preseason now and Reid is required to be there. Where he is, that's where I'll be, and fortunately for me, Vintage Soul is easily relocated. I'm glad I decided not to rush into opening a storefront, and as it is, I have a waitlist of commissioned pieces from the wives of some of Reid's friends on the team.

"Both nights we were here, for the rehearsal dinner and the reception, I didn't realize the property was this large, or at least that so much of it belonged to your family."

Reid is leaning forward with his forearms propped up on the veranda railing. His injuries healed at a rapid pace, and he's training hard just to prove he can. I'm proud of him.

He's wearing a white button-down with the sleeves rolled up, and he looks mighty good.

"How would you have known? First off, it was dark, and second, we were preoccupied with other more pertinent things."

"True," he mumbles, nodding in agreement.

Tearing my eyes off of him, I follow the trail that leads through the dogwoods down to an old bench. When we were little, we would sit out there on late summer nights and watch the fireflies rise up out of the tall grass, but since we lost Clare, my father's kept the field mowed down and it looks more like a grassy lawn. It's still beautiful, just different. Then again, I suppose we all are now—different.

"I can still see Clare and me running through the field. Do you see over there?" I point toward a cluster of trees about a quarter mile away. "Those are peach trees. We spent way too many days and nights lying under the trees and getting sticky while eating peaches, but boy were they delicious."

"The trees look small." He squints a little at the brightness of the midmorning sun.

"They are."

"Take me out there?" He stands up straight and turns to me.

"Now?"

I haven't been back in the field since the night Clare died, and he realizes this as he sees the panic on my face.

Pity flashes through his eyes then is replaced with astute understanding.

"Come on." He takes my hand and pulls me to the stairs. "It's July now, so the peaches will be ripe. Show this city boy what it's like to pick fruit and eat it right off the tree."

"You've never picked fruit before?"

He looks at me like I'm crazy and then grins. "Nope, not like this. We need to go out there and make some new memories, if you catch my drift." He winks at me, his grin stretching into a full-blown smile.

"I swear, is that all you think about?" I shake my head in exasperation as I follow him.

"Of course not. I think about food and football, too. Thing is, you're my wife—I'm allowed to think about it and do it as much as I want."

"I'm not your wife yet." I break free and take off running for the trees.

Next month, Reid and I are getting remarried.

I didn't think it would take him long, but even I was surprised that he asked after only two days. Just like the first morning we were at the beach, I wandered into the kitchen for a cup of coffee, and there on the island was a new paper airplane. I was beyond delighted to see it sitting there, and then when I peeled back the folded edges and saw those four words—*Will you marry me?*—my heart could have burst. With my hands flying to my mouth and tears in my eyes, I spun around, ready to run back upstairs, only to find Reid down on one knee holding the most stunning solitaire diamond ring I've ever seen. It was one of the greatest moments of my life, and it couldn't have been more perfect if he tried.

We talked about going down to the courthouse and making it quick and painless, but that didn't seem fair to those who love us and went on this journey too. His mother was beside herself with excitement, and that alone makes waiting a few more weeks worth it. We chose the beach, back on Anna Maria Island, because that's where we fell in love.

"Would you hold up? For someone so small, you're pretty fast," he calls from behind.

"Oh, is Mr. Wide Receiver having problems keeping up?"

"No." With that he blows by me, laughing the whole time.

"Show-off," I call after him, and he slows, turning around, running backward. He's so handsome with his hair flopping in his face and his eyes gleaming with playfulness, sometimes I feel like I need to pinch myself to prove this is real.

Eventually, we reach the trees and spend the next hour eating peaches, horsing around, and yes, making new memories. We're both a little dirty, but neither of us cares, and as we lie in the grass and stare up at the clouds, I feel a contentment I haven't experienced in a long time.

"Didn't you once tell me you and your sister used to lie in this field and stare at the clouds as they floated by?" His arm is tossed over his forehead as he blocks the sun and stares up into the sky.

"We did, but I think every kid does that." I pick a dandelion that's between us and lightly run my fingertips over the white fluffy top.

"We didn't, Nate and I. There were no fields for us to lie in."

I turn and look at him as I think about this, and I guess he's right. Where would they have done this in the Bronx? "Not even in a city park?"

"Nope. Never even occurred to me to lie down somewhere and look at them. If we were out, we were too busy playing sports, running around." His free hand reaches over and snatches the dandelion from me. He brings it up to his face and examines it.

"Clare and I spent hours outside describing what each one looked like, imagining where they were going, and chasing them as they floated by."

"You chased the clouds?" One corner of his mouth quirks up.

"We did. She always marveled as they passed over, whereas I always pretended they were taking me with them. She loved our life, and I hated it, but you know this."

"No offense, princess, but your life was very privileged. You might have hated it, but others would have killed for it—for this." Using his other hand, he pulls the fuzzy seeds and I watch as they drop and stick all over him. Swearing, he sits up, wiping at them, and I can't help but giggle.

"I suppose." I'm not stubborn enough to disagree with him; there's no point. I know we were afforded things others weren't, but as with everything, there was a cost, and I paid the price tenfold.

"The paper airplanes," Reid blurts out, dropping back down next to me, turning to look at me.

"What about them?" I ask as he reaches for my hand.

"Nate and I used to find as many business flyers as we could, and we would fold them into paper airplanes then throw them off the balcony of our apartment. Some would catch in the wind and some would nosedive to the ground, but we always sent them chasing the clouds. We were convinced that one day, one would soar so high, the clouds would reach down and take it with them to some far-off exotic place."

"See, we're not so different after all."

He gives me an incredulous look but says nothing, appeasing me.

Past him, my eyes catch on a slip of pale blue and I freeze.

"Do you believe in heaven?" I ask in a low voice, unshed tears instantly burning.

"Of course. Do you?" He turns to look at me, but I can't tear my eyes off her. It's been weeks since I've seen her.

"Yes. Do you believe in angels?"

"Honestly, I haven't given it much thought, but I would say yes, why not."

"Do you think I'm crazy because I can see my dead sister and she talks to me?"

"We already discussed this." He studies my face. "But, no. Who am I to say what you do or don't see? I believe in miracles, and those happen every day."

"Good, because I see her now."

Clare smiles, and I smile back.

His eyes grow wide as he turns his head and looks around us. "Where is she?"

"Right there, ten yards in front of us." I point to the exact spot.

Slowly, Reid and I stand. He brushes the dirt off of us as I continue to stare and grin. Reality is, I know she's not really there . . . but then again, maybe she is.

"I wish you could see her," I whisper to him. I know he's looking hard in the same direction I am, but he never will. His fingers thread through mine as he gently embraces me.

"I do see her," he whispers in my ear.

I turn to look up and find his expression is affectionate, tender, pure acceptance.

"I see her *in* you and *through* you, and not because of the way you look, but because of how you are. From all the stories you've told and all the memories shared, it's the kindness that radiates from you that I'm certain radiated from her as well."

His words touch a delicate part of my heart, and I'm rendered near speechless.

"I still wish you could have met her."

"Me too, princess. Me too."

Silence falls over us as I turn back to look at Clare and she stares at us. Never, not once since I started seeing her after her death have I been nervous to talk to her, but today I am. There's something different; something's about to change.

"So, you're finally making that move," Clare says, popping her hip out and placing her hand on it.

A laugh bursts out of my mouth and Reid startles next to me.

"Yeah, I guess you could say I am."

"Good for you."

"Nice dress," I state, stepping away from Reid and closer to her.

"I think so." She giggles, twirls, and the skirt flares out. It's the strapless bridesmaid's dress I had picked out for her and torn from a magazine. She wore it at our wedding and I remember thinking she looked so beautiful then, but she's even more beautiful now.

"Why am I the only one who can see you?"

She tilts her head and thinks about her answer. "I don't know, but then again, I don't make the rules."

"Will I see you again?" I have to ask, have to know.

She shrugs her shoulders and gives me a small smile. She doesn't answer my question, but deep down, something tells me this is it. I knew it was coming; it was only a matter of time.

She looks past me, and I know she's looking at Reid. Warm salty tears flood my eyes as I so desperately wish my past could meet my future. To have them both in the same place at the same time—it's like a dream come true, although it never really will.

"You're going to be all right," she says, returning her loving gaze back to me.

I know with absolute certainty she's right, but then again, I also know, "I already am."

She smiles as the breeze around us lightly picks up, blowing her white blonde hair across her face.

I never thought I'd be ready to let her go, to say goodbye, but now that we're here, in the field, I realize it couldn't have happened anywhere else. It's idyllic. It's destined.

"I know," she says. "With these new superpowers I have, I know all kinds of things."

I laugh at her wit; it's so Clare to try to keep moments like this light and serene.

"Are you going to share and tell me these things?" I ask, hopeful for more of anything she's willing to give.

"No way. Earning them is like a rite of passage, but you'll see one day—one day really far from today." She takes her time enunciating each word. Smiling, her crystal blue eyes bounce back and forth between me and Reid.

It's hard to hear this because her life was cut short, but I can't help the swell of emotion that blooms knowing my time with him is near infinite. It makes surrendering to his love that much more effortless, and I'm grateful for this little gift she just gave me, gave us.

"I miss you every day," I tell her.

"I know, but, Camille, I'm always with you. Don't ever forget that."

"I won't. I promise."

Words come to an end and silence fills the space between us. I soak up and cling to every detail of her I can, from the way her hair moves to the shine in her eyes and how her skin glows from the sunlight.

Minutes pass as the image of her starts to turn translucent and waver. I know I've stopped breathing. This is about to be it, and I watch as a cool wind swirls around my legs and then hers, flapping her dress in the breeze. Leaves from the trees next to us rustle, and the grass around us sways.

One by one, the white feathers of the dandelions in the field float up around us, and with one final kiss, blown straight to me, her image fades and scatters away with the seeds. It feels so dramatic, so final, and that's because I know it is.

I expected there to be an emptiness within, a great gaping hole, but there isn't. Instead, through the tears, I blink and feel fulfilled—filled with friendship, support, and love, a love only a twin sister can give. Just because she's absent doesn't mean these things are, and I smile knowing they'll never be gone, just like her.

As I let out a sigh, the wind dies down, and I turn around to find Reid standing just a few feet away. His back is ramrod straight, his arms are folded over his chest, and his brows are pulled low over his eyes. He looks confused, very wary, and I couldn't possibly love him more.

Walking back, I stop in front of him and see that dandelion seeds are sticking all over him, in his clothes and in his hair. That's when I know this was real, and inside I smile. Leave it to Clare to find a way to have the last word.

"Are we going to talk about this?" he asks, briefly glancing over my shoulder to what I know is nothing but an empty field, and I just shake my head.

Tears continue to fall, but I smile up into those light green eyes I know are all mine and say, "Not today, but one day."

"Are you okay?" he asks, searching my face for any tell that might show I'm anguished or distressed. He won't find it, though, because after years, the burden has lifted and I feel released.

"I'm better than I've ever been," I say, and I mean it.

The muscles in his face relax as he bends down and kisses my forehead. My eyes slip shut as I lean into him, finally knowing I'll always be able to give him the best version of me. Our life won't be restrained or suppressed by regrets or loss. We'll live it to its fullest, because that's what we both deserve.

Clare and I once asked Grandfather how we became identical twins and he said, "One egg, two hearts." He said there was so much love in that one little egg, it had to split in two. The love couldn't be contained, it had to be shared, and that's what I plan to do.

To love oneself is to love life.

Months ago, I found myself asking two questions: who am I, and what's important to me? I left the beach knowing what's important, and with certainty and clarity, I now know who I am.

When you hide who you are, you deny the world your gifts, and I have so many to give. I love the me I'm becoming, the me I was meant to be, but not just for myself—for Clare, too.

She would want this for us, and I do, too.

Pulling me closer, Reid tucks me up next to him as he drapes his arm over my shoulders. I wrap mine around his waist, and we begin to make our way back to the house together, hip to hip. Not much is said—I think we're still both so lost in our thoughts—but as I look around, I realize Reid's right: it is quiet here. It's peaceful, or maybe it's that I finally feel peace within me. Either way, I'm owning it.

"So, Prince Charming . . ." I start as we find ourselves back on the path between the dogwoods. He huffs with amusement, but I think it's fitting; after all, he does call me princess. "I was thinking we need to make a stop at the store before we hit the road."

"What for?" he asks suspiciously.

"Gummy bears, of course."

"You do understand that just because they say they're fat free, they're not actually calorie free or sugar free." He gives me side-eye as he speaks.

"Shhh. Are you trying to ruin them for me? You know how much I love them," I say with mock horror, teasing him.

"Yeah, but not as much as you love me." He smirks. He's tempting me with those lips, and if he's not careful, he might find himself making more memories with me behind the bushes.

"This is true." I pinch his side and he grunts. "By the way, after today, I've decided on our next honeymoon we're going to spend half the day lying around on the beach and watching the clouds. It's a rite of passage that you must call out any animals and objects you see in the sky. Everyone must do it at least once."

"Does this mean we're going to be chasing them, too?" He chuckles.

"No, I'm done chasing clouds." I grin.

"And why is that?" He looks down at me.

"Because the only thing I'm interested in chasing is you." I poke him in the chest.

"Is that so?" His expression fills with complete devotion.

"Yes."

Behind him, the sun provides a backdrop of light, and it's stunning. He's stunning.

"Well, I hate to break it to you, but you've already caught me."

Yeah, I guess I have.

Linking my fingers in his belt loop, I think about how he's caught me, too. Who knew marrying a stranger would turn into the greatest love? A love I plan to spend the rest of my life holding onto, and never ever letting go.

The End

From the Author

Thank you for reading *Chasing Clouds*. If you enjoyed this book, please consider leaving a spoiler free review.

Acknowledgements

OVER TEN YEARS ago my husband and I were driving from Chicago to Tampa and somewhere in Kentucky I remember seeing a billboard that was all black with five white words, "I do, therefore I am!" I'm certain that it was a Nike ad, but for me I found this to be completely profound.

Take running for example. Most will say that a runner is someone who runs five days a week and runs under a ten minute mile pace. Well, I can tell you that I never run five days a week and on my best days my pace is an eleven minute mile. I have run quite a few half marathons and one full marathon. No matter what anyone says . . . I run, therefore I am a runner.

I've taken this same thought and applied it to so many areas of my life: cooking, gardening, quilting, and yes . . . writing.

I may not be culinary trained, but I love to cook and my family and friends loves to eat my food. I cook, therefore I am a chef!

My thumb is not black. I love to grow herbs, tomatoes, roses, and lavender. I garden, therefore I am a gardener!

I love beautiful fabrics and I can follow a pattern. My triangles may not line up perfectly . . . but who cares, my quilts are still beautiful when they are finished. I quilt, therefore I am a quilter.

I have been writing my entire life. It is my husband who finally said, "Who cares if people like your books or not? If you enjoy writing them and you love your stories...then write them." He has always been my biggest fan and he was right. Being a writer has always been my dream and what I said I wanted to be when I grew up.

So, I've told you who I am and what I love to do . . . now I'm going to tell you the why.

I have two boys that are three years a part. My husband and I want to instill in them adventure, courage, and passion. We don't expect them to be perfect at things, we just want them to try and do. It's not about winning the race; it's about showing up in the first place. We don't want them to be discouraged by society stereotypes, we want them to embrace who they are and what they love. After all, we only get one life.

In the end, they won't care how many books I actually sell . . . all that matters to them is that I said I was going to do it, I did it, and I have loved every minute of it.

Find something that you love and tell yourself, "I do, therefore I am."

Acknowledgements

To my three guys, thank you for having patience with me and for giving me the time to dream up and write another beautiful story. I love each of you immensely and cannot imagine a life without you.

To my sweet friend Megan. This book is for you because you never stop believing in me, supporting me, and cheering me on. Not one word hasn't been touched by you and the story wouldn't be the same without you. From the bottom of my heart, thank you for everything.

Author Elle Brooks, my book bestie, thank you for being you. Whether it's sending me PMA vibes, while listening to me moan on and on about this story or sending me gif's to storm the tower, you always know just what I need. This book isn't complete without a toast, so cheers to us with our pink Moet Champagne!

Author Karla Sorensen, thank you for your friendship, our daily chats about anything and everything, and for being the ultimate sprinting partner. You kept me going, even when I wanted to slow down, and I'm so grateful. Much love... xoxo

Author Kandi Steiner, thank you for always being the first to help with industry advice, volunteering to blurb my stories, and well, for just being awesome. I am inspired by you daily and look forward to endless lunch dates.

Julie from Heart to Cover, thank you for putting up with me. You create the face to my stories and this cover is just so beautiful. I appreciate every minute you spend working on teasers, revisions, and reading my words.

Caitlin from Editing by C. Marie, thank you for leaving my voice as you worked your magic to make this manuscript as perfect as it is. I look forward to working with you again and again.

Emily from Lawrence editing, thank you for proofreading and polishing this story to make sure it's reader ready.

Elaine, from Allusion Graphics, thank you for being my formatter and for creating the inside look. Every time I open *Chasing Clouds,* I'll think of you and smile. Thank you for what you do . . .

Lauren from Perrywinkle Photography, thank you for the beautiful cover image. It fits the story perfectly.

To the book bloggers: Thank you! The book community on a daily basis still awes me. I am indebted to each of you. Thank you for the endless amount of support and interest you have shown for my stories. It's through you that my dreams continue to come true.

And finally . . . to the readers: THANK YOU. I really hope you enjoyed reading Chasing Clouds as much as I loved writing it. As an author, every review, every inbox message, and every comment means the world. Keep writing them and keep sending them, I read them all! Until next time! Take care . . . Kathryn xoxo

Ways to Connect

http://kandrewsauthor.com/

https://www.facebook.com/pages/
Author-Kathryn-Andrews/792608227420971

http://www.amazon.com/Kathryn-Andrews/e/
B00MZEDHMC/ref=ntt_athr_dp_pel_pop_1

Instagram: @kandrewsauthor
http://www.instagram.com/kandrewsauthor

Twitter: @kandrewsauthor
http://www.twitter.com/kandrewsauthor

https://www.goodreads.com/author/dashboard

Other Books

The Hale Brothers Series

Drops of Rain
(Book 1)
Amazon US: http://amzn.to/1iLoqe7

Starless Nights
(Book 2)
Amazon US: http://amzn.to/1uTYTnh

Unforgettable Sun
(Book 3)
Amazon US: http://amzn.to/1JCF7oR

Blue Horizons
Amazon US: http://amzn.to/1U35BUE

The Sweetness of Life
Amazon US: http://amzn.to/2fAfdK7

Made in the USA
Columbia, SC
12 December 2018